Praise for
BEVERLY LEWIS

"No one does Amish-based inspirationals better than Lewis."
—*Booklist*

"Author Beverly Lewis has come up with a new magic formula for producing best-selling romance novels: humility, plainness and no sex. Lewis' G-rated books, set among the Old Order Amish in Lancaster County, Pennsylvania, have sold more than 12 million copies, as bodice rippers make room for 'bonnet books,' chaste romances that chronicle the lives and loves of America's Amish."
—*Time* magazine

"Much of the credit [for the growth of Amish fiction] goes to Beverly Lewis, a Colorado author who gave birth to the genre in 1997 with *The Shunning,* loosely based on her grandmother's experience of leaving her Old Order Mennonite upbringing to marry a Bible college student. The book has sold more than 1 million copies."
—Associated Press

"As in her other novels, Lewis creates a vividly imagined sensory world. . . . And her well-drawn characters speak with authentic voices as they struggle to cope with grief and questions about their traditions and relationship with God."
—*Library Journal*
(about *The Parting*)

BEVERLY LEWIS

the MERCY

BETHANYHOUSE

MINNEAPOLIS, MINNESOTA

Cover design by Dan Thornberg, Design Source Creative Services
Art direction by Paul Higdon

Published by Bethany House Publishers
11400 Hampshire Avenue South
Bloomington, Minnesota 55438
www.bethanyhouse.com

Bethany House Publishers is a division of
Baker Publishing Group, Grand Rapids, Michigan

Printed in the United States of America

Library of Congress Cataloging-in-Publication Data
Lewis, Beverly.
    The mercy / Beverly Lewis.
        p. cm.—(The rose trilogy; 3)
    ISBN 978-0-7642-0938-3 (hardcover : alk. paper)—ISBN 978-0-7642-
0601-6 (pbk.)   ISBN 978-0-7642-0939-0 (large-print pbk.)
    1. Amish—Fiction. 2. Pennsylvania Dutch Country (Pa.)—Fiction. I. Title.
PS3562.E9383M47 2011
813'.54—dc22   2011023959

Scripture quotations are from the King James Version of the Bible.

To
Dr. Nan Buchwalter Best,
always Cousin Betsy to me.
With love.

By Beverly Lewis

THE ROSE TRILOGY
The Thorn • *The Judgment* • *The Mercy*

ABRAM'S DAUGHTERS
The Covenant • *The Betrayal* • *The Sacrifice*
The Prodigal • *The Revelation*

THE HERITAGE OF LANCASTER COUNTY
The Shunning • *The Confession*
The Reckoning

ANNIE'S PEOPLE
The Preacher's Daughter • *The Englisher*
The Brethren

THE COURTSHIP OF NELLIE FISHER
The Parting • *The Forbidden* • *The Longing*

SEASONS OF GRACE
The Secret • *The Missing* • *The Telling*

The Postcard • *The Crossroad*

The Redemption of Sarah Cain
October Song • *Sanctuary* (with David Lewis)
The Sunroom

Amish Prayers
The Beverly Lewis Amish Heritage Cookbook

www.beverlylewis.com

BEVERLY LEWIS, born in the heart of Pennsylvania Dutch country, is the *New York Times* bestselling author of more than eighty books. Her stories have been published in eleven languages worldwide. A keen interest in her mother's Plain heritage has inspired Beverly to write many Amish-related novels, beginning with *The Shunning*, which has sold more than a million copies. *The Brethren* was honored with a 2007 Christy Award.

Beverly lives with her husband, David, in Colorado.

PROLOGUE

January 1986

A solemn pallor covers the landscape of our lives since Bishop Aaron Petersheim was removed from his ministerial duties.

Silenced, the brethren call it.

The Lord's fingerprint on a man is a fearsome thing. According to my father and those who question whether God's will was accomplished, Aaron is blameless. Yet his reaction to the silencing is astonishing. Our longtime neighbor friend appears to be genuinely at peace, as if nothing has changed.

"A man cannot determine his son's destiny ... whether Plain or fancy," my father uttered

as he rose from the breakfast table just this morning. *"Neither is he responsible for the actions of a wayward child."*

Because I'd wheeled my mother back to the bedroom to rest and *Dat* and I were alone in the kitchen, I assumed he was talking to me, my hands already deep in the soapy dishwater. He must've realized how much I've gleaned from the neighborhood grapevine. Folks are not only wagging their tongues but their heads, too. 'Tis mighty peculiar, this harsh discipline doled out to our beloved bishop.

Despite that, no one breathes a word anymore about Nick Franco, his foster son. It's as if Nick never lived amongst us here on Salem Road, rubbing shoulders with neighboring farmers or sharing the Lord's Day at Preaching. As if he never existed.

Even so, while all of us feel downtrodden about the ousting of Aaron, I'm honestly taken aback by the fact he doesn't seem affected by what's happened. He simply goes about his farm chores with a cheerful attitude, caring for the animals, butchering, and chopping wood for the cookstove. Sometimes with help from his sons-in-law or his male cousins, like a man shunned but permitted to stay, work, and worship with the People. It's the oddest thing I've ever encountered . . . except for my married sister's return from the world.

Another dumbfounding situation, for sure and for certain.

Hannah—or Hen, as most folks know her—is becoming reacclimated to her former Plain life here, all while caring for her *Englischer* husband in hope of his sight—and their love—returning. But the way I see it, she'll lose any ground she's gained the minute Brandon recovers. Next to the situation with our one-time bishop, my sister's dilemma is the most perplexing I know.

On top of everything else, Rebekah Bontrager has quickly become Silas Good's new sweetheart-girl. That wouldn't be so peculiar, except that Silas was my fiancé until we recently parted ways. Truth is, nothing was the same between us after Rebekah arrived from Indiana—and all three of us knew it.

Just last week at Thursday market, I was minding my business and selling my handmade faceless dolls to tourists when who but Rebekah came right over to talk to me. She approached the market table rather boldly.

"*Denki for releasing Silas from his betrothal,*" she said softly, her brown eyes mighty sincere. "*It was awful nice of you, Rose Ann.*"

I merely nodded. *Ach,* I hardly knew what to say back to her. But what Rebekah added startled me even more.

"I wish you the same happiness." She lightly touched my hand.

I couldn't help but smile, though I didn't see how that could possibly be, given most all the fellas my age were already married or engaged. Somehow I held even the slightest bitterness toward her at bay . . . what little there was. No point in that.

"Kind of you," I said.

Rebekah's shining face was a *wunnerbaar-gut* reminder that Silas and Rebekah are surely meant to wed. Honestly, I doubt I ever looked or felt so happy when I was engaged to him, fine fellow though he is. Well, maybe I did for a time, but that's water over the wheel now.

Before breakfast this morning, I was out behind Dat's barn, where the wind had flattened the snow cloaking the pastureland. I noticed deer tracks and followed them over toward Petersheims' property. My boots crunched into the frosty snow as I remembered the many wintry adventures Nick and I enjoyed, growing up here on these heavenly acres. All those years together, we were each other's closest friend. And I admit to having wondered why my father, or whoever found the money tin buried down in the ravine, hasn't mentioned the letter I wrote one month ago . . . the one that revealed my feelings for our former bishop's son. I suspect it was Dat who somehow discovered the letter, although I'll probably never know. Even if he wasn't the one who removed it from *Mamm*'s old market box, not a soul in the community has fessed up to it. How awkward would it be if someone did?

Sometimes I hope the Lord himself mercifully reached down and removed my impulsive letter from the battered tin. That would explain its disappearance, for sure.

I lie awake at night, hoping whoever *did* take it stopped before reading the letter clear through. Oh, what I wouldn't give to have my private thoughts about rebellious Nick locked away once again, safe inside my poor heart!

PART ONE

Mercy and truth are met together;

righteousness and peace have kissed each other.

—PSALM 85:10 KJV

CHAPTER 1

A brutal blizzard howled across Lancaster County in the night, dumping nearly a foot of snow on Salem Road and the surrounding farmland. The heavy snowfall quickly concealed the existing banks of crust and grime along the roadside. Icy ruts that ran between the stable and the barnyard were now hidden.

Rose Ann's oldest brothers, Joshua and Enos, hurried into the house from the barn along with Dat as snowflakes flew thick early Friday morning. The brims of their black felt hats were nearly white as the men came inside for hot coffee, red-faced, their eyes alight at the aroma. Eagerly they warmed their big, callused hands around the cups, chattering in *Deitsch* about the upcoming Gordonville Spring Mud Sale.

Mamm sat primly in her wheelchair, wearing a green choring dress and long black apron, her brownish-blond hair pulled back into a perfect round bun at the nape of her neck. Her *Kapp* was perched on her head, the strings draped over her shoulders. From time to time, she gazed lovingly at Dat where he sat beside the gas lamp on this dreary day.

The winter solstice had brought with it exceptionally cold temperatures and plenty of snow, as foretold by the neighbors' chickens, which last fall had shed their feathers from the front of their bodies before the rest. Corn husks had been mighty thick at the harvest, too, and Aaron and Barbara Petersheim reported spotting caterpillars that were inky-black at both ends last summer. All of that had indicated a severe start to the bleakest season.

Quite unexpectedly, a bolt of lightning crisscrossed the snowy backyard from the west, ripping through the bitter storm. The smell of sulfur instantly pervaded the atmosphere, making Rose tremble. *Ach, such a rare thing in the wintertime. Is it an omen?*

"Did ya see that?" She rushed to the window.

The wind howled noisily, too loud for her to hear the rumble of thunder sure to follow.

"Never point at lightning," Josh told her, a

twinkle in his eyes as he came to stand beside her.

"That's silly." Rose stared through the tufts of snow that clung to the window, looking out into the swirling world of white.

Enos chuckled. "Most superstitions are just that."

But nothing could have predicted what Rose saw while standing at the icy window, peering out in the direction of the lightning strike. It was the unmistakable plume of . . .

Could it be?

Smoke was rising from the roof of the woodshed. She squinted and frowned. *How can this be, in the middle of winter?*

Then suddenly, as if in answer to her unspoken question, the shingles on the woodshed burst into flames. "Ach, boys! Dat . . . oh, hurry, Dat!" Rose waved at the flames, stumbling for words. "Fire!"

Josh and Enos grabbed their black winter hats and darted out the back door, not bothering to put on work coats or woolen scarves. Dat hurried along, too, instructing them to dump buckets of snow onto the flaming roof, although they already seemed to know what to do.

"Rosie," Mamm called, her small voice high pitched. "Stay right here with me, won't ya, dear?"

Quickly, Rose moved to her side and took hold of her trembling hand. "Thank goodness it wasn't the barn."

"Or the house," Mamm added, eyes wide.

"*Jah,* 'tis just the ol' woodshed," Rose said. "They'll have it out in no time."

"But the fire's so high," Mamm said. "How will they—"

"Don't fret, now." Rose bowed her head and folded her hands. In another moment she heard Mamm's soft murmurings as she asked the Lord God and heavenly Father to protect her sons and husband.

Rose stayed right next to her mother. Just the thought of not being able to walk and being trapped near—or in—a fire gave Rose the shivers.

After she'd added her own silent prayer, Rose raised her head to watch her brothers and Dat form a small line to douse the woodshed roof with snow. Josh was up on the tall ladder, but Rose could tell by the look on Dat's face that he was not fearful.

A dozen or more buckets were filled with the heavy snow and thrown onto the woodshed roof as the wind wailed and snow flew in all directions.

Rose and Mamm watched anxiously as the men dumped even more snow than was necessary on the now-smoking roof, just to be sure. Or perhaps, was it for fun?

Then, of all things, Enos threw a snowball at Joshua, who ducked, then leaned down and scooped a handful of snow as the boys laughed and carried on rambunctiously.

"Ach, such silliness." Mamm gave a relieved sigh, her hands no longer shaking.

"Thank goodness the fire's out."

"Praise be," Mamm said softly.

Rose moved the wheelchair away from the window. She observed her mother more closely. *Dear long-suffering Mamm.* It wouldn't be much longer before she and Dat would travel over the Susquehanna River to York for Mamm's back surgery. Only another thirteen days. Mamm seemed rather stoic about her situation as she counted the hours, hoping the constant pain from her buggy accident years ago could be alleviated soon. She had been given an epidural pain medication to decrease inflammation in the nerve endings, but the relief lasted mere days, so the doctor had dismissed such treatment as unsuccessful. In a case like Mamm's, he said, surgery was warranted.

"Folks daresn't ever use wood struck by lightning to build a barn or house, ya know," Mamm said, a glint in her golden-brown eyes.

"Lest that building be struck by lightning, too."

Another superstition, thought Rose, wondering about all the strange sayings she'd heard as a girl. Her sister, Hen, had mocked such Amish old wives' tales in her teens. Now, however, Hen had come nearly full circle, realizing too late that there was more to the Old Ways than superstition. Her sister wished with all of her heart for her English husband to join church with her. Far as Rose could tell, that seemed downright hopeless.

As if sensing whom she was thinking about, Mamm asked how Brandon was feeling today. "Hen says he still can't see a stitch." Rose paraphrased her sister's remark from earlier that morning, when Rose was over in the *Dawdi Haus* where her sister lived, helping make bread. The small house was attached to their father's large home.

"Isn't it odd?" Mamm replied. "Whoever heard of a man goin' blind after a blow to the head?"

"According to the doctor, Brandon had some swelling in his brain." *It is strange for the blindness to go on this long,* Rose thought. *But these are strange times. . . .*

"You and Hen seem to be getting along nicely, ain't?" Mamm said. "Like when you were girls."

"Jah, I missed her something awful when she lived in town."

Mamm dipped her head. "We all did."

Rose told her Brandon was itching to talk to his business partner again. "Land development is booming, Hen says. And with Brandon still out of the office, he and his partner have discussed that they might have to hire someone to cover for him. Just till he can return to work."

Till his sight returns . . .

A little frown crossed Mamm's brow. "Surely that won't be long."

Rose wondered what would happen when Brandon could see well enough to drive a car once more . . . and to live on his own in the house he and Hen had once shared. *Separated again.* She shuddered.

"He must have cabin fever after all this time in the Dawdi Haus." Mamm sighed. "I won't stop prayin' for him."

"Might still be weeks yet," Rose reminded her of the original doctor's assessment. She stared outside and watched the snow continue to fall. "It's surprising he's not as outspoken against stayin' here as Hen first thought."

Mamm's face brightened. "Could it be he's getting accustomed to our ways?"

"Not to discourage ya, Mamm, but I doubt it. He seems pretty low, almost despairing.

More so each time I visit Hen and Mattie Sue."

"Poor man. Who can blame him?"

It was odd hearing Mamm speak so sympathetically about Brandon when he had chosen not to have any contact with their family during the years of his marriage to Hen. But since he was Hen's husband, what else *could* Mamm say?

Abruptly, Mamm said, "I hope you're plannin' to attend the next Singing, dear."

Rose hesitated. "Haven't decided, really." She felt sure Dat had told Mamm about the parting of ways between her and Silas Good. Close as Dat was to Silas's father, he must have been one of the first to know, particularly when he had helped to encourage their relationship.

"I understand your reluctance." Mamm paused and glanced at her. "But ya might want to think about going . . . you know, make yourself available right away."

For a new fella, she means.

Thoughtfully, Rose nodded her head. "Just wouldn't be the same."

"Rosie . . . honey-girl, you'll get over Silas soon enough," Mamm surprised her by saying right out.

"Well, it's not Silas I was thinkin' about."

Rose caught herself too late, and Mamm's astonished eyes held Rose's gaze.

Rose looked away and wheeled her mother closer to the cookstove, to ward off the chill of the room . . . not all of it from the cold.

Just that quick, Mamm changed the subject. "It's the second time that ol' shed's been hit."

"I thought lightning didn't strike twice in the same spot." But as soon as she said it, Rose knew better. Where people's lives were concerned, lightning sometimes struck repeatedly. Bishop Aaron and Barbara had to know this, bless their hearts. Their family had been struck nigh unto *three* times now, including the loss of their only sons: Christian, their natural-born son, who'd died in a so-called accident, and Nick, who ran off to the world not long afterward. And Aaron himself had suffered a direct blow, as well, when his divine calling was taken away from him as a punishment for Nick's refusal to join church—a sign of his foster son's willfulness against God and the People.

So much pain . . .

Rose disliked thinking about all that had happened since Christian's untimely death . . . and Nick's sudden leaving.

Only the dear Lord knows what may befall us, just around the bend.

CHAPTER 2

Hen finished smoothing her light brown hair and reached for the white prayer Kapp on the hook near the sink mirror that morning. She placed it reverently on her head and pinned it near the back with bobby pins, thankful all the while for the cozy bathroom but a few feet from the kitchen. Her father and several of her brothers had gotten permission from Bishop Aaron to add it some years back, most likely in preparation for her parents to live here someday, once Rose Ann married and occupied the main farmhouse. Or if one of Hen's married brothers agreed to take over the farm and live next door with his wife and children.

Had it not been for the indoor facilities, Brandon would never have consented to convalesce here after his hospital release following his recent accident. An outhouse would be intolerable to a worldly man such as Brandon Orringer.

Hen glanced at the bathtub-shower combination, smiling. *All the comforts of home.* Her eyes came to rest on the gas lantern set on the wooden shelf. *Well . . . almost.*

As it was, her wounded husband complained about the lack of central heat in the drafty house . . . and that not a single telephone could be found inside. He even complained that he had to shave with a razor and shaving cream—*"hit or miss for someone who can't see,"* he said. Overall, though, he seemed as comfortable as could be expected, given his present situation. And that was her goal: to make Brandon feel at ease until he recovered.

Who would ever guess he would live on an Amish farm? Hen corrected herself. No, it wasn't as if Brandon was actually going to live here. That wasn't his plan at all. He would promptly return to their beautiful modern home in town once his sight returned and his right arm mended.

When he no longer needs me.

Hen shuddered to think about the terrible car accident that had resulted in broken ribs and a serious fracture to his right arm, one that had required two surgeries. And the dangerous concussion and associated brain swelling still caused him some confusion. Yet it was the blindness that plagued him most.

There were times when she found herself watching him rest on the settee in the front room or interact contentedly with their curly-haired Mattie Sue at the kitchen table. Hen was startled by the irony of it all, the three of them thrust back together when on the cusp of divorce.

But how did God view the situation? She contemplated their old conflict regarding modern versus Plain living. *Did the Lord allow the accident to happen?*

She had been brought up to believe that God's sovereignty was to be revered, not questioned. Young fellows like Christian Petersheim suffered untimely deaths; dutiful women like Hen's own mother encountered unexplained buggy accidents. And too many Amish babies were born with deformities due to genetic disorders, sometimes more than one child in the same family. Yet people like Brandon, and Hen's friend Diane Perliss, too, would never be convinced that such things were actually permitted by God. *His will.* Yet it was how the People viewed everything that happened in their lives.

Hen heard Brandon calling from the front room and poked her head out. "Be right there." Quickly, she dried her hands and snuffed out the lantern. Hearing his voice within the confines of these Amish walls still made her heart leap. The sound of it wrapped around the secret hope she carried with her each day that their marriage might still be saved. The inner stirring had moved her forward since he'd agreed to come here, pushing her along like a plow furrowing hard soil.

She made her way to the small room where her husband and four-and-a-half-year-old daughter were snuggled together on the upholstered settee with Mattie Sue's library book spread across their laps. Wiggles, the cocker spaniel puppy Brandon had purchased last fall, nestled there, too.

Brandon's light brown hair looked mussed as he raised his head and turned his face toward her. He must have heard her come into the room. "I hate to ask you this, Hen, but . . ." He hesitated.

She braced herself.

"I really need to get to the office today."

Again? As it was, she'd taken him to Quarryville twice already this week. "By car?" Surely he knew by now how she felt about driving.

"Hen, seriously, I'm never getting into a buggy again. A person could freeze to death!" Brandon paused. "Besides, it's humiliating."

She didn't mean to be difficult. It was just

that she had come to resent the modern conveniences that had once taken her away from her Plain lifestyle. Anymore, she resisted anything that smacked of the outside world . . . and she deeply cared what her father thought, too. There was much to make up for with her parents, and she knew her dad was troubled by the presence of her car on his property. So much so that he'd requested Hen park it behind the barn.

"You know . . . maybe it would be better to hire a driver for you, Brandon."

Appearing surprised, he shook his head. "But you don't have plans today, right?"

"Not away from the house, no."

"So couldn't you drive me to town for a few hours after lunch if the snow lets up? There's no need to hire anyone."

Is it my job to see to your every wish? Almost as soon as the words came to mind, Hen chastised herself. Hadn't she wanted with all of her heart to help him? She recalled the great relief she'd felt when Brandon consented to let her tend to him here, the day she'd driven him away from the hospital, leaving his nurse and wheelchair behind.

She looked at Mattie Sue, caught up in her picture book, her little pointer finger running under the words she already recognized.

Sighing, Hen relented. "All right—I'll drive you . . . in the car."

Mattie Sue's big eyes blinked fast as she glanced first at her daddy, then back up at Hen. "Mattie, honey," Hen said, "maybe you can go help *Aendi* Rose for a bit."

"No, Hen," Brandon protested. "You don't have to wait for me at the office. Just return here. Or bring Mattie Sue along if you have errands to run."

"And then return for you later?"

Brandon rubbed the stubble on his chin. It looked as though he'd opted not to shave today. "Whatever works better for you, yes."

Wiggles whined to get off the settee, and Mattie helped him down, holding him gently as Hen had taught her to do. He scampered up the stairs and Mattie followed, taking her book with her.

Hen looked back at Brandon, sitting there alone on the settee. She wondered what the doctor would say about his progress next Tuesday, when they went to yet another follow-up visit.

Brandon broke into her thoughts. "I can't believe you had your bishop stop by earlier, Hen."

"He did? In this weather?" This surprised her. "I knew nothing about it."

"He came by while you and Mattie Sue were out feeding the mules or whatever."

"Why did he come?" asked Hen.

Brandon shrugged. "We had some coffee . . . he asked me how I was getting along. Nothing important." His words were clipped. "He wanted to apologize, I think."

"About what?"

"He thought we'd gotten off on the wrong foot years ago. Surely you remember how he ran me off when we were dating."

Hen was shocked. "He said that?"

"In so many words."

She could hardly believe this.

"A waste of time, if you ask me. His and mine." Brandon muttered something she couldn't make out. "So you had nothing to do with the visit?"

"Nothing whatsoever."

He grimaced. "I'm a sitting duck, Hen. Forced to consort with your—"

"Ach, was it so bad?"

"We have nothing in common. Nothing to talk about."

She eyed him. "So what did you do after he said those nice things?"

"Drank more coffee."

"Neither of you talked further?" Hen imagined the awkward scene and found herself smiling a little.

"Not at first," Brandon said.

She perked up her ears. "Then, one of you must've found *something* to say."

Brandon rose and slowly made his way to the table. He stood there, his back to Hen. "I finally asked him outright something I've been thinking about since his preacher pals gave him the boot."

Hen gasped. "Oh, Brandon, you didn't."

"The man's lost nearly everything—his sons, his job, his standing in the community—everything that matters to folk in Amishville, you know."

She cringed and lowered herself into a nearby chair, holding her breath. What on earth had Brandon said to their former bishop?

Her husband drew a long breath. "He didn't seem to mind the question—acted like he didn't care. Said God could be trusted no matter what happened."

The response struck Hen as pure Bishop Aaron. "The man is as even-keeled as anyone I've known."

Brandon appeared to consider that. "But if your people here are so patient and kind, why was he treated so badly?"

"We're not perfect." She paused. "We make mistakes. And some of us find it more difficult to forgive than others."

"Then why would you want to be Amish

again? There are imperfect people living out in the *real* world, you know. Christians, for one. You don't have to wear a prayer bonnet or ride around in a horse-drawn buggy to follow God."

Hen wasn't sure what to make of hearing her unbelieving husband talk like this. "I was raised this way."

He shook his head. "Well, *I* wasn't."

Hen felt her hackles rising. "So that's all you got out of Aaron's visit?"

"I didn't say that."

She looked at her handsome husband, his fractured ribs still wrapped in a brace beneath his long-sleeved green-striped shirt, his right arm in a cast and sling.

"I just . . ."

She waited.

"I wanted to understand."

"And did you?"

"It made me think. That's all." Brandon shook his head in frustration and chuckled bitterly. "All I have time to do anymore is think."

Hen tried to imagine what it would be like, suddenly going from the frenetic pace Brandon had maintained at the office to simply sitting, without a TV or even a radio to listen to.

"Besides . . . I think Aaron might visit

again," Brandon added. "He commented on your wonderful blend of coffee."

She pondered that. "I could ask him not to come, if you'd rather."

Another lengthy moment of silence ensued. Finally Brandon shrugged. "You know me and coffee."

Hen broke into a smile, and she was momentarily glad he couldn't see her.

Brandon cleared his throat. "I really need your help getting around, Hen." His tone had changed. It was softer, almost tender—like it used to be.

She recalled his rushing home for lunch between appointments, back before Mattie Sue was born . . . eating soup and sandwiches with her as they talked about ordinary things like getting the lawnmower blades sharpened or making two mortgage payments in a month to get ahead. The memory gave her the same promising feeling as when she'd watched her father take Mattie Sue into his arms and hoist her onto his shoulders as he strode out to the stable their first day here.

She'd been too hard on him. "Just remember that I'm here for you, Brandon. That won't change," Hen said, then silently whispered a prayer of gratitude for Aaron Petersheim's impromptu visit.

CHAPTER 3

It was apparent to Rose that her cousin Melvin Glick hadn't slept much the night before. He and his father stood with the other men in line on the far right side of the brick farmhouse early Sunday morning. The deep pockets beneath Melvin's eyes marred his usually pleasant countenance. Rose inched forward toward the women's entrance to the temporary house of worship, Hen and Mattie Sue beside her. As was her sister's way since returning home nearly four months ago, Hen did not sit with Rose during the meetings, because she was not a baptized church member—and could not become one unless Brandon joined church with her. Thus Rose would sit close to the front, while Hen sat in the back with Mattie Sue and the visitors and youth who hadn't yet bowed their knee to make their lifelong pledge to God and the church.

Rose glanced at Melvin again and saw that he was staring at Rebekah Bontrager, just ahead of her in line. Well, goodness! Though she hadn't told it around, hadn't word already rolled through the grapevine about Rebekah and Silas Good?

Hours later, during the shared meal after Preaching, Rose again spotted Melvin gazing longingly at Rebekah, who sat with Silas's unmarried sisters, Sarah and Anna Mae. He looked quickly away when he realized Rose had spotted him.

Ach, he's got it bad.

Hen had joined Rose at the table, where they enjoyed the cold cuts and homemade bread, peanut butter, and snitz pie. The meal after the Sunday gatherings was fairly light, intended mostly to ward off hunger pangs for the ride home. The tradition benefited the farming families who had to eventually return home to feed their animals or for afternoon milking. Rose was tempted to reach for another piece of bread and some strawberry jam, her favorite, but she disciplined herself, not wanting to grow as stout as some of the older women around the table.

What'll my life be like as a Maidel *if God doesn't send along another beau?* She recalled

Mamm's encouragement to attend tonight's Singing. But there were only a handful of fellows her age that weren't spoken for, and her cousin Melvin was one of them. Of course, he didn't count. Even if he weren't her cousin, she wouldn't even think of pairing up with someone so obviously smitten with someone else.

Hen broke into Rose's thoughts. "Brandon won't be home till later tonight," she said softly. "Again . . ."

He had been gone all day last Sunday, too, Rose recalled. "Did his business partner stop by for him?"

"Jah, he and Bruce headed off this morning, no doubt to get caught up on some work. He told me the plan at breakfast." Hen paused, looking away. "It made Mattie Sue cry."

Rose felt bad for her dear niece, but she'd never really expected her brother-in-law to attend one of their Preaching services. "Bruce will look after him, jah?"

"I'm sure he will, but it makes no difference to Mattie Sue," Hen said. "Brandon has no interest in keeping the Lord's Day holy—and she knows it."

"Well, Mattie Sue knows he's never attended church with you before."

"Still." Hen nodded thoughtfully as she spread peanut butter on her bread. "She's got to be feeling uncertain about things, about the future." She sighed. "Just as I am."

"Understandable," Rose murmured. Her sister looked as wilted as a daisy before a good rain. Wilted and dejected. *What must it be like to be unequally yoked with an unbeliever?*

"I thought maybe Bishop Aaron's visit might've helped Brandon . . . somehow."

"*Bishop* came to see him?"

"Jah." Hen smiled sadly. "I guess I'll always think of him that way, too."

"S'pose we all will." Rose went on to say she'd seen Aaron coming toward the house on Friday, braving the snow. "Thought he might have headed over to see our grandparents."

"No, he came seeking out my husband. Still hard to believe." Hen added, "And Brandon says he might come see him again."

Rose found this heartening, though altogether unexpected— from even a soon-to-be former minister toward an Englischer. It was as if Aaron hoped to win Brandon to the church somehow. She wondered what other bishops might do in a situation like this, knotty as it was.

"I wish Brandon wouldn't go off with his business partner and work on a Sunday, of all things."

"Well, it's not like either of them is Amish."

Hen's face drooped further. She looked as

sad as when she'd first arrived at Dat's farm, back in early October.

Rose hated to think what it would do to her sister when Brandon left for good, as surely he would once he was well. Hen had to live with this niggling concern. Most likely went to bed with it and awakened with the thought each and every day—a continual reminder, like the constant ticking of a clock.

"Brandon's talked about putting the house in town up for sale," Hen said through tight lips.

"Well, why?"

"He'd get a smaller place if we end up . . ." She shook her head, her hair gleaming in the light from the window. "The house is in his name, so I guess he can do what he wants with it."

Rose searched her sister's solemn face. "Ya honestly think he'd sell it?"

"Possibly."

"But . . . while he's recovering . . . and can't see?" asked Rose. "That doesn't make sense."

"Since when does any of this make sense?" Hen sighed. "I guess it's not my place to worry—I mean, look at me."

"Because you don't live there?"

Hen nodded, blinking back tears.

Rose slipped her arm around Hen. "Oh, sister . . . I'm so sorry."

Hen turned away from the table to blow her nose. "Even though I don't want to move back, thinking of Brandon's selling our house really bothers me. And I don't know what will happen with Mattie Sue—what the court will decide if he still pursues a divorce."

"Well, let's trust it won't come to that. Surely God's workin' on his heart."

Hen made no reply. She sat there like an empty husk, not moving and scarcely breathing, or so it seemed.

Was it a good thing to encourage Hen to embrace hope? Rose knew what God expected of a marriage vow—that it was to be kept, honored. Yet would the tender shoot of hope sprouting in Hen's heart lead her to more heartache?

∼

It wasn't because she felt ready to pair up again at Singing that Rose picked her way over the snowy road that evening, nor did going have anything to do with Mamm's suggestion the other day. She'd decided to go because she wanted to visit with her girl cousins. Besides, she was tired of being largely stuck in the house due to all the snow and cold.

Right away cousins Mary, Sadie, and

Sarah greeted her just inside the upper-level barn door. The three sisters told her about a farm and house sale the second Saturday in February, at the elder Kings' on Ridge Road. "It's within walking distance of your house, Rosie," Mary said, insisting Rose just had to go. Sadie and Sarah nodded their heads in agreement.

"There'll be lots of perty dishes for sale," Sarah added.

"And anyway, ain't so *gut* to pine away for a fella," Sadie whispered suddenly, glancing over at the cluster of young men across the barn.

"Not to worry," Rose replied, but even as she said it, she knew there were times when she felt rather blue. Still, she wouldn't wish Silas Good back. That was quite settled between them, and while her cousins certainly knew more about her situation than she would've expected, the girls might not realize that Rose had been the one to break things off with Silas.

Sarah asked her to sit with them, and Rose happily agreed. Pretty Sarah had been seen riding with their younger preacher's nephew lately, and her heart-shaped face flushed whenever she allowed her gaze to follow the particularly handsome fellow across the way. *Too young for me,* thought Rose, going with her cousins to the table and getting settled in before the unison singing started.

After a time, Rose noticed Silas among the older young men. He looked her way and smiled politely—a different sort of smile than when they'd courted. For that she was relieved; it made things easier for her . . . for both of them. Truly it seemed he felt not a speck of lingering regret over their parting.

When the young men made their way to the opposite side of the table, Rose would have been blind not to notice blond Hank Zook and dark-haired Ezra Lapp looking at her. Good friends since childhood, Hank and Ezra both sat across the table from Rose and her cousins. Younger though they were, Rose suspected both boys might be feeling a little sorry for her. She'd noticed in the past that Ezra especially was quick to befriend any girl who appeared not to have a ride.

Then and there, she decided that no matter what Ezra said or how pleasantly he smiled at her, she would not go riding with him tonight. Appealing as it might be to accept an invitation from a potential beau rather than walk home through the snow and ice, Rose wouldn't allow herself to be the object of pity.

Sure enough, when the hour had grown quite late, Ezra did seek her out, and Rose politely declined. She was more surprised when Hank asked her, as well, so much so that she agreed to go with him as the other fellows and girls paired up and left the barn. Silently, she fell into step with Hank, wondering if, lonely though she was, she was doing the right thing as they walked to his waiting carriage.

"Mighty cold tonight, ain't?" Hank offered to help her into his open buggy.

She nodded, hoping he'd brought along plenty of woolen lap robes. *Like Silas always did. . . .*

Once they were settled inside, she realized it was snowing again. *A blessing,* she thought. Like all farmers, her father had taught her to accept the weather with gratitude no matter what the Good Lord sent their way. She was glad, however, for the extra layers of clothes she'd worn beneath her coat and dress, and thankful for her outer bonnet, which shielded her face from the heavy flakes that were coming fast now.

"I sure hope ya didn't think I was too *vorwitzich*—bold—comin' over and talking to you, Rose Ann."

"Thought nothin' of it."

Hank exhaled, clearly relieved. "I won't keep you out too long, since it's so chilly."

She thanked him. Of course, had it been Nick, he would've simply bundled her up. But she caught herself. She'd never gone courting with Nick. Why was she thinking of him?

But as Hank continued to talk, Rose's mind kept wandering back to the days when she and Nick were best friends. Even though he'd been a troublemaker from day one—or so the People said—he had been her truest companion. Just then she wondered what Hank might think if he knew what she'd written in her secret letter to Nick. *Consorting with such a fellow.* Some even suspected him of murder. What would *any* fellow think if he knew how Nick had held her in his arms?

Hank's voice interrupted her musing. "My mother knows your English friends, the Brownings. Mighty nice folk, she says."

Rose told him that she, too, thought a lot of Mr. Browning and his daughter, Beth. "We looked after Beth while her father was gone last month."

"Tending to his ailing father . . . who died, jah?"

"That's right."

"And Beth's special, is what I hear."

She was glad he'd mentioned her. "She is special, and she was such a help to our family. My Mamm is going to undergo a serious surgery because of her encouragement."

Hank listened but didn't seem particularly interested. And after a while, as he moved on to talk about other, more mundane things, Rose wished he would just take her home. He wasn't Silas or Nick—and didn't hold a candle to them when it came to handling a horse, either. She smiled to herself about the latter.

By the time they reached Dat's farm, Rose was not only shivering but quite weary of Hank's chatter. He'd droned on and on about the kind of farming operation he hoped to have someday. Was it to impress her? She didn't know, but his talk was dreadfully dull and she wondered if this was the reason he was still single at nineteen.

She was quite ready to climb down from the open buggy. *"Denki. Gut Nacht."*

Hank jumped out of the carriage and hurried around to her. "I'll see ya next time," he said, but she'd already turned to make her way toward the house, glad she'd worn her boots. She waved her hand in a brief farewell and hoped he wouldn't ask her to ride with him ever again.

CHAPTER 4

$\mathcal{R}$ose was glad Dat took her to work on Wednesday morning, since the roads were so treacherous. He steered the horse and buggy carefully into Gilbert Browning's snow-packed driveway, where they spotted a U-Haul parked along the side of the house.

"Looks like Mr. Browning's mother's things have arrived." Rose leaned forward in the carriage and saw Beth's aunt Judith Templeton—sister of Beth's deceased mother—coming out of the front door, carrying empty boxes. Rose recognized her from a wallet picture Beth had shown her some time ago. The sweet-faced, middle-aged woman looked as kind as Beth had always described her to be.

"Must be why the bishop asked if I could help him build a bedroom off the main level," said Dat.

"For Mr. Browning's mother?" This was the first Rose had heard it.

"Jah, just last week we talked about it."

"Well, I wonder if she'll be comfortable in the sitting room, at least for now," Rose said, thinking aloud. "Surely he won't expect her to manage goin' up and down the stairs to the bedrooms."

"Maybe you can help with that." Dat turned and smiled. "No matter what your hands find to do, Rosie, you always make quick work of it."

Her cheeks warmed slightly and she thanked him for bringing her. "I can walk home, if that would help."

"No . . . no, it's much too far in the cold and snow."

"I don't mind, Dat."

"If it was plowin' season, I might think twice. But I'll come for ya at eleven."

She nodded, grateful. "Tell *Mammi* Sylvia I'll cook supper tonight, since she's—"

"Ach, Rosie, I'll leave that to you." Like most men hereabouts, he wasn't one to poke his nose into women's work.

"All right, then. See ya later." She watched him back out to the narrow country road.

The sun moved out from behind the gray cloud cover, shards of light piercing through the gloom. Gut, *the ride home won't be so cold for him,* she thought. Even so, the trip would feel long—the road was heavily snow-packed, and deep runnels made by the carriage wheels had frozen and melted and refrozen, making the way extra jarring.

Hurrying inside, Rose was anxious to warm up. And immediately upon stepping inside the Browning home, she felt the lovely, even heat of the front room and kitchen, altogether unlike her father's house.

Beth spotted her and gave her a quick hug. "Hi, Rosie!"

"Nice to see you again." Rose glanced out the window. "Looks like you've got company—your aunt, jah?"

"Oh yes, Aunt Judith. And Grandma's coming in two days . . . on the train."

Soon, Judith stepped indoors, as well, wearing a hooded coat and scarf. Beth introduced Rose to her aunt. "Remember how I talked about her?" Beth asked.

"I certainly do." Judith removed a glove to shake Rose's hand. "I'm very pleased to meet you."

"Beth speaks so highly of you," Rose said.

"Isn't she sweet?" Judith hugged Beth and looked fondly at her.

Beth blushed. "Oh, Auntie . . ."

Judith gave her another quick squeeze, then said she needed to get back outside to help Beth's father unload a few more boxes. "I'll be inside soon for some hot cocoa." Judith smiled warmly at Rose. "It's really wonderful meeting you, Rose."

"And you, too." Rose was delighted. "What a nice lady," she told Beth.

"She's sweet as honey pie, Mommy used to say."

"Well, I can see why."

Beth reached for Rose's hand and led her into the narrow sitting room on the opposite wall of the front room, where the staircase ascended to the right. Most of the furniture in the room had been removed, except for a daybed replete with pretty pillows and matching coverlet, and an upholstered rocking chair and night table. "Grandma's going to sleep on the daybed here," said Beth, brightening even more. "And did you know what?"

"Let's see . . . your grandmother will soon be getting a bedroom of her own?"

Beth moved her head up and down. "You guessed it."

"I s'pose ya know who's goin' to add on to the house, too, ain't so?"

Beth's face was like a gleam of sunshine on the snow as she nodded. "You know what I think?"

"What?" Rose played along.

"We'll seem like Amish."

"Why's that?"

"It'll look like a barn-raising, won't it?"

"Oh, you mean when the men come to add on the room?"

Beth nodded. "Only it won't be a barn—just a big bedroom." Beth laughed. "Like a tiny Dawdi Haus."

Mr. Browning came in the front door and wandered into the sitting room. He talked about the excitement surrounding the new addition, the fact that, weather permitting, the foundation would be poured tomorrow, and all the preparations for Beth's grandmother's moving here this Friday. The to-do list he gave Rose today had plenty to tackle to ready the house for her arrival.

Rose wondered how long Aunt Judith would stay but didn't feel it was her place to ask. "I'm sure you and your father will take *gut* care of your grandmother," she said to Beth.

"You'll like her, Rosie . . . I just know it."

They walked through the living room and into the kitchen. "How would ya like to go to the quilting bee with me tomorrow morning?" Rose asked. "You could help entertain some of the children there while we work on more quilts and tied comforters for the shelter."

"Oh yes!"

"We'll ask your father if it's all right, then."

Beth beamed with happiness. "I like

playing with the little ones. Will Mattie Sue be there, too?"

"I'll be sure to bring her." Rose smiled.

In the kitchen Beth picked up a pile of mail while Rose went to the broom closet in the back hallway, where she found the bucket and mop. "Oh goodness. Just look at this!" Beth said, tearing open an envelope. Then, catching herself, she said, "Oops, this letter's not for me."

Wondering what was up, Rose carried the bucket to the sink, glancing over her shoulder at Beth. "What're ya sayin'?"

"I opened Daddy's letter by mistake."

"You didn't mean to," Rose reassured her, knowing Beth sometimes acted impulsively.

As if she'd done something wrong, Beth inched toward her, carrying the partially opened letter in her hand.

"You don't understand," Beth whispered, leaning against Rose's arm while hot water gushed into the bucket. "It's from my mother's nurse, Jane Keene."

Rose couldn't help but wonder why Beth was whispering.

"Miss Jane is the kindest lady I know." She stopped. "Except for you, Rosie."

Rose didn't inquire about Jane, but there was clearly more on Beth's mind. "Maybe it's a belated New Year's card. Could that be?"

Beth shook her head, her short dark hair swinging back and forth against her cheeks. "Jane wasn't just nice to my mother and me. . . ." She paused.

"What do ya mean?"

"Oh . . . uh, I don't know."

Turning, Rose looked into Beth's innocent face. "I think you do."

"Miss Jane loved our family . . . *all* of us."

"And I can see why." She smiled at Beth. "Something to be happy about, ain't?"

A light went on in Beth's eyes. "I didn't think we'd hear from her ever again."

"Why's that?" Rose turned off the water and lifted the pail out of the sink.

Beth shrugged, bashful now. "I better go and give this to Daddy." Beth headed for the front room, where she pulled on her jacket and wrapped her red scarf around her neck before she cautiously made her way outside, the letter from Jane Keene in her hand.

What on earth? Rose wondered, unable to get Beth's guarded expression out of her mind.

CHAPTER 5

When Rose returned home from the Brownings', Dat let her out of the buggy before he went to unhitch the horse. Rose saw Mattie Sue emerge from the Dawdi Haus with her father, leading him down the snowy walkway, chattering all the while. She talked about the horses—Alfalfa, George, and Upsy-Daisy—but it was the colts that seemed most exciting to Mattie Sue as she guided Brandon out toward the stable.

Rose was touched by the way her young niece called her father's attention to the unevenness of the path. It was ever so dear the way Mattie Sue held his hand and glanced up at him every few seconds.

How she loves him!

What would it do to her to live apart from him, if and when Brandon's sight returned and he was to go back home? Or what if Brandon had his way and eventually got custody? How would Mattie Sue fare without seeing her mother every day?

It was hard for Rose to imagine such a thing, having grown up with both parents, surrounded by her many brothers and Hen. They'd loved and laughed and worked together from dawn to dusk. Oh, the *gut* times they'd had! No, she couldn't let herself think such thoughts about Hen's family. She just couldn't.

Turning to head to the house, she looked over her shoulder, again moved by Mattie Sue's tender care of her daddy. But it was the fact that Rose hadn't ever seen Brandon go with Mattie Sue—or anyone—to the barn that made her wonder. Was he ready to warm up to his surroundings, and maybe even Rose's family, at long last? She hoped so but wouldn't stand there speculating further with the cold seeping into her. Opening the door, she stepped inside, glad Mammi Sylvia was stoking the black cookstove with plenty of logs. She walked straight to it, removing her mittens and rubbing her hands together, and observed Mamm reading the old German *Biewel* in her wooden wheelchair.

Rose assumed Hen had gone to work at her part-time job at the fabric shop up yonder, leaving Mattie Sue in charge of occupying Brandon for these hours. She didn't have to voice her thoughts, because her grandmother confirmed her hunch and told Rose to keep an eye out for Mattie.

"I just saw her and her father walkin' together," Rose said, eyeing Mamm, who looked deep in concentration as she read the Scriptures. "How long is Hen workin' today?"

"Till before supper." Mammi reached for a box of salt in the freestanding cupboard near the stove. "Seems her husband and Mattie Sue will be joinin' us for the noon meal."

Rose wondered if she felt uncomfortable at the thought of Brandon's feet beneath their family table, Englischer that he was.

Rose took off her boots and pushed her toes into some old slippers she kept nearby during the coldest months. "I'll help you finish cookin'," she offered.

First, though, she went over and touched her mother's shoulder, still aware that Mamm hadn't spoken or even raised her head. She smiled down at her. "You're so quiet," she whispered.

Mamm blinked back tears as she looked up at her.

"Mamm, are you all right?"

Her mother smiled weakly. "Not to worry. I'm just pondering this passage." She pointed to Galatians chapter six, verse two: *Bear ye one another's burdens, and so fulfill the law of Christ.* "Still awful worried for Barbara. She's nearly heartbroken over . . . well, what's happened to our bishop, comin' so quick on the heels of everything else."

It was like Mamm to think of others before herself. Rose guessed poor Barbara must carry the burden of her husband's silencing. How could she not?

"I want to have them over for supper . . . show our support," Mamm said, glancing up at her own mother, Rose's Mammi Sylvia. "Just don't know what we'll talk 'bout . . . ya know."

"There's always the weather," Rose said, going to wash her hands before testing the vegetables in the stew pot. She wouldn't for the life of her mention the power Nick held in his hands regarding his foster father—if he were to join church and become an upstanding Amishman. After being gone this long, there was little chance of that.

Mamm returned to her reading, caressing the Bible's cover like a mother stroking a child.

When it was time for dinner, Mattie Sue cheerfully guided her father in the back door and into the kitchen. She helped him stuff his gloves into his coat pockets, then hung up his jacket and scarf before leading him to the bench, where she plunked down right next to him, looking mighty pleased.

Her mother's child. Rose carried the pan of corn bread to the table. Then she went back to the drawer for the black ladle and placed it deep in the tureen of delicious stew. Looking at Mattie Sue sitting there with her father, Rose wondered whether, if the tables were turned and if Hen were the one suffering from the aftereffects of a serious accident, Brandon would care for *her,* despite their vast differences?

Rose hated to judge, even in her thoughts, but she had a hard time picturing that.

"My partner, Bruce Kramer, is stopping by to drive me to Quarryville later," Brandon stated. "I'll take Mattie Sue along."

Dat and Mamm glanced at each other. "Does Hen know?" asked Dat.

"I told her this morning, before she left," Brandon replied, his unseeing eyes blinking rapidly.

"Aw, we can't leave Wiggles alone," Mattie Sue said, her face wrinkled in concern. "He'll cry, Daddy."

"Then he'll have to cry," Brandon said quietly, turning to Mattie Sue. "Dogs need to learn to be alone sometimes."

"We'll watch your puppy for ya," Mamm

volunteered from across the table. "We'd be glad to."

Dat straightened in his chair. "Mattie Sue can stay here, too, while you're gone," he said.

Brandon surprised Rose by nodding in compliance. "I thought it was time she saw my office. But we can do that another day."

Rose sighed, grateful there wasn't going to be an argument between Brandon and Dat. She took her seat next to Mamm and her grandparents, opposite her niece and brother-in-law, and bowed her head when Dat gave the silent table blessing. *O Lord God and heavenly Father, bless us and these bountiful gifts, which we do gratefully accept from your loving and gracious hand....*

At the end of the prayer, Dat cleared his throat, and Rose raised her head, glad to see Brandon had kept his hands in his lap during the prayer. Hen had said recently that he typically fumbled about for his silverware during the table blessing, even though Mattie Sue always reminded him to pray before eating.

Mattie Sue must've noticed her father's more reverent attitude, because she looked with wide eyes across at Rose, then up at her father. "We're having stew, Daddy," she announced.

"Nice and thick," Rose added, letting him know he could manage this meal pretty easily.

"Smells great." Brandon offered a rare smile. "So does the corn bread." He touched his slice lightly with his left hand after Mattie Sue told him where it was on his plate. His right arm would still be in a cast for a few more weeks, according to yesterday's doctor visit. Hen had given the family an update last evening.

"Daddy's getting along real *gut*," Mattie Sue told them, grinning at him. "Ain't so?"

Brandon colored slightly at the comment, then thanked Mammi Sylvia, who filled his bowl with the vegetable beef stew. It certainly was heartier than usual; Mammi must have had Brandon in mind when she made it.

Mamm leaned forward slightly in her wheelchair. "Son, it's so nice to have you join us for dinner," she said softly, pausing before she added, "You're welcome anytime."

"Denki, Mammi Emma," said Mattie Sue.

"My daughter and I appreciate it, Emma," Brandon said, a small smile on his lips as he seemed to recognize Mattie Sue's efforts on his behalf.

A lull followed when the only sounds were the clinking of spoons against bowls and the soft thud of water tumblers on the table. Then Brandon surprised Rose by speaking again. "Emma," he said, "I understand you're scheduled to have back surgery next week."

"That's right."

"I do hope it goes well."

"Denki, so kind of you, Brandon."

He paused, his spoon buried in the stew. "How have you managed the pain . . . all these years?" His words came cautiously.

"Well, I have to say it hasn't been easy." Mamm breathed out in a little hiss, as if she was trying to keep herself in check, suffering right at that moment. "Think of taking a crumb from a piece of bread and nibbling it, one small piece each bite," she replied. "Sometimes you just have to live an hour or so at a time, trusting the Lord will help you through. I don't know any other way, really."

"My wife can't tolerate pain medication," Dat added, "which makes things even more difficult."

Mattie Sue piped up. "But Beth's prayers— and her dream—helped Mammi Emma want to go to the doctor again. Ain't so, Mammi?"

"Now, Mattie Sue." Brandon touched her arm.

"No . . . no, it's all right," said Mamm quickly. "She's quite right." She explained how Beth Browning's dream of her healing had spurred her to seek out professional help at long last. "The dear Lord used that girl's dream—and prayerful spirit—to open my eyes."

Rose held her breath at Mamm's words. Truth was, they were all praying for God to open Brandon's eyes, as well. And not only his physical ones.

"You've been so gracious in your suffering," Brandon said. "Hen says you've never been anything else."

"The Lord helps Emma each and every day," Dat stated. He patted Mamm's hand.

"Surely does," Mammi Sylvia said, shaking her head.

"Don't see how she could've managed this long otherwise," *Dawdi* Jeremiah added, holding his bowl out for seconds. Rose quickly reached for the ladle.

"I don't, either." Brandon shook his head, as if in awe.

Rose hadn't expected this sort of response from Brandon at all. And for the rest of the meal, he seemed subdued. Several times, Mamm talked to him exclusively, attempting to draw him out.

Rose smiled to herself, grateful for Brandon's kindly responses to Mamm's sweetness.

Has Brandon's heart begun to soften?

CHAPTER 6

While she worked at Rachel's Fabrics, Hen found herself recalling yesterday's follow-up doctor visit. It had offered Brandon some encouragement, but not what he'd wanted to hear: Patience and rest were strongly emphasized. *"Clearly more time is needed,"* the doctor had insisted.

"I feel trapped . . . like this will never end," Brandon had confided to Hen afterward. His vulnerability had surprised her, and she reached to touch his arm as she drove him home.

"I don't blame you, hon. If this had happened to me, I don't know what I'd do." Now, recalling the short-lived moment, Hen realized they had been almost companionable.

Most days the strain between them was an enduring undertow. Both seemed reticent to address the fact their togetherness might be only temporary.

She caught herself sighing frequently, especially on days when she worked at the fabric shop—the very thing she'd fought so hard to do. Yet the hours at work put even more distance between herself and her wounded husband. Hen considered their dilemma as she shelved dress material or rang up orders at the cash register.

It seemed Mattie Sue was their one and only link to happiness, their only chance to fleetingly reconnect. Mattie Sue would surprise them by saying the sweetest or funniest thing at the dinner table or as Hen and Brandon tucked her into bed. And helpless not to burst into gentle laughter, they found enjoyment for a second . . . only to return to tiptoeing around each other and their volatile issues. Hen was holding her breath in so many words, waiting for the day when Brandon could once again lay eyes on her "dowdy" dress and apron.

Now, before heading back to Salem Road, she stopped in at the Quarryville library. With the cold, she'd resorted to driving her car again today. Brandon had suggested she reconsider selling it, at least while he was staying with her. So, to be more agreeable, she'd put the sale of her car on hold. After all, Brandon already had to adapt to Amish life in so many other ways.

While she stood in the checkout line at the library, Hen sorted through the books her sister had requested—each one featured a young woman pining over a forbidden or lost love. *Poor Rosie, will she ever find happiness?*

Hen wouldn't think of faulting her sister for wanting to lose herself in a sweet love story. There were times when she, too, was tempted to escape into a good book. *How might my life have turned out had I married a nice Amish boy?*

But it was too late to rewrite her own story. She must be true to her marriage vows.

Later, after placing the library books in the front seat next to her, she started the car and drove through Quarryville, aware of the horses and buggies on the main street.

While stopped at the traffic light, she glanced over at the parking lot for Brandon's land development office and noticed him getting out of a car. She watched her husband wait for his friend and partner to help him into the building. Where was Mattie Sue? She looked at the car, thinking she might be in there. But no, her daughter hadn't come. *Why not?*

Perhaps Mattie Sue had been invited to stay at the main house. Maybe some of the younger Petersheim grandchildren had come to visit. She hoped so. She hadn't known what to make of Brandon's plan to take her to his office in the first place.

Turning her attention back to her husband, Hen was struck again at just how dependent he was on others. Her heart ached for him as she recalled his words at the doctor's office.

"How soon will I see?" he'd asked, and Hen's jaw clenched as she waited for the kindly doctor's answer.

"It's rare for cortical blindness to hang on as long as yours, but we still expect sight to return within a few weeks," the man had replied.

The day before the appointment, Brandon had told her he'd contacted his attorney brother when last at the office. Hen worried his plan for their divorce was still on his mind. She'd hoped by now that he might have reconsidered legally dissolving their union.

She recalled her father's pointed question to them last fall, before Brandon's accident. *"Did ya ever think there might be something each of you can surrender?"* He maintained it was the only way to save their marriage.

Yet while each knew precisely what they wanted the other to give up, neither Hen nor Brandon had budged. So here they were, merely marking time, still at square one. *With or without Brandon's sight,* Hen thought as the light changed to green.

~

While Rose and Mammi Sylvia were busy making laundry soap that afternoon, Rose's older brother Mose dropped by to talk with Dat in the front room. Father and son greeted each other warmly, then continued talking at a volume easily heard in the kitchen. Dat was saying he'd gladly help Mose's brother-in-law organize a farm sale in the next few weeks, while in return, Mose offered to assist Dat and Aaron with the building project over at the Brownings' place. "It's only right."

This seemed agreeable to Dat. And later, when Mose and Dat came into the kitchen, Mose poked his head between Rose and her grandmother. "Say, Rosie, we'd like ya to come for dinner next Sunday noon."

It seemed odd to be invited clear out of the blue, especially singled out like this. But since it was a no-Preaching day and she knew of no family plans, Rose accepted.

"Ruthann's goin' to make her famous pecan sticky buns for dessert," he added on the way to the back porch. "She'll have them all warmed up for ya."

"Yum," Rose said, thinking of the mouthwatering rolls. "No one makes 'em better."

"Don't be late," Mose said, his eyes twinkling.

She wondered why he was teasing her. "Who else is comin' to dinner, Mose?"

"Well, the children will be there, of course." He grinned and Rose suspected he and Ruthann had cooked up something for her with a fellow.

"Anyone I might *not* know?" she dared to ask.

Mose chuckled. "Now, Rose, don't ya go spoiling all the fun. But ya might want to wear your for-*gut* dress."

Her brother opened the back door and waved at her before she could get any more out of him. Truth be told, she was actually a little curious.

Rose finished helping Mammi Sylvia strain the melted fat through the muslin, storing it in the usual stoneware. Then as Rose prepared to add the lye to some cold water they'd already set aside, she surprised herself with the realization she didn't mind Mose and Ruthann's setup. Not at all.

After Hank Zook, almost anyone would be interesting!

~

Hen was surprised to see the front room all redd up when she returned from work. Mattie Sue's books and toys had been picked up and put away. She kept her coat on to check the stove and saw that the wood had burned down to mere embers.

Where's Mattie Sue?

She went to the back door and looked out. Rubbing her hands together, she recalled Brandon's plans to take their daughter to the office today. But she hadn't seen Mattie Sue earlier with Brandon outside his office.

A nagging worry rippled across her mind, and she stared out at the snow-covered yard. Then, squelching it, she felt sure Mattie Sue was over with her grandparents next door. Where else, since she hadn't gone with Brandon as planned? Hen would go over and check to ease her mind right away.

As she opened the back door to do just that, Hen's father waved to her from the sidewalk. "Didn't want ya to be anxious about Mattie," he said, a knowing look on his ruddy face.

"Was starting to wonder."

"She's been with Rose most of the day." He paused, coming to the door. "By the way, Brandon's taking a real interest in your mother."

"Oh?"

"He stayed around after the noon meal. I was surprised Emma didn't even bother to take her usual rest, she was so happy to accommodate him with a visit before he left for town."

Hen found this interesting. "I hardly know what to say."

"Your mother was awful glad he stayed."

"It's wonderful he did."

He gave a nod. "I'll go an' tell Mattie you're home." He waved again and Hen closed the door.

"Well, for goodness' sake." Hen couldn't imagine what Brandon and Mom had to talk about, although in some sense they did share a life of confinement. Could it be they'd found some common ground?

Turning from the door, Hen pondered this and what a chance to get to know her mother could mean for Brandon. She tried not to get too excited, yet it was promising.

She decided to unwind a little by making a nice hot meal for her family. Immediately Hen set about cooking one of her husband's favorites, wishing she'd planned ahead better for the dessert. Still, she was glad to have on hand all of the ingredients for a good cut of Swiss steak and gravy, as well as scalloped potatoes. Come to think of it, she hadn't made this meal since Brandon had first come to the Dawdi Haus to visit.

Not once, Hen thought sadly, determined

to dote on him in whatever time they had left together.

Hen listened at supper as Brandon described his morning trip to the stable with Mattie Sue as an adventure.

He reached across the table to clasp their daughter's hand. "What a good little tour guide we have here."

Mattie Sue bobbed her head, eyes dancing. "I showed Daddy all around the barn, Mommy . . . the new calves, too."

"I learned about feed, watering, birthing . . . you name it," Brandon added.

"My dad must've been there, as well," said Hen.

Brandon nodded.

"I wanted to go to the hayloft, but Dawdi said we had to wait till Daddy can see again to climb the ladder," Mattie Sue said.

"Sounds like you had a *gut* time, then?" Hen asked.

"We're goin' again, ain't so, Daddy?"

Hen held her breath, wondering if Brandon might reprimand Mattie Sue for using the familiar dialect.

"I don't see why not," he replied. Then he announced, "I wore your father's oldest work boots today."

"Daddy looked like an Amish farmer!" Mattie Sue giggled. "They fit him, Mommy."

Brandon laughed. "Let's just say I clunked around in them."

Mattie Sue looked so fondly at her father across the table, it broke Hen's heart.

More details of the barn tour came out over the next half hour as they devoured Hen's chocolate chip cookies. After drinking her milk, Mattie Sue excused herself and went to the back door to look out at the rising moon. "Goody, it's snowin' again!"

Brandon remained seated at the table. "Well, remember Dawdi Sol said it would."

Dawdi Sol? Brandon had never before permitted Mattie Sue to refer to Hen's grandparents in Pennsylvania Dutch, let alone utter the words himself. Hen was so surprised, she almost missed what Brandon said next.

"While we were in the barn, your dad read sections to us from this year's *Farmers' Almanac*," he stated.

Dawdi and *the almanac all in the same day?*

Hen knew better than to hope this meant her husband was interested in Plain living. It would be downright foolish to think so.

Mattie Sue went to wash her hands without being told, which pleased Hen, leaving her and Brandon alone at the table.

He turned toward her again. "Thanks for dinner."

"Glad you liked it."

He paused as though he had more on his mind but then fell silent. Was he reluctant to mention his visit with her mother?

She felt suddenly shy as he quietly rose and left the room. They rarely talked about anything important anymore, except for his health concerns. *He never asks about my day.*

Watching Brandon settle into a chair near the woodstove, Hen missed more keenly than ever what they'd had when first married. *How we used to be . . .*

CHAPTER 7

Thursday's quilting party turned out to be a comforter-knotting bee, since they were quicker and less expensive to make. Rose was happy to see Laura Esh, the cheery hostess, once again, and her daughters, Linda and Mandy, who seemed delighted Rose had brought Mattie Sue and Beth along. Mattie quickly joined three little ones who had already planted themselves beneath the large table set up in the front room.

After a substantial snack of doughnuts, cookies, and pie, they set to work. Linda talked excitedly about the moving sale this Saturday at the elder Kings' home. The house itself was not being sold, but many linens, dish sets, and some small pieces of furniture would be. The Kings were downsizing so they could move into one of the attached Dawdi Hauses while their youngest son and his new bride settled into the main farmhouse with their own household items.

Listening to Linda talk, Rose couldn't help wondering what it would be like for the Kings' son and daughter-in-law to move into the main farmhouse.

"He'll run the dairy farm with his father," Linda said, reminding Rose of Silas Good's plans with *his* father. The parallel was much too close, and whatever stirred in her heart just then caused Rose to abruptly excuse herself and leave the front room, amidst a few stares. She found herself alone in the summer kitchen, and she folded her arms around her middle to suppress her sobs.

Ach, I'm just feeling sorry for myself! I know Silas wasn't for me.

She paced the length of the room till she heard someone enter. Turning, she saw that Beth was there, holding out her arms to her.

"I saw you leave, Rosie." Beth hugged her and leaned her head on Rose's shoulder.

Rose shook her head, determined not to cry yet unable to speak.

"Whatever's wrong . . . I'm so sorry," Beth said.

Rose scarcely knew herself why she was so upset, but eventually she was able to thank Beth for being so considerate. "You're awful sweet," she said with a kiss on her friend's cheek.

"Here's a tissue," Beth said, pulling one from her own pocket.

Rose wiped her eyes and face. When she'd regained her composure, she returned to the main kitchen to pour some hot cocoa. Beth went back to the children and sat cross-legged on the floor while Rose sipped her drink. Watching her with the little ones, Rose experienced a twinge of hope that one day she might have children—perhaps a large family like Dat and Mamm's.

Sighing, she wished she'd never poured out her heart in a silly letter not so long ago to a young man she would never see again. And even before breaking it off with Silas, too. *What sort of girl am I?*

Yet she longed to be loved and dreaded the thought of growing old alone. Surely God had someone in mind for her. *But who, when nearly all the single fellows in the district are too young for me?*

She thought again of Mose and Ruthann's dinner invitation. Who better to trust as a matchmaker than her own big brother and wife? Privately, Rose determined to be as softhearted and open-minded as possible on Sunday. *The day can't come soon enough.*

~

Rose Ann made creamed chipped beef and served it over boiled potatoes that evening. It would be just Dat, Mamm, and herself at the table tonight, since Dawdi Jeremiah and Mammi Sylvia were having supper in their own kitchen, on the other side of Hen's place. Two of Dawdi's cousins from out of town were visiting overnight, so Mammi Sylvia would have her hands full.

In Mamm's kitchen, Dat was more *bapplich*—talkative—than usual. Rose listened intently as he remarked again about the time Brandon had spent here yesterday with Mamm.

"You two have quite a lot to discuss," Dat said. "Seems so."

Mamm nodded, her expression tight with pain. "I wanted to make him feel comfortable. He needs someone who understands him."

Mamm surely didn't mean to imply that Hen didn't understand. But even as caring as Hen was toward Brandon, Rose wondered if Mamm might be in a better position to reach his heart. *And Bishop Aaron,* thought Rose, hoping their neighbor-friend might visit Brandon again soon.

"You have a kindly way with our son-in-law," Dat said with a smile, returning his attention to his plate.

"I see such awful hurt on his face," Mamm whispered.

"Healing is surely needed—for body, mind, and soul."

Rose was touched by her parents' remarks and glad it was just the three of them tonight. Normally they would not speak so openly.

"Whenever the Lord brings him to mind, I go right to prayer," Mamm said. "'Specially at night, when sleep is far from me."

Dat looked at her with affection, eyes moist in the corners. "Emma, I daresay you're a saint."

Mamm shook her head. "Now, Solomon dear . . ."

Rose smiled in wholehearted agreement with her father's assessment. Few folks she knew were as faithful in prayer as her mother.

They ate their fill, talking about how nice it was that Mattie Sue had been able to spend today with Rose and Beth at the quilting. "Mattie's so eager for when she's old enough to make a quilt of her own," Rose said.

In due time Rose cleared the table. Dessert was peanut butter pie and hot coffee, but Mamm pushed her plate away after only two bites. Rose sensed she was struggling with more discomfort than usual. Dat must have known it, too, and got up to wheel her to rest in their room.

When he returned to finish both his piece of pie and Mamm's, he made small talk with Rose. "Sunday is Groundhog Day, but I don't need an animal to tell me whether we'll have us another six weeks of winter," he said with a grin. "Seems pretty clear to me that spring's a ways off. All the snow's a blessing from heaven." A good amount of snow in January and February made for a glorious springtime.

Stirring sugar into her coffee, Rose ventured to ask, "How do ya think Mamm will do after the surgery?"

"As the Lord allows . . ."

She pondered that. "Same thinking as the bishop's 'bout his silencing, jah?"

"Aaron's one trusting soul. A person can learn from a godly man like that."

She didn't press further, knowing this topic was as much a thorn in her father's heart as the ongoing pain in Mamm's frail body.

Dat steered the conversation to the household sale at the Kings' place Saturday. "Would ya like to go along?"

Rose recalled what her cousins had said at the Singing about the pretty sets of dishes and all, as well as Linda Esh's mention at the quilting today. "That'd be right nice, Dat."

"Well, I'm sure you're still fillin' your hope chest, ain't?"

She smiled. *Ever thoughtful Dat.*

They talked of all the farm and mud sales coming up in early spring. One thing led to another and Dat mentioned the construction soon to begin on Gilbert Browning's new addition. He asked about Beth then, inquiring how she was doing since Mr. Browning's return from his father's funeral.

"Oh, you should see how happy she is over her grandma comin' to stay."

"Having Gilbert's mother around might just be the thing the Brownings need."

"Jah, I should think it'll help get Mr. Browning's mind off his wife's and father's passings," Rose said, truly praying that would be the case.

"Well, a man needs something to occupy his mind and his hands at such times."

His heart, too? Rose wondered. She had hoped Beth might tell her something more about the letter from Jane Keene, but Beth had been mum on the topic today.

"It's good he's got Beth to care for," Dat said. "Such a jewel of a girl."

"That she is. Beth told me yesterday she hasn't quit prayin' for Mamm." Rose said it quietly, aware of the stillness in the house.

Her father looked away, blinking his eyes. "I trust your dear Mamm will be greatly helped by the surgery. I've never seen her so hopeful."

Nodding in agreement, Rose waited while Dat finished his coffee. He used his fork to get the crumbs from the piecrust on his plate before leaning back in his chair, eyes closed, weary of the day.

Dat's eyes fluttered open after a time and he looked at Rose, a somber expression on his face. "I s'pose there's been no word from Nick lately."

The words jarred her. "Why . . . no, Dat." Nick had flown to the world. As far as she knew, he hadn't written to even Barbara Petersheim.

Then her heart stopped. Would her father admit to finding her letter to Nick in the battered tin box?

She held her breath, waiting.

He folded his arms across his chest, concern on his face. " 'Tis a real pity, the way things turned out."

"Does the bishop hold out hope for his return?"

"Never says. But what father gives up on a son?"

Rose was relieved; he wasn't probing about any lingering feelings she might have for Nick. "Anyone who knows the bishop would think Nick was mighty blessed to grow up in his home," she said, realizing just then that something had changed in her. She wasn't gritting her teeth or fighting back tears, and because of this, Rose assumed her heart was no longer tender toward her old friend . . . at least not as it had been. *Unwise to hang on to such a dream.*

"Aaron will be all right." Dat rose to carry his coffee cup to the sink. "He'll minister the way he did long before the divine lot fell on him, is my guess."

Her father's meaning was lost on her, but nothing more was said. The way Rose saw it, her brother Mose's kind invitation had come just at the right time. *Jah, in many ways, Sunday will be a brand-new day.*

CHAPTER 8

$\mathscr{B}$randon hadn't actually complained about his shoulder pain, but he had mentioned it in passing after supper. Not wishing to embarrass him but wanting to help ease his discomfort if possible, Hen went to stand behind his chair at the table and offered to massage his shoulder. "If it would help," she said.

"Thanks . . . great." He leaned back.

He'd often said he'd never turn down a massage from her. As she'd always done when rubbing his back and neck, Hen began gently, then worked deeper, kneading the area. "Too hard?" she asked, close enough to smell his shampoo.

He sighed, not speaking.

It wasn't easy being this near to him— the closest they'd been in months. While she massaged his shoulder, she daydreamed, recalling their newlywed days—of having teased him about wanting to take an occasional bath. And when he did, she would offer to shampoo his hair. From then on, whenever he was discouraged about his work or anything at all, Brandon would take a long soak in the tub and ask her to wash his hair. Something about having his scalp massaged made him relax, he said.

She smiled at the fond memory, wondering what he'd say about that now. But no, she couldn't . . . wouldn't. Her breath must've caught because he turned and asked if she'd said something.

"No," she replied as he leaned against her hands, the knots easing as she worked.

After a time, he sensed she was getting tired and reached up to pat her hand. "Thanks," he said. "You've done enough, Hen. I appreciate it."

"Glad to help." She stepped back, feeling sad somehow. Such wooden-sounding words compared to the tender ones back before things started to fall apart—before she'd changed her mind about living his English life.

He sat there silently while she moved away to the sink. Hen really wanted to inquire about all the time he was spending in town at the office—he'd gone in again today—but would not probe. Still, he was going to work more often now, and she was concerned he wasn't getting sufficient rest. The doctor had strongly urged him to take long naps, as well as to go to bed early at night—the best way to recover from the brain injury. At the time, Brandon had seemed willing to comply.

Brandon broke the silence. "Hen, I've made some plans."

She tensed at his serious tone.

"If my sight doesn't return soon, I'm thinking of visiting my parents in New York for the remainder of my recovery. I've already talked to them about it." He paused. "And about bringing Mattie Sue along. They could help look after her . . . she'd have her own bedroom."

"How long are you thinking?" Hen could hardly manage the words. But she knew it wasn't realistic for her to expect him to stay here with her and Mattie Sue forever.

"However long the blindness persists, I guess."

"And if your sight doesn't return?"

He drew a long breath. "Haven't gotten that far."

"Well, then, you can't take Mattie Sue out of state if you don't know when you're coming back . . . or if you are."

He ignored her. "I didn't want to just spring it on you. Besides, Mattie Sue would love it—and it would make things easier on you, as well."

Easier? His words fell like stones against her heart. *He's determined to do this.*

"Must you take our daughter?" She worked her jaw, realizing her hands were clenched.

"It wouldn't be a permanent arrangement."

"How can I know that, Brandon? You aren't being fair. How can you possibly think you are?"

He sighed. "That's why I hesitate to talk to you anymore. Things always deteriorate to this."

"To what?"

"This, Hen. What you just did."

Was it so wrong what she'd voiced? Was she not allowed to express her feelings, just as he did?

"You're finger-pointing," he said. "I'm weary of it."

"If that's what you think I'm doing, Brandon, you're wrong." She looked over at the settee, where Mattie Sue was sitting and playing with Wiggles next to her, oblivious to what was being said in the kitchen.

You can't even take care of yourself . . . how

can you expect to care for Mattie Sue for even a short time?

"As you may recall, Hen, we were in the process of filing divorce papers when the accident occurred."

The sting of his sarcasm! She did not say what she thought: that perhaps the head-on collision had happened to get his attention on what really mattered in life—faith, family, friends. That was too much even for her to say in the heat of an argument.

Besides, wasn't she equally at fault? After all, she had been the one to leave him to return to her Amish roots . . . but only at his insistence. *And when I left, I took Mattie Sue with me.* Oh, the whole thing was a disaster! They had both caused themselves this grief—made a mess of things.

"I refuse to fight with you any longer." Brandon got up from the table, favoring his right arm in its cast, and headed toward the staircase. He no longer inched along as he had the first few weeks; he knew his way around the little house. "It's early, but I'm calling it a night," he added.

"Daddy, aren't you gonna tell me a story?" called Mattie Sue.

She must've heard us, Hen worried.

"I'll spend extra time with you tomorrow, honey." His hand was on the banister.

"Your daddy's tired." Hen's voice trembled. *And very upset* . . .

"Good night, Mattie Sue. I'll see you in the morning," he said.

She came running over, followed by a yipping Wiggles. "It's too soon to go to bed, Daddy."

He leaned down to gently kiss her cheek. "I love you, sweetheart." He straightened. "Now, be good for Mommy, okay?"

"Can we go out to the barn again soon?" Mattie pleaded.

Hen intervened. "Let's see how Daddy feels tomorrow, sweetie."

Mattie Sue blinked, a frown crossing her brow. "I don't want you to leave. I don't—"

"Honey, Daddy needs to rest," Hen said, going to her daughter and taking her hand. "Come and show me your book."

Mattie Sue sniffled and looked over her shoulder as she went. "I want Daddy to stay here . . . with us."

Going to the sitting room with her daughter, Hen wondered what Brandon's attorney brother might be drawing up, without her knowledge. Even something temporary would involve her, wouldn't it? So why was she being kept in the dark?

Hen tried not to let Brandon's earlier comments spoil this time with Mattie Sue. She was mentally prepared in the event her daughter changed her mind and didn't want to be read to. But surprisingly, Mattie Sue settled right down with Hen for the story of her choosing. Hen opened the book and began to read the first page, struggling to keep her voice from cracking.

~

Rose Ann perused the fine china and other housewares at the Kings' Saturday moving sale. A half dozen tables were set up to display the many lovely items, some clearly antiques. Several cousins waved to her from the other side of the porch, where teacups and saucers and other pretty, colorful for-*gut* dishes were laid out. Enjoying herself, Rose wished Hen might've come today, too. Rose had even said something to Dat about inviting her. But Dat had felt it best for Hen to be with Brandon, particularly since Saturday was the only day Brandon stayed around much anymore. By that, Rose assumed Dat was concerned about the amount of time they were spending apart. She had noticed Brandon's business partner coming and going more often here lately, even on Sundays.

"Hullo, Rose Ann," a cheery voice called to her.

She turned to see Rebekah Bontrager

smiling broadly, wearing a plum-colored dress and matching apron. The color made her cheeks look peachier than usual. Rebekah had obviously sewn several new dresses for herself since she'd returned to be a mother's helper to Annie Mast and her identical twin babies, Mary and Anna. Anymore it felt as though Rebekah had never moved away to Indiana in the first place.

"*Wie bischt?*" Rebekah asked.

"Just fine . . . you?"

"Busier than ever. The babies are more wakeful now." Rebekah pushed one Kapp string back over her shoulder. "Annie and I really have our hands full."

"Does Annie's mother help some?"

Rebekah nodded. "And Annie's sisters come over quite often, too."

Rose wondered how long Rebekah would stay at Masts'. Would she remain there until her wedding to Silas next wedding season?

"Have ya seen any nice dishes—a service for, say, twenty or more?" asked Rebekah, changing the subject.

"Sure, there's plenty over there." Rose had contemplated two such patterns for the longest time but wasn't sure it was a good idea to stock up on a bunch of dishes when she might end up single. However, with the prospect of something happening tomorrow at Mose's, she wondered if she should've purchased the dainty blue, yellow, and green floral service for twenty-five that she'd admired. It was a pattern she had rarely seen and really liked. But purchasing it would be making a real leap of faith, for sure and for certain.

"Denki, Rose . . . I'll see ya later." Rebekah meandered past the glass saltshakers and candy dishes, the hem of her dress swishing as she went.

Returning to her browsing, Rose caught sight of a set of eight beautiful teacups and saucers. The bright red roses looked hand painted, which made her heart skip a beat. How she loved dishes, especially ones with brilliant hues. It occurred to her that these might cheer Mamm's heart after her surgery—plus her birthday was near Valentine's Day, a day Englischers celebrated with chocolates, fancy cards, and roses.

Rose opened her purse to see if she'd brought enough money. *I'll surprise Mamm,* she thought, picking up one of the dainty cups and carrying it to the youngest King girl, Martha King Esh. "Can you tell me anything about these?"

Though Martha had been married for two years, she was close to Rose's age. "They're awful perty, ain't so?" She smiled cheerfully.

"I've never seen anything quite like them."

"Can ya guess where this set came from?" asked Martha.

Rose shook her head.

"They were passed down in the family from the early settlement here—belonged to a distant cousin who left the Big Valley area. I'm sure you've heard of Yost Kauffman— maybe your own great-*Grossvadder*. Look on the back, and you'll see a date."

"Yost Kauffman was my great-uncle," Rose said. *So Martha and I are related in some distant way.* She looked on the underside of the cup and saw a faded date she couldn't make out: 1800-something. "Why would ya want to sell them?" she asked, thinking the price should be higher.

"All of us girls already have our own things from our weddings. And there's just too much here for *Mamma* to care about or keep up with, ya know. My father wants everything cleared out at this sale."

Rose wondered if the really bold color of the roses might be another reason. There were no other dishes this striking on display here.

"They're ever so delicate and nice for having tea." Martha smiled again. "Whether you're married or not."

Martha didn't mean any harm by her comment, but had Rose been in Martha's shoes, she would've been more tactful. At least she hoped so.

Rose turned the matching saucer in her hand, appreciating its beauty.

"Take your time deciding." Martha glanced over her shoulder at the many women streaming into the porch, all chatting and smiling and waving at kinfolk.

Rose noticed Rebekah standing over yonder, near the dishes Rose herself had admired earlier. She watched Rebekah to see if she was interested.

"Martha, I'll take the tea set . . . and possibly some more dishes, too," Rose said.

As Martha started to wrap one of the teacups in plain brown paper, Rose glanced again at the stack of dishes near Rebekah, wishing she hadn't pointed them out to Silas's girlfriend. Rose didn't feel envious, but she was curious what it was like to be Rebekah. Did she and Silas have a hope of a happy life together—just as Hen and Brandon had seemed to at the outset of their courtship? Years ago, when Hen had first met Brandon, Hen described the butterflies in her stomach whenever Brandon's eyes met hers. Rose had never forgotten the glow on Hen's face when she told her this. Nor had Rose herself forgotten the magnetic draw she had felt the times when Nick had surprised her by taking her into his arms.

She shook off the remembrance. No sense clinging to it.

Her thoughts returned to the present as, wonder of wonders, Rebekah moved away from the place settings Rose had her eye on. "Ach . . . sorry, Martha, just a minute." Rose made her way carefully past the long table to Rebekah Bontrager. "Aren't ya interested in that dish set?" she asked her.

"*Nee*—no, the color looks too faded."

Rose glanced at the dinner plate on top. "I think it's s'posed to be that way." She hesitated. "If ya don't mind, then, I'd like to buy them."

"Sure." Rebekah nodded. "Look them over carefully first for any cracks, though."

"*Gut Gedanke*—good thought."

"Nice seein' ya, Rose Ann."

"You too." Rose headed back to Martha, ready to pay for her new collection of dishes. *An investment in hope . . .*

CHAPTER 9

*R*ose's bedroom was situated toward the back of the house, away from the road. It was two rooms away from the largest bedroom in the house—the vacant one where her parents had slept prior to the mysterious market day accident that left Mamm paralyzed.

The pretty oak bookcase Dat had made for Rose stood at one end of the rectangular-shaped room. Rose liked to line up her library books there, sliding them into the middle shelf, spine out, pretending they were her very own collection. Each week, or at least every other week, she returned from the Quarryville library with yet another armload of historical romances—the very best kind of book, she'd decided some years ago.

This being the Lord's Day, she knew better than to indulge in reading fanciful writings, even though her mother no longer harped about it. Perhaps it was because Rose was of age and her hobbies were her own. Still, she knew Sundays were meant for the Lord. They were not for reading love stories, except those from the Bible.

Lying in bed, nestled amongst pillows and her warmest quilts, Rose wondered in her sleepiness if any future husband would care if she had the lovely bookshelf in their house. And not only that, but filled nicely with books on all five shelves. Would he?

Whoever he might be. She smiled hazily, her mind moving away from sleep. Had she become so lonely she would simply settle for whoever came along after Silas Good?

I can't let that happen. She threw off the covers and inched out of the comfortable bed. Swinging her legs over the side, she was glad for the rag rug that lay beneath her feet. She pushed her bare feet into her slippers, shivering in the dawn's early light as she ventured onto the cold floor.

Finding her bathrobe, she snuggled into its warmth and opened her top drawer to find her long johns. Rose was so chilled, she put them on under her nightgown, then headed down the stairs to the bathroom just off the kitchen. It hadn't struck her till just this minute that it was a no-Preaching Sunday. Right quick, she remembered her noontime plans with Mose and Ruthann. She was fairly certain the invitation had much to do with whatever fellow would be sitting across the table from her, but even if not, she could happily entertain herself with her little nephew and nieces. All under the age of five, Jonas, Barbara Ann, and Sally were sweet children.

Rose closed the bathroom door and began to run the bathwater, hoping her father wouldn't mind when he came to shave his upper lip later and discovered precious little hot water left. That had become a problem with Brandon's almost daily showering next door. Talk about having to make do with a spoonful of water! She laughed at her own joke, thinking now of Hen and the man she loved, living on the other side of this wall, trying to put things back to the way they had been before Mattie Sue was born.

Lately, Rose had seen glimpses of something between them—a measure of sweetness. With all of her heart, she hoped they would in time rediscover how much they cared for each other, if for no other reason than for Mattie Sue's sake. *And the Lord's,* Rose thought, splashing cold water on her face.

While she brushed her teeth at the sink, she wondered if the groundhog had seen his shadow and gone back to his burrow for six more weeks of winter. She smiled at the notion that a marmot could predict the end of the coldest season.

She finished her bath quickly, her excitement for the day taking her full attention now. Mose had also dropped a hint to Dat that Rose wasn't the only guest coming to dinner today, confirming her suspicions. But just who could it be?

Wouldn't Cousin Melvin call me silly for wondering? She knew without a doubt he would. But then, so would her old friend Nick. *Ach, for double sure!*

After Rose was dressed and had breakfast under way for her parents, she looked through her basket of finished dolls for market to find one or two for her nieces. She noticed one on which she'd purposely stitched a downturned mouth after hearing from Dat about Nick's going to college. Even now, she felt distressed when she thought of it, knowing the world had grabbed him and would never let him go.

Of course, she wouldn't think of taking the sad-faced doll along to give to Barbara Ann or Sally. Instead, she picked out two matching faceless dolls—twins, really. Of course, except for the color of their dresses, all the girl dolls she made looked quite alike.

After a breakfast of cornmeal mush and

tasty sausage, Rose washed and dried the dishes, then went in to read the Bible to Mamm, two chapters from Matthew that focused on some of the parables. Mamm especially liked the one about the kingdom of heaven being likened unto a treasure hidden in a field.

"God's treasures are our truest gifts," Mamm said in a near whisper. "Things not of this world."

Rose knew what her mother meant: gifts such as comfort, peace, joy, love . . . and healing. "Beth Browning told me she's still prayin' for you, Mamm."

Her mother's eyes welled up with tears. "What a dear young woman." Mamm wiped her eyes with a hankie.

Rose closed the Bible. "Beth seems wise beyond her years in some ways." *Like an old soul.*

"I'm glad you're still workin' over there, dear."

Rose was, too. "Well, I'd hate to lose touch after everything Beth's done for us. . . ."

"I need to close my eyes for a while," her mother said. Her face was pinched and her hands clenched, no doubt from pain.

"I'll let you be, Mamm." Rose placed the Good Book next to her mother's pillow, where she liked it.

"Have a nice time today," Mamm said

softly. "Your father told me 'bout Mose's plan . . . well, some of it."

Ah, so both her parents knew.

"Mammi Sylvia will be over to set out some bread and cold cuts. And I made some lime Jell-O, too," Rose told her mother.

"Your father will take you over to Mose and Ruthann's," Mamm said with a fleeting smile.

Playing along, Rose replied, "Awful *gut* of Dat." She leaned down to kiss Mamm's cheek and left the room, holding her breath and wondering why.

~

Hen had been reading a Bible storybook to Mattie Sue when the knock came at the back door. She looked up and was surprised to see their neighbor Aaron.

Is he coming to visit Brandon?

She placed the book on Mattie's lap and rose to answer the door. "Welcome, Bishop . . . come inside and get warm."

Aaron nodded his thanks and removed his black hat, hanging it on a nearby hook. He glanced about, then smiled at Mattie Sue, who still sat in the small adjoining room with her puppy dog. "Is your husband resting?" he asked Hen.

"At the moment."

"Well, I don't mean to be a bother." The bishop reached again for his hat and was about to put it back on.

"No . . . I think Brandon would be pleased to know you're here." Hen offered him some hot coffee and a sticky bun, which put a smile on Aaron's wrinkled face as he moved toward the table.

Hen poured coffee for him, then placed the plate of cinnamon rolls on the table. "There you are." She excused herself to go upstairs and found Brandon sitting on the side of his bed, looking as if he'd had a good nap. Waiting in the doorway until she knew he was fully alert, she saw that he needed a shave under his neck. For the most part he had been doing a pretty good job with a razor and shaving cream, purely by feel. She hadn't offered to help him, although she'd thought of it several times.

"Hen, I know you're standing there."

"Wondered if you felt up to having a visit with Bishop Aaron."

Brandon raised his head. "Didn't hear him come in."

"Jah, he's sitting at the table having coffee."

"Tell him I'll be right down."

"Sure." She turned to go.

"Hen . . . thanks for letting me know."

"Of course." She turned back toward him.

"Is my comb nearby?" he asked.

She spied it on the dresser and went to retrieve it for him, curious whether there was something more on his mind. She returned to the bed and placed the comb in his hand. "I'll tell him you're getting up."

"Thanks."

She hurried back downstairs in time to see Mattie Sue put Wiggles in the bishop's lap. "Brandon will be down in a minute," she announced as she went to pour coffee for herself and her husband.

"How's he feelin'?" Aaron asked, petting the cocker spaniel with callused hands.

"His arm and ribs are healing, but he still can't see."

"Well, resting's mighty *gut*."

"The doctor says so."

Mattie Sue moved closer to the table. "Daddy's starting to like the farm," she said.

"Jah. Just takes some getting used to," Aaron said.

Mattie Sue looked ever so solemn.

"Now, honey-girl, don't be frettin', all right?" Aaron winked at her. "The Lord cares 'bout your daddy. Don't ya forget, now."

Mattie Sue's face broke into a thoughtful smile.

The puppy jumped down from Aaron's

lap and followed Mattie Sue back to the front room, where the two of them cuddled and played.

When Brandon came downstairs, he shook Aaron's hand and apologized for keeping him waiting. But Aaron wouldn't hear of it. "I'm the one pokin' my head in on ya," he said.

Hen put the sugar bowl on the table right where she always did, so Brandon knew where to reach for it. Then she motioned for Mattie Sue to go upstairs with her, so the men could talk privately on this most beautiful Lord's Day morning.

CHAPTER 10

On the way to Mose and Ruthann's late that morning, Rose and her father passed Deacon Samuel Esh's farm, prompting Rose to ask about the vacancy their former bishop's silencing had left in their church district. Her father explained that another bishop—Bishop Simon Peachey, from this side of Bart—had been appointed by Old Ezekiel, the oldest bishop in the county. "He'll oversee our district for the next six months."

Six months . . .

"What'll happen then?"

"Aaron's ordination will be lifted."

"Completely taken away?"

Dat was quiet for a time. "Certain higher-ups evidently had their say-so." He glanced her way, a solemn look on his face.

"And nothing can keep that from happening?"

"Short of a miracle, no."

Rose knew little about the inner workings of the ministerial brethren. But she knew how much stock her father had always put in Aaron Petersheim. "It's not like he's sinned or is being punished. Or has he been set up as an example?"

"I can't be certain."

Rose didn't want to press further, not as hurtful as all this had been. Besides, Dat was under enough stress with Mamm facing surgery. He wore the concern on his face, even though he continually trusted the Lord for all things pertaining to his family. Mamm was his beloved wife and longtime sweetheart. If things went awry and she was left worse off, Dat would surely blame himself.

"En Sinn un en Schand," he said, referring to Aaron's possible ousting.

"We can still pray," she said. "For God to rule . . . and overrule before August first."

"Ach, ya must never put time limits on the Lord," Dat admonished her. "Leave things to His will."

When they arrived at Mose's, another family buggy was parked at the side of the house. Rose wasn't sure who else had come, but Dat seemed to recognize the horse as one of the Millers'.

"Which Miller?" There were so many in the area.

"Arie's father."

Hen's best friend's father . . .

Rose thanked him for the ride, saying she'd get a ride home with Mose later. Dat grinned at that. "I'll see ya later, then."

"All right," she said, suddenly feeling a bit shy. Was she truly ready to meet someone new?

Making haste to the back door, she found Leah Miller in the kitchen playing with Ruthann's youngest, eighteen-month-old Sally, while Leah's mother, Ruth, talked with Ruthann near the cookstove before waving her good-bye. "Hullo," they all greeted Rose. Looking happier than she had since her beau Christian's death, Leah carried curly-haired Sally over to Rose.

"How've ya been?" Leah asked Rose, bending to rub noses with little Sally.

"Just fine . . . and you?"

"Oh, busy helpin' Mamma mend and sew."

"Awful nice of Mose and Ruthann to invite us, ain't?" Rose said, smiling as Sally played with Leah's Kapp strings.

"Heard there might be another guest comin'," Leah whispered.

Rose didn't make a peep. Just as she'd thought, this was not going to be a normal family gathering.

"Seems your brother and wife are bent on matchmaking."

Do they feel sorry for us? It was the first they'd ever attempted such a thing. Regardless, it seemed unfitting for Mose to invite two single girls and only *one* fellow!

~

Hen was aware of the ebb and flow of conversation downstairs, but she couldn't make out what was being said. Brandon and Aaron seemed to be getting along agreeably, even laughing occasionally—something quite remarkable.

"Mommy, why's Daddy goin' to New York?" Mattie Sue asked out of the blue. They had been sitting on Hen's bed while Mattie Sue played with Wiggles and Hen read her Bible.

"Your grandpa and grandma Orringer live in New York."

Mattie Sue frowned. "I wish he'd stay here . . . with us." She cuddled Wiggles next to her face.

"I know, honey." Hen tickled Mattie Sue

under her chin. Wiggles began licking her finger and Mattie let out a stream of laughter.

"Wiggles wants to stay with us, Mommy."

"The puppy told you?" Hen kissed Mattie Sue's cheek, laughing softly.

Mattie Sue looked up at her with trusting eyes. Then she surprised her and said, "Beth prays about everything, doesn't she?"

"I think you might be right."

"Well, then, I want to pray like that, too." Mattie Sue got down on her knees beside the bed, bowed her head, and folded her hands. Wiggles licked her cheek and Mattie Sue giggled the start of her prayer.

"Now, honey. Why don't you wait till you're more serious?"

"Dawdi Sol says God can see inside my heart, so He knows what I'm going to say, jah?"

As a child, Hen had been taught the importance of being reverent while praying. "Still, it's best to pray when Wiggles isn't making you laugh," she urged.

Mattie Sue rose, gathered Wiggles into her arms, and carried him off to her own bedroom. She closed the door and returned to Hen's room empty-handed. Smiling at her, Hen opened her arms and held her near. "We must always trust the Lord. He knows our hearts . . . and does all things well, according to His plan and purpose."

Mattie Sue's face shone with joy. "Then will Daddy see again soon?"

"The doctor believes so."

Mattie Sue stayed nestled in her arms. *Dear little girl, so in need of reassurance.* "God loves Daddy," whispered Hen. "Never forget, honey."

Brandon raised a brow when Hen returned to the kitchen with Mattie Sue in tow. The bishop had left for home, and Hen was curious about how the visit had gone. But her very presence in the kitchen seemed to annoy her husband.

She went to the table and stood near his chair. "Would you like some more coffee?"

"I'm fine, thanks."

"All right."

As he continued to sit there, she made some fruit salad for the noon meal. Glancing over her shoulder, she asked if he was all right. "Can I get you anything to snack on, maybe?"

"Not now, thanks."

He was clearly deep in thought; if only she knew how to ease his anxiety. What had he and the bishop discussed?

Mattie Sue went over and leaned her head against Brandon's good arm. "I'll read to you,

Daddy," she said. "Would that make you feel better?"

"No, honey. Not now."

"Later on?" she asked.

He kissed her forehead. "Maybe."

Hen watched the scene play out before her. Mattie Sue clearly felt rejected, yet she tried to be a big girl and not complain or whine. Their daughter had come a long way since Hen had worked with her on obedience and respect for elders . . . parents, especially.

Brandon leaned his good elbow on the table, wiping his eyes as Mattie Sue left the room.

Hen finished making the fruit salad and pressed down on the lid till she heard it snap. Then, nearly tiptoeing, she went to stand beside her husband. She placed her hand on his shoulder without speaking.

She felt ever so awkward. "I'm here if you want to talk." She didn't wait for his reply but turned to go with Mattie Sue into the sitting room to read to her. All the while, Hen kept glancing over at her poor husband, who looked more distraught than ever.

～

Rose enjoyed giving Barbara Ann and Sally their little dolls, tickled to see their eyes sparkle with joy. "Denki," Barbara Ann said in her tiny voice, and Sally tried to do the same. Rose received a wet kiss on the cheek from both girls.

Afterward, Rose entertained four-year-old Jonas in the sitting room near her sister-in-law's kitchen. He was inquisitive, much like Mattie Sue, who was the same age. She and Jonas were enjoying a game of checkers when Rose heard the back door open and Mose's voice. She kept playing, even though she wanted to gawk to see who'd come. *Be calm, Rosie . . . this fellow, whoever he is, will probably like Leah Miller anyway.* At any rate, she planned to let Leah have all of the attention. After all, the poor girl had suffered terribly, losing her beau to death.

In a few minutes, Ruthann came into the room. "*Kumme,* the meal's all ready."

Just that quick, Jonas abandoned the game and hurried to the kitchen. Feeling quite nervous, Rose followed him to the sink, where she helped him reach the towel to dry his hands.

When she turned toward the table, Rose realized there wasn't one but *two* young men seated across from Leah. Tall, dark-headed, and blue-eyed, they looked enough alike to be twins. Upon second glance, Rose was sure they were exactly that!

By the time she was seated on the wooden bench next to Leah, it was time for the table blessing. Mose bowed his head and they joined in the silent prayer till Mose made a little cough to signal the end of the prayer.

Without delay, Mose introduced Rose and Leah to the fellows. Then he said, "We're glad to have Ruthann's twin cousins visiting from Bart—Isaac and Jacob Ebersol."

So Rose's hunch was correct, although it was apparent by the shape of their faces they were not identical. And Isaac's eyes were a lighter blue than Jacob's.

"Nice to meet yous, Leah and Rose Ann," Isaac said first, quickly adding, "My friends call me Ike."

"Our mother still calls him Isaac, though," Jacob said, his winning smile directed at Leah. "And I'm mostly Jake."

Rose wasn't sure what to think, but Leah glanced at her, as if quite pleased.

The children were quiet, and it amused Rose that even young Jonas was smart enough to sense something was up. He kept looking first at Isaac, then at Rose . . . then at Jake, and over at Leah. She wondered what sort of prompting Mose had given Jonas.

As they passed the serving dishes, Mose took the lead, asking questions to encourage conversation between the four young people. It felt awkward but not as bad as Rose had feared, and the young men were polite and respectful. During the course of the meal, Rose learned that the brothers were twenty-one, regular attenders of their local Amish church, and gainfully employed. Isaac worked for an English farmer down the road from his father's house, and Jacob was in partnership with his father, raising tobacco.

Discreetly, Rose observed Isaac, then Jake, wondering which fellow, if either, she found appealing. It was too soon to tell, of course, but she couldn't help wondering if Leah was doing the same. Which brother did she like? After all, what if they happened to like the same one? And what if Isaac liked Leah, but Leah preferred Jacob?

Ach, what a pickle indeed, if it comes to that!

It wasn't until after the meal, when the twins asked Leah and Rose to go riding with them, that Isaac mentioned having twelve siblings, including another younger set of twin sisters. *Thirteen children!* She'd known other large families, but none quite so large as the Ebersol twins' extended family—their church district was made up of nearly all first cousins.

"Every courting-age girl in our church is somehow related to us," Isaac said, holding the reins.

Rose understood now why Mose and Ruthann had invited her and Leah to meet these fine young men.

"Do ya like ice cream, Rose?" asked Isaac, his eyes twinkling. He seemed to have the livelier personality of the two.

"Oh jah, we make it all the time." She was conscious of Leah and Jacob in the second seat behind them as they rode.

"Even in the winter?" asked Isaac.

"Why, sure, don't you?"

Leah tittered under her breath and poked Rose gently. *She must think I like him,* thought Rose, not giving Leah the satisfaction of turning around.

"We wait till spring to make it," Isaac said, glancing back at Jacob, who nodded.

"The ice cream maker tends to freeze up in the winter." Isaac chuckled at his own joke.

Leah laughed softly, but Rose wasn't sure if Isaac was kidding or not. She sat quietly, thankful the young men had brought their two-seater family carriage, instead of a cramped courting buggy.

"We could get some ice cream some-where," Isaac suggested.

"Ach, but not on Sunday!" Jacob replied.

Rose turned, giving Leah a surprised look.

"It's the Lord's Day," Jacob reminded his brother. "Isaac just forgot."

Neither Leah nor Rose said a word.

"Another time, maybe?" Jacob suggested quickly.

Rose wondered if this was their way of lining up another date with her and Leah.

"Jah. . . *gut* idea, brother." Isaac urged the horse faster. "Only next time, we'll bring two buggies, ain't?"

Rose felt her cheeks blush in spite of the cold. In so many words, Isaac was asking on behalf of both of them. She smiled at Leah, who seemed right happy next to Jacob in the second seat. And by the time they said good-bye to Leah, whom Jacob walked partway up the lane, Rose realized that he had chosen Leah.

"A nice pair, jah?" Isaac said, turning to face Rose.

"Seems so."

He was quiet awhile. Then, as if gathering the nerve, Isaac said at last, "What about you and me goin' riding sometime together? Would that suit ya?"

She liked him well enough, not only because he had a good sense of humor, but also for his confidence. She was relieved the day was turning out so nicely. "That'd be right fine," she said, wanting to know him better.

"Next Saturday evening?"

"Jah, Saturday," she replied.

His face broke into a grin. "*Gut,* then."

Rose couldn't help smiling in return as

they waited for Jacob to hop back into the buggy. *Dat would like Isaac, I'm sure of it.* Then, reprimanding herself for jumping too far ahead, Rose settled back in the seat, very glad Jacob had chosen Leah.

CHAPTER 11

*H*en had tried hard to be pleasant when Bruce Kramer came to the back door hours earlier, asking for Brandon. Now it was late afternoon and Brandon and Bruce were still gone. Her mind raced: Was her husband actually going to put their pretty house up for sale? Was he also finalizing plans to visit his parents in upstate New York? *Taking Mattie Sue along?*

Pondering the latter, she felt she must have some legal recourse. But she remembered what had happened the last time she'd gone to an attorney's office to fill out forms, though at Brandon's request. Her husband had been involved in a terrible accident!

Was God trying to tell me something? For weeks now, she'd asked herself that, as well as whether the Lord was trying to get Brandon's attention, too. They'd both lived so selfishly.

Mattie Sue was stirring over on the settee as she awakened from her nap. "Mommy, can we go an' see Aendi Rose?" she asked, rubbing her eyes.

"Rosie's visiting Uncle Mose and Aunt Ruthann today, honey."

Mattie Sue seemed to consider that for a moment, then asked if they could visit Hen's grandparents instead. Hen had seen two buggies parked next door and wondered which relatives had stopped by. "That'd be nice, sure. But you need to walk the dog first."

"Okay, Mommy." Mattie Sue put on her warm coat and tied on her outer bonnet. She took the leash off the hook nearby and Wiggles came running. "Here, boy . . . time for you to go out."

While Mattie and the puppy were outdoors, Hen thought of leaving a note on the door for Bruce to read to Brandon, if he should arrive before they returned. She watched Mattie Sue follow Wiggles, remembering how she'd yearned for a rural setting like this— with her daughter enjoying the farmland surroundings. Never, though, did she imagine Brandon would purchase the puppy Mattie Sue had begged for.

Hen pulled on her woolen shawl and found

her black bonnet, which exactly matched Mattie's smaller one. *Will she follow the Lord in holy baptism when the time comes?* But Hen knew it was impossible to project too far into the future. Not the way things were now.

In a few minutes, when Mattie Sue returned with Wiggles, she asked, "Will Daddy know where we are?"

"I wondered the same thing. You're very thoughtful, honey." She picked up the note and waved it, laughing.

"I'm just like you." Mattie Sue smiled up at her.

Would Brandon think so? Hen thought with a start. *Have I been kind enough to my husband?* She hadn't considered this back when she was so determined to work at the fabric shop against his wishes. Had she ever really taken into consideration his feelings these recent months, English as he was?

"Let's go!" Mattie Sue said, glancing over her shoulder at Wiggles, who'd already settled down near the warm cookstove.

Hen could hardly wait to fill her lungs with fresh, clean air as they followed the snow-swept sidewalk to Hen's grandparents' little house around the back. The day was crisp and cold, and Hen wished they'd had Preaching service today. With Brandon away, the house felt much too quiet.

When Hen and Mattie Sue arrived at Dawdi Jeremiah's, Hen discovered four of her mother's older cousins—two couples—and several of their own great-grandchildren there visiting, all of them dressed as if for church. They smiled their delight at seeing her and Mattie Sue—the children ran over to greet Mattie, even though they'd never met her before. The older folk sat in a semicircle in the kitchen near the cookstove with Dawdi Jeremiah and Mammi Sylvia, also wearing their best clothes. Several of the cousins mentioned how big Mattie Sue was getting, but as was true to their way, no one remarked on how pretty she was.

"We've been makin' the rounds this afternoon—saw Aaron and Barbara . . . then stopped in to see your parents awhile," plump and rosy-cheeked Annie Kauffman said. She was one of Mamm's many first cousins. "We were planning to drop by and see you next, Hen . . . and here you both are!" Annie's blue eyes twinkled.

There was not a hint of curiosity from any of them regarding Brandon's whereabouts. Hen's father must have mentioned Brandon had gone to town, like he did most Sundays. Still, Hen felt no sense of judgment from them, and she was grateful for that. It was hard enough knowing her husband had no interest in keeping the day holy.

"Aaron and Barbara are expecting another grandbaby come spring," Annie's sister Nancy announced.

"Verna?" asked Hen.

"No, one of the twins—Anna."

She's two years younger than I am. Hen spotted Mattie Sue with one of the toddler girls, Becky Mae, who was babbling away in Deitsch where she sat under the kitchen table. The two were tapping spoons to their hearts' delight.

Hen watched Mattie Sue playing so sweetly with the tiny tyke and, just that quick, tears sprang to her eyes. Goodness, she didn't even know why.

~

After an hour-long visit, Hen and Mattie Sue returned to the house. Brandon still had not arrived, so she set about making potato salad. She'd cooked the potatoes yesterday, just as Mammi Sylvia and Mamm had always done, cooking ahead for the Lord's Day. After that, she sliced cold roast beef for sandwiches, hoping Brandon might be home in time for supper.

She had just finished cutting up home-made dill pickles for the sandwiches when she spied Rose Ann at the back door and waved her inside. "We were about to sit down for a bite to eat. Would ya like to join us?"

Rose glanced about, as if noticing Brandon wasn't home. "Why, sure, I'll stay an' eat with you." She opened her arms for Mattie Sue, who came running over. "I've missed seein' ya."

"Me too," Mattie Sue said. "And I miss Beth, too."

"Well, Beth's grandmother is prob'ly getting settled in over there," Rose explained. "Maybe Beth can visit after some days pass. Would you like that?"

Mattie Sue lit up. "We can go in the pony cart again once the snow's all gone."

Rose laughed. "Well, that might not be for a long time yet."

Hen was nodding. "Ain't that the truth!"

They sat down together and prayed the silent prayer, then began to eat. Hen couldn't help noticing the sparkle in Rose's eyes. Mom had told Hen privately that Mose and Ruthann were "definitely planning something" with two fellows for Rose and her friend Leah Miller today. And there was no doubt in Hen's mind that whatever Mose had had up his sleeve proved to make Rosie happy. *Will she tell me about it?* Since Brandon's arrival,

Hen hadn't been as available to Rose for sisterly talks.

"Will ya play dolls with me after supper, Aendi Rosie?" asked Mattie Sue.

"After your Mamma and I do the dishes." Rose locked eyes with Hen, which confirmed that she'd come for more than just the meal. For that, Hen was ever so glad.

As soon as Hen drew the water and swished the dish soap around, Rose began to share about her visit to Mose and Ruthann's. "I met someone today." Her voice was soft at first.

"Anyone I know?" Hen smiled, knowing her sister most likely wouldn't reveal his identity.

Rose looked toward Mattie Sue, who was presently occupied in the sitting room. "I'll only say that he's not from round here."

"Out of state?"

"Well, no. But not from our church district."

"A town nearby?"

Rose nodded. "A forty-minute buggy ride."

"Will ya write letters, then?"

"We haven't even had our first date yet, Hen."

"Sorry . . . guess I got ahead of myself."

Rose laughed quietly. "Better slow down, or you'll have me married next thing."

"So, you *really* like this fella?"

"I wouldn't be tellin' you if I didn't." Rose smiled at her. "And you'll keep it mum, jah?"

"Cross my heart." Hen looked at her. "Now you're blushing, Rosie."

"I 'spect I am."

"When will you see him again?"

"He wants to take me ridin' next weekend." Rose picked up another plate and dried it. "I've said yes, but the youth in our church district will wonder if I don't go to Singing—on Sunday."

Hen nodded. "Prob'ly so . . . but they'll just have to wonder, ain't?"

"Oh," she groaned. "I hope I'm doin' the right thing."

"Well, if you're not . . . I don't know who is." Hen meant it.

"I don't want to displease the Lord . . . or Dat and Mamm."

"As long as you're thinking that way, you'll be fine." She wondered if Rose was still brooding over Nick. Oh, she hoped not!

"It's not too soon to be courted by someone new, is it?" asked Rose.

"Well, that depends how you parted with your former beau," Hen suggested.

"The feelings were mutual, believe me."

"Well, then, you could pray about it."

"I do every day."

"And so do I—for you! But I'm talking about praying for God's choice in a mate—such an important decision." *As if I should be talking* . . .

They finished up the dishes in no time, and Rose hung the tea towel to dry. "How's Brandon doin' since he went to the doctor last?"

"Between you and me, I think he's become pretty frustrated. For a while there, he was starting to see shadows and glimpses of light."

"And now?"

"Only taunting flickers." Hen sighed. It was so hard to talk about this, even with her sister. "I just wish he'd rest more. It really worries me."

Rose seemed to hesitate, then asked, "What if he's blind forever?"

"I'm sure he fears that. It must be driving him nearly crazy."

"It would anyone."

Hen reached to embrace Rose. "Each and every morning, I wake up hoping this is the day he'll see again. It just breaks my heart."

"I pray for that, too. Even though it would change everything for you and Mattie Sue, ain't so?" Rose stepped back, still holding

Hen's arms. She glanced out the window. "Ach, someone's here. Must be Brandon."

Hen looked to see Bruce's car pulling up.

"Daddy's home!" Mattie Sue went running to the door, Wiggles right behind her, barking and wagging his little tail.

Hen clasped Rose's hand as she watched her daughter. "She loves him so much," she whispered.

"Ain't hard to see that." Rose's eyes softened and held her gaze. "What about you, sister?"

The question took Hen off guard. She paused a moment and realized the truth: She *did* love her husband. She'd never stopped. "Jah, I love him, Rosie. I truly do."

"Oh, Hen. I feel for ya . . . honestly." Rose kissed her cheek and went to grab her shawl. "I'll be seein' ya," she called, rushing to get out the door before Brandon entered.

"Come again soon."

Rose said she would and waved good-bye.

Hen put on a cheery face as she heard two sets of footsteps and Brandon's voice outside. "Thanks for your help," she heard him tell Bruce.

Her husband managed to get inside without Bruce's assistance. Mattie Sue greeted him, hanging on to his strong arm as she guided him into the kitchen. Hen had heard somewhere that when one aspect of the senses was hampered, the others were heightened, but she didn't know if that was true for Brandon.

Mattie Sue helped him remove his coat and scarf, jabbering about visiting Mommy's grandparents and meeting a new little cousin named Becky Mae. "She was teeny tiny, Daddy, but she could talk Amish even better than me. Can you imagine that?"

"She doesn't know any different, right?" he replied.

Mattie Sue continued, still talking about little Becky Mae while Brandon smiled. Hen, too, was eager to go and welcome him home, but try as she might, something held her back.

CHAPTER 12

*H*en had risen before dawn, wanting some time alone. She'd read several psalms before praying once more for her husband's sight to be restored, no matter the eventual consequences for her and Mattie Sue.

In the stillness of her room as Brandon slept in the spare room down the hall, she shared her frustrations with God—and her worries and fears. Leaving Brandon and coming to live here hadn't been the wisest thing she'd done. Hen knew that. But now that she was quite thoroughly enmeshed again in the Old Ways, she was no more ready to abandon them and simply walk away.

"Please lead me on the right path, dear Lord," Hen prayed as she did each and every day. "And create in me a pure heart before you."

~

After breakfast Monday, Solomon trudged through the snow on Salem Road, bypassing his usual shortcut to Bishop Aaron's house by way of the back meadow. Like Rose—and Emma, too—he would always think of his kindhearted neighbor and friend as Bishop. In his thinking, nothing had changed.

Breathing in the icy air, Sol was glad for the brim of his black felt hat as the snow fell in heavy flakes, sticking to his old work coat. The silence around him was uncanny. When he set out walking this stretch any other season, the air was filled with the chirping and buzzing of birds and insects. Now the only sound was his boots crunching against the snow as he watched thousands of white flecks descend the sky and cover the landscape.

Deep winter—such weather for Emma's surgery. Sol wondered if the ice and snow would impede their travel to York. Of course, plenty could change between now and next Thursday, that was certain. He'd lived long enough to know that things were constantly changing—for both good and bad.

When he arrived at the bishop's, Barbara was reading her Bible in the corner of the kitchen, wrapped in an afghan. Aaron, too, was reading, but Sol couldn't quite make out what. Most likely it was the *Farm Journal,* with its listings of upcoming auctions and whatnot.

"Mornin', Aaron . . . Barbara," he said after knocking lightly on the back door and being told to "Kumme in."

Aaron knew why he was there and proceeded with him to the kitchen table, where Sol showed him the building permit, then laid out the approved plans for Gilbert Browning's addition.

"We can get goin' on this first thing tomorrow." Sol filled him in on Gilbert's mother's recent move there. "She and the family will get cramped mighty quick, I daresay."

"I've already talked to several young men from the church," Aaron said. "We'll make fast work of it, ain't?"

"That we will," Sol agreed. He was looking forward to working alongside his friend and other menfolk. "Oh, and I'll be with Emma on Thursday, when she has her surgery, then back and forth to York for quite a few days. We'll just have to see how things go."

"There'll be plenty of prayers goin' up for her that day and onward," Barbara said from the corner of the kitchen.

"Denki," Sol replied. "Means a lot." He added, "And Emma wants yous to come over for a meal before then. I'd like that, too."

"Why, sure . . . but only if we can bring along some food," Barbara piped up again.

Sol knew they'd be helping out some with meals later on, as well, once Emma was released from the hospital and home from rehabilitation. "We miss your spiritual wisdom, Aaron."

His friend said nothing to that, but Barbara said several families wanted to gather with him for just that reason. "They've asked him to preach or teach privately. Nearly like a Sunday school—like some do out in Ohio and Indiana . . . in places."

This was the first Sol had heard of it. "I can see wanting that. But be careful, lest those who silenced ya in the first place oust you altogether."

Aaron's meek countenance said it before he did. "Oh, there'll be no secret Bible studies. Except maybe another one with your son-in-law."

This surprised Sol. "You mean Brandon's open to talking 'bout Scripture?"

"Seems to be. 'Course now, remember that even the apostle Paul had to be struck down blind before he'd bend his knee."

At Aaron's offhand description, Barbara let out a little disapproving gasp. Other than back when Nick and Christian were at odds, Sol hadn't heard Aaron talk so.

"Hen's husband is full up with questions," Aaron added. "Has nothing to draw on spiritually."

Sol suspected as much. "No church affiliation, then?"

Aaron pursed his mouth. "I suggest ya pray for him. He's struggling as any of us would be, searching for meaning in all this."

"Denki for takin' time to help him," Sol said. "And we do pray."

"I sometimes wonder if the Lord is permitting this silencing for a larger purpose . . . as something He's using to draw Brandon to experience the mercy and grace of our Lord."

Something good will come of it, Sol thought.

They were silent for a moment as Sol refolded the blueprints. "Why don't you come for supper tomorrow night?"

"Are ya sure?" Barbara asked.

"Rose and Sylvia will do the cookin'—no need to bring anything."

Barbara smiled secretively, and Sol guessed she'd do as she pleased, which more than likely meant a pineapple upside-down cake was in his near future!

~

Mattie Sue scampered to the barn to help Hen's brother Joshua feed the calves while Hen and Brandon remained at the table. Unlike other days, they'd lingered over a breakfast of bacon, eggs, and homemade waffles . . . the latter at Mattie's request. Hen wasn't accustomed to making so much to eat in the morning, but because they'd gotten a later start than usual, it seemed like a good idea. Especially because Mattie Sue was so eager for her daddy to "eat like an Amish farmer." Both Hen and Brandon had erupted in a good laugh at this.

Presently, Hen offered Brandon another cup of coffee. He stirred it and waited for it to cool. "I plan to stay home to rest most of this week," he told her.

This was a relief, but it surprised Hen.

"I've been pushing it and need to follow the doctor's advice if I'm ever going to get better," Brandon admitted.

She agreed, glad he was willing.

Sitting there, he began to talk about Aaron's latest visit, mentioning that the bishop had some upcoming building on his mind. "I didn't realize this before, but I guess the Amish really can—and do—raise a barn in a single day. That's right up my alley."

"It *is* amazing," she replied as she reached for her own coffee. "So Aaron's sounding chipper as ever—just as I remember. For all the years I've known him, I have never heard him speak a negative word."

"I still don't know how he does it, staying optimistic with things as they are."

"So you must've talked further on this?"

Brandon sighed and she waited for him to reply.

"Like he said before, he's thankful for the opportunity to trust God and believes he has no right to question." Brandon rested his left hand on his right, fingering the hard cast. "He also insists my blindness is part of God's plan. Which, of course, is nuts."

"Aaron lives his life in accordance with the Good Book," Hen replied softly.

Brandon blinked and squinted, as if struggling to see again. "Well, that's pretty messed up, if you think about it."

"Not if you accept Scripture as truth."

He chuckled offhandedly. "Aaron actually quoted a verse from the Old Testament about that."

"Was it this? 'O Lord, I know that the way of man is not in himself: it is not in man that walketh to direct his steps.'"

"Yes, that's the one." He ran his hand over his stubbled chin. "He honestly believes that the lousy things that happen are God's will. That God allows bad things to happen."

"The sovereignty of God," Hen said softly.

"Call it whatever you want. The way I see it, Aaron's in denial about his situation—that ridiculous silencing. He's going to crack, you'll see. Just like I'm going to if I don't get my sight back soon."

Hen bit her lip to prevent a retort from escaping. *Best just to let him vent.*

Brandon squinted again, as if trying desperately to break through the thick veil that blanketed his sight. "My whole life has been turned inside out. I can't get a grip on anything." His voice broke with emotion and he fell silent.

Getting up, she quickly went to him and wrapped her arms around him. He leaned his head against hers for the longest time, and if she wasn't mistaken, he was silently weeping. "Even though we accept the providence of God, that doesn't mean we can't pray," Hen ventured. "I know that Aaron's praying for you. All of us are."

"Much good it's done."

"That's where trust comes in." She released him, standing near.

"We have to accept whatever happens as God's will, right?"

She swallowed hard. "I realize this must be terribly hard for you."

"Hen?" Brandon raised his head.

"I'm here." She looked at him, and for just a moment his manner was so vulnerable, even tentative, she could scarcely remember his former arrogance. She rested her hand on his good arm.

"I appreciate that . . . more than you know."

She hadn't ever expected to hear this and didn't know how to respond. Wiping back tears, she said nothing.

"Are you crying?" He turned to face her. "You are, aren't you?"

She didn't want to admit it. After all they'd been through, Hen still didn't want to let her guard down and show him her helpless side. "I'll be all right . . . really."

He held out his hand. "I can't do this alone, Hen."

"You don't have to."

"But I don't want to keep putting you out like this. It's not fair. You have your life here."

Not without you and Mattie Sue, she thought, pulling away. "I'll be fine, really."

"Right." He sighed. "Because *you* can see to drive and move about at will. Yes, I'm sure you'll be fine even if my nightmare never ends." His tone had abruptly changed.

Another silent moment passed. At last, Hen voiced the question whose answer she dreaded. "How soon will you go to New York?"

"Not before your mother's surgery," he

said. "I won't leave until you know the outcome."

"Thanks, Brandon—that's kind of you."

"Will you go to the hospital with your
mother?" he asked.

"All of us are going. Well, most of us."
She explained that her grandparents would
stay behind. "Maybe they can watch Mattie
Sue that day."

"How will everyone get there?"

"Dad's already lined up a good-sized van.
Maybe we'll need another one, if the bishop
comes along . . . and he just might."

Brandon nodded. "I suppose I'd want to
have a man like Aaron around if someone was
operating on *my* back."

She stared at him, surprised at his remark.

"I'd like to go with you to the hospital,"
he said suddenly.

"Oh, Brandon . . . honestly?" She lost it
then, letting the tears flow.

"Yeah, I'd like to cheer your mom on
somehow . . . I guess being there is the best
I can do."

She nodded silently, unable to speak.

"You all right?"

Hen squeezed his hand and tried not to
sniffle.

"From what your mother's told me, this

surgery is very serious. There's a tremendous amount of risk involved."

"Jah," Hen managed to say. She gathered herself and blew her nose. "I never thought I'd—"

"Shh," he said. "You don't have to say it." He reached for his coffee cup.

"I wouldn't have asked you to go along, Brandon."

He sipped his coffee, then stopped and blinked his eyes repeatedly.

"Are you seeing something?"

"For a second, there were some streaks of light."

"And now?"

"Gone again."

Hen felt sure Brandon's sight would come back if he rested consistently. "Why not lie down now and relax for a while?"

He agreed. "After that, I'd like to go over and visit your mother if she's up."

"I'm sure she'd enjoy that."

He nodded. "So would I."

Hen waited to clear the table until he'd finished his coffee. Meanwhile, she thanked the Lord for the fleeting light Brandon had just experienced. *May he also cling to the light of your truth in due time,* she prayed.

~

Rose was on her way to the house from the barn when she looked up to see her grandfather turn into the driveway with the team. He waved to her slowly and called her name. "Rosie-girl, won't ya come help me unhitch George?" She picked up her skirt and hurried over, always glad to lend a hand.

"Mighty nice of you," he said, getting out of the carriage with a long groan. "Ach, the ol' bones are creakin' more than usual. Cold sure has gotten the best of me."

"Where've you been, Dawdi?"

"Heard from Gilbert that Jeb's been under the weather lately. So I went over to have a look-see."

"Oh?" She wondered if Mr. Browning and Jeb had become friends. The elderly man in the ravine could certainly use a good one.

"Your grandmother cooked up a hot dish of chicken and homemade noodles."

"Bet he was glad to see *you* comin'!"

Dawdi Jeremiah chuckled. "Was he ever."

They brought the driving lines forward out of the buggy, then hung them on the ring in the middle of the harness. "Sure do think the People may have misjudged him all these years," Dawdi said, unhooking the back hold strap on his side.

"Why's that?"

"Even though he was feelin' poorly, Jeb

was mighty sharp today . . . has been every time I've talked to him recently."

Rose pondered that. Most folk, her father included, spoke of the elderly Englischer as being a bit soft in the head, though they never said so unkindly. It was merely a matter of fact. "Well, that's interesting."

Together, one on each side, they unfastened the tugs and inserted them into the harness around the back. Then, holding the shafts, they led the horse out.

"The man's mighty frail, for certain. But he ain't feeble-minded like some think," Dawdi said, guiding the horse away to the stable. "He does tend to keep to himself, though," he said over his shoulder.

Her grandfather was always one to look for the best in folk—and usually found it. Rose recalled the years of her friendship with Nick. She and Dawdi Jeremiah were similar in that way, considering both Jeb and Nick were reckoned outsiders. *Englischers through and through.*

CHAPTER 13

Come Tuesday evening, Solomon was glad for Emma's suggestion to have Aaron and Barbara break bread with them. He took heart at their neighbors' interest in Emma's imminent surgery.

At the meal, Barbara drew Emma out in conversation. And much later, when Emma asked Sol to take her back to their bedroom— even before Rose Ann served Barbara's pineapple upside-down cake—Barbara went and sat with her in the room, relinquishing dessert.

Meanwhile, Aaron talked cordially with Emma's parents and Sol and Rose Ann while enjoying black coffee and the tasty dessert his wife had gone out of her way to make. All of them keenly realized this would be the last time such a gathering would take place for quite some time. At least until Emma was released from the rehab facility where she would go following her recovery from surgery. Sol was mighty thankful all of them had shared in the meal and the fellowship. Emma, too, had expressed her delight that they'd come.

Solomon talked with Aaron about his family's plan to go to York early on Thursday morning. "Nearly all the boys and their wives are comin'. Hen's husband wants to be there, too." *Of all things.*

Sylvia's head popped up, and Sol assumed that she was as surprised as he'd been about Brandon's decision.

" 'Tis unexpected, I daresay," said Aaron.

Jeremiah didn't comment, only nodded his head right quick, looking mighty tired. His gray hair was awfully sparse on top—Sol hadn't really noticed till just now. Smacking his lips, Jeremiah raised his coffee cup and with pleading eyes asked Rose for more. She cheerfully did his bidding.

"Next thing, there might be a whole caravan of vehicles heading over to York for Emma," said Aaron thoughtfully.

"She's well loved. We'll all be there pullin' for her," Sol said.

Just then Barbara came back into the kitchen. "Emma's fallen asleep," she said quietly, then asked what the talk was about so many going to the hospital in York. Sol explained how they planned to fill the waiting room during the surgery.

Barbara's eyebrows rose. She looked at Aaron. "I'd sure like to go. All right with you, Aaron?"

Her husband set down his coffee. "Well, now, I was thinkin' the same thing. But only if it'd bring some solace to ya, Sol."

Solomon blinked back tears. "Havin' my family and both of yous there, during this dangerous surgery . . . well, that'd be wonderful-*gut*."

"Then consider it done." Aaron nodded his head, his long beard nearly brushing the table's edge.

Barbara offered to help Rose and Sylvia clear the table and put away the leftovers, but Rose wouldn't hear of it and urged the two older women to sit and enjoy themselves, which they did.

Aaron moved with Sol to the front room and mentioned again how pleased he was Brandon would be joining them on Thursday. "Seems he's become interested in the family," he observed.

"Sometimes it takes a bolt of lightning, ya know?" Sol replied.

In that moment, Sol knew he would miss seeing Brandon round here—walking hand-in-hand with Mattie Sue in the barn and elsewhere—when he left to resume his modern life back in town. Sol truly would.

~

After the dishes were done, Mamm awakened refreshed and was able to join them again. Aaron and Barbara had stayed for Bible reading and prayers, and Aaron offered to read from the *Christenpflicht.* The good bishop was so moved by the evening prayer he'd chosen, he unashamedly wiped his face with the back of his hand.

Once their neighbors said good-bye and headed out to the road to walk home, Rose slipped upstairs, just itching to open the letter that had come for her, postmarked Bart. She guessed it was from Isaac Ebersol. Who else?

Unless it's from his twin. She closed her door, snickering at her own little joke, and settled down on the edge of the bed to read.

Dear Rose Ann,

Greetings! Jake and I enjoyed meeting you and Leah Miller, as well as visiting with our cousin Ruthann and your brother Mose. It was real nice of them to invite us to dinner there.

I hope the weather holds out for me to see you again. Even if I have to hitch up one of the horses to a sleigh, I'll find a way to get there. We never had to miss school for

*big snows growing up—same as you, I'm
sure. Just so the drifts don't rise too high
on the horse, jah?*

*Well, I'll see you this Saturday, Rose. I'll
pull up the road a ways from your home
and wait for you at dusk.*

Your friend,
Isaac Ebersol

Funny. She could almost hear him talking.
Rose leaned back on the pillow and held up the
letter, rereading it. She'd never had a friendship with a fellow who lived five long miles
away. She realized she was quite happy about
the whole thing—their meeting last Sunday,
his letter coming so quickly—and she looked
forward to seeing him next weekend already.

Jah, this could be real nice!

~

It was late, but Hen couldn't turn off her
brain. While waiting for sleep to come, she kept
reliving her growing-up years, thinking of all
the spring and summer seasons she'd worked
with her mother and Rose outdoors. Hours and
days of pressing her hands into the rich, dark
soil of the vegetable garden—the flower gar-
dens, too, that edged the perimeter of the front
porch and house. All the pruning and attempts
to tie back the clusters of shoots and vines in
preparation for eventual blossoms. Rose Ann

had been better at this. When it came to gardening, especially with flowers, Rose seemed to know what to trim and what to keep in order to make plants flourish.

Rose knows how to keep her own life in check, too. Hen rolled over and faced the far wall, where the faintest amount of light from outside slipped around the window shade.

She had always been nervous about the sounds of the house at night and of the feeling that pervaded the nighttime hours. Unlike anyone else in her family, for her, darkness meant peril. Had it stemmed from her mother's accident that dismal day on Bridle Path Lane? She did not know. But Hen was afraid of the dark.

Sleep evaded her. As the minutes slipped by, she wondered where she'd ever gotten the notion that the house was in any way different at night than in the daylight. One thing was sure, she felt more at ease with Brandon sleeping across the hall. Not that she'd ever been as fearful in the Dawdi Haus as she had been in town. No, her father's farm made Hen feel more contented and peaceful.

Hen didn't know when she'd dropped off to sleep. Now, in her haziness, she was aware of someone's hesitant footsteps in the hallway. She strained to hear the familiar shuffle—Brandon moving slowly, finding his way on the stairs. Perhaps he was going after some cookies in the kitchen, which he'd been known to do at night.

Or was she even awake?

Dozing off again, Hen didn't hear him return; she was so weary from the long day.

Then, as if in a dream, she felt a presence in her room. She squinted into the darkness. Was it Brandon or a figment of her imagination? Had her husband stumbled into her room by mistake, disoriented because of his inability to see?

She waited before saying anything, lying very still. The room was darker than earlier tonight when she'd suffered from insomnia. She recognized Brandon's silhouette. He was sitting on the edge of her bed, facing away from her.

"Brandon, are you all right?" she eked out.

"Did I wake you?"

"I'm fine. Did you lose your way . . . getting back to your room?" She felt silly asking, but what else could she say?

"No, I knew." His voice sounded as sleepy as hers. "I'm sorry, Hen. I want to apologize for being so pointed. I should've asked how you felt about Mattie Sue going with me to New York . . . if I go."

She could hardly believe this. "I forgive you." The words floated out effortlessly.

"I've been difficult, Hen. And for that I'm sorry, too."

"Brandon . . ."

"No, really. Having me here underfoot has been tough on you and Mattie Sue."

She insisted he was no trouble, that she didn't mind at all.

He continued talking. "To put it bluntly, taking care of me has been much harder here than it would have been at our house in town. Don't try to deny it." He paused a second. "I mean, how *do* you manage to live day after day, minus all the comforts you used to love and appreciate?"

She had to be honest. Besides, surely he knew. "I really don't miss any of that." Hen stopped for a moment, weighing her words. "I love it here. I only wish you did, too."

Brandon was quiet a long while. "Well, the place does have its charms for anyone anxious to get away from it all. I just would have liked a little more choice in the matter."

Hen sat up in bed. "I realize this has been very painful for you. Coming here . . . the accident."

"You've no idea, Hen. I relive that crash dozens of times a day, trying to figure out what I could have done differently. I'm close to despair at times—and even worse some days—waiting for what I always took for granted to return." He hung his head.

She heard him sigh. Rising, she didn't bother to put on her bathrobe. She crept around the bed, her feet bare on the ice-cold floor, and sat next to him, slipping her arm around him. She had not forgotten the shape of his frame, the strength of his limbs, the muscles in his back and neck. "I'd like to pray for you, Brandon. Would you mind?"

He surprised her by agreeing.

She asked God to heal him—to comfort and strengthen him in this time of need. "And make your will known above all else, dear Lord. Amen."

They sat silently for a moment, and then he touched her face. He pressed his forehead against hers. "No one else would've taken care of me the way you have, Hen."

This acknowledgment moved her deeply. "I care about you, Brandon . . . I truly do."

He drew her near and kissed her gently. Again his lips found hers but lingered now, so fervent was this kiss. The darkness in the room seemed suddenly to lessen—no longer something to fear but to relish as Hen yielded to her husband's tender yet strong embrace.

CHAPTER 14

*R*ose had been aware of the hammering going on Wednesday morning while working at Brownings'. It made her smile, knowing her father and Aaron were building the addition.

Back home now, Rose kept busy hemming a dress for one of her new dolls. Mattie Sue was her little shadow, watching every stitch.

"Will ya tell me a story, Aendi Rose?" Mattie Sue finally asked.

"What sort of story?" Rose glanced down at her.

Mattie Sue hesitated, as though thinking it through. "How about a story about Nick."

Startled, Rose asked, "Nick? What do you want to know?"

"Why'd he go away? Mommy said he did something really bad."

Rose sighed. *Oh goodness.* She didn't know how to explain what she knew about Nick's life prior to his coming here, and she certainly wasn't going to address why he'd left.

"I miss him." Mattie Sue fooled with the hem of her apron. "Did he like growin' up in the country . . . around the animals?"

"Sure, he loved it here."

"What was he like when he was little?"

Mattie Sue was certainly fond of Nick, just as he had been of her, but Rose truly wondered what prompted her niece's interest today. "Well, honey, he didn't come to live with the bishop till he was ten years old, ya know."

"Where was he before that?"

"With his mother." Rose braced herself for more questions, but surprisingly, Mattie Sue said nothing more, going to the window to look across at the Petersheims' two-story barn. She pressed her nose against the glass, making circular breath marks while Rose finished hand sewing the little black apron.

"I can tell you about Nick coming to live next door," Rose offered at last.

Mattie Sue turned and hurried back to Rose. She sat down, dangling her short legs from the bench. "Did he ride a horse then?"

"Jah, and sometimes he rode bareback, too, but he wasn't s'posed to. He was disobedient."

"Did he ride before he came here?"

"He lived in a big city, so I doubt it."

"Did he tell ya 'bout that?"

"Some." Rose didn't want to reveal much on that topic. She looked at the day clock on the wall over the sink. "Mammi Sylvia will be comin' in a bit to help make supper, so now's a *gut* time for a story."

Leaning her head against Rose's arm, Mattie Sue curled up.

"Once upon a time—"

Mattie Sue giggled. "Goody! I like this one."

"How do ya even know?" Rose laughed softly, carefully threading the needle through the black fabric.

"Daddy always starts like this."

Rose glanced over her shoulder toward the sitting room and the stairs. And the bedroom beyond, where Mamm was resting soundly when she checked earlier. *Her last day to rest before the surgery,* Rose thought nervously.

"Don't stop," Mattie Sue urged.

"All right." She kissed the top of Mattie's head. "Once upon a time, there was a boy named Nick, who often left the table before the second grace. He was told if he didn't stay put, he'd have to spend time with his older sister, milking cows by hand. Of course, that was the last thing the city boy wanted to learn.

So he started sitting still till the second prayer was finished."

"He learned to obey?"

"Well, in that case he did."

"I'm learnin' that, too," Mattie Sue said almost proudly.

"Anyway, one day Nick found a wounded raccoon in a tree hole and carried the furry little creature all the way home to show his sisters, who squealed with glee."

Mattie Sue perked up. "He *did*?"

"He ended up setting the raccoon's leg in a little wooden splint and nursing the poor critter back to health. In his free time, Nick even built a big cage just for her, though he let the raccoon go free after a couple of months."

"Did he name her?"

"Oh, he was always namin' the animals. That one he called Rosie."

"But that's *your* name."

"Jah . . . 'tis." Rose wasn't about to guess why Nick had chosen her name. Maybe he was sweet on her even then.

"Tell me another story 'bout Nick," pleaded Mattie Sue, clapping her hands. "This is fun!"

"Well, let's see. I could tell you about the time he and I went fishing and caught enough catfish for both our families to fry up for supper. Nick cleaned the whole bunch of them, which pleased the cooks no end."

Mattie Sue had a faraway look in her eyes. "Nick's awful nice, ain't?"

Rose smiled.

"I heard him talkin' to Pepper once."

"He loved that horse, for sure."

"More than anything, didn't he, Aendi Rose?"

Rose stopped her sewing to look down at Mattie Sue. "Well, he also loved the bishop and Barbara. And their grandchildren. He sometimes told them stories, ya know, but mostly they'd have a tellin' amongst themselves—and he'd listen in."

"Nick told *me* a story once."

"A happy one?"

Mattie Sue straightened and leaned forward on the table. "He wanted to go to school. It was his dream."

"To college?"

"I think so."

Rose's heart sank. *That's a sad story.*

"It made his brother real mad."

"Maybe Christian didn't want to hear that story," Rose said.

"Nick said Christian's name wasn't right for him."

Rose remembered all too well how adamant Nick had been about that. *"They should have named him Cain.*" She shivered with the memory.

"Nick's story came true, ya know," Rose said. "He's attending college right now."

Mattie Sue frowned and looked at her.

"That's why he left here." *One reason.*

"So that's not a pretend story, then?"

Rose shook her head.

"Nick said there's a hobgoblin in the ravine. Is *that* true?" Mattie's eyes were wide now.

Rose shook her head. "Oh, that's just a joke."

Suddenly, she heard Mamm calling and put down her sewing. "Be careful not to bump the needle, all right?" she instructed Mattie Sue. With that, Rose went into the bedroom, where she found her mother in tears. "Mamma, what is it?"

"I had an awful dream."

She knelt beside the bed and clasped her mother's hands. "I'm right here, Mamma." Rose didn't really want to hear about the dream. Not after her talk with Mattie Sue.

"I dreamed I was still in pain even after the surgery," Mamm said, clinging to her hand.

Rose refused to give in to fear. "Let's trust the Lord for the outcome," she whispered. "He knows what's best, jah?"

Mamm smiled through her tears. "Beth's dream was heaven-sent, ain't?"

Rose remembered everything about the dream that inspired Mamm to see the York specialist after so many years of resisting medical treatment. "We're following what God put on Beth's heart . . . for you, Mamma. Near everyone I know is beseeching the Lord God for you," Rose said. "You can rest assured of that."

"I heard ya talking 'bout Nick, just now. 'Least I thought it was him."

Mamm had such good ears.

"Has the Lord put it on anyone's heart to pray for him?" she asked.

"I'm sure Barbara and the bishop do," Rose ventured. She, too, had prayed many times for her friend, though she wasn't ready to say so.

"Lyin' here, night after night, giving my pain up to God," Mamm said, squeezing Rose's hand, "I pray for Nick."

"Do ya, Mamm?"

"Well, the Lord cares 'bout him. He's lost, ain't so?"

It was hard not to remember the times Mamm had spoken out against him, back when he lived amongst them. Rose agreed Nick was in need of God's help. But even if he were to return and make a full confession, he would forever carry the mantle of responsibility for his brother's death . . . even though the People would offer forgiveness.

Despite that, all this talk about Nick had stirred something in her, something she'd thought was buried. Maybe she *wasn't* ready to start seeing a new fellow. Rose had placed Isaac Ebersol's letter on top of Nick's in her dresser drawer on purpose. But now she really didn't know what to think.

Just when I was looking forward to meeting Isaac come Saturday. Yet Rose honestly wondered if he, or any young man, could ever make her forget Nick Franco.

CHAPTER 15

*R*ose scanned the semiprivate waiting room at the York hospital Thursday. Except for Brandon, everyone wore Plain garb. Her family and the Petersheims huddled together for support on this day Mamm had been so anxious for. The day brought its own set of concerns, though hopefully the surgery would bring about the longed-for result of a life free of chronic pain. *Like going through a long tunnel to get to the other side,* thought Rose.

Each member of the family had taken a turn with Mamm prior to her being wheeled through the double doors and down the corridor. They gave a gentle hug and promised to uphold her in prayer. Dat had squeezed Mamm's hand more than once, telling her they would stay put for the duration of the surgery—possibly four to six hours—waiting for the doctor's report. *"Don't worry none, jah, Emma? God is with you,"* he'd said. *"Ever near . . ."*

Now five hours had already passed and Mamm was still unconscious behind those big doors, and no one had come out to say she was all right. "Are things goin' as expected, do ya think?" Rose whispered to Hen, who sat next to her.

Hen shook her head slightly, apparently deep in thought.

Dat looked as though he might be wondering the same thing, over there across the room with Rose's brothers and the bishop. Mose and Josh talked quietly in Deitsch while Eli flipped through magazines, restless as anything. The many ham-and-cheese sandwiches and soft pretzels Mammi Sylvia had kindly sent along with them were long gone, consumed by nervous eaters.

As for herself, Rose had lost her appetite. She wished for one of her library books from home—a lighthearted love story might help her block out this tense moment. But then again, such reading material might've offended her father on such a solemn day, and she wouldn't have done that for the world.

She sat between Hen and sister-in-law Suzy, who'd come in her husband Enos's stead, as he'd awakened with a fever and congestion and didn't want to expose Mamm or other hospital patients. There they waited—six of her brothers, Suzy, and Hen with Brandon. It was a peculiar situation, given that Suzy had always found it difficult to forgive Hen's marriage to an outsider. Even now, Suzy was unable to disguise her displeasure, refusing to so much as even look at Hen or Brandon.

Brandon, on the opposite end of the plaid sofa, was more talkative than usual, conversing particularly with Aaron. He seemed more relaxed than normal this morning, yet Hen's face was drawn and somewhat pale. Barbara, Mamm's closest friend, seemed the least distressed of all of them, offering a real source of comfort.

Still looking about, Rose took in the artificial greenery, including an off-kilter tree that ascended behind one of the overstuffed leather chairs. She wished Mattie Sue had been able to come along. Each day Mattie spent with her daddy was one less day to pine for him, if and when he should leave the farm and return to their home in Quarryville.

Next to her, Suzy again opened her basket of embroidery, fidgeting. She smelled like lilacs, and Rose wondered why her sister-in-law had worn cologne today. Had she forgotten they might be cooped up together in the same room? The air in the space felt mighty stale and close.

Rose folded her hands in her lap and glanced back at the doors over yonder, wondering when someone—*anyone*—would have the courtesy to push them open and tell them what was happening on the other end of that long hallway.

Sol had been biting his nails—one of them nearly down to the quick. He watched the clock on the wall, its minute hand jerking forward second by second. It felt like ages since they'd taken Emma away from him, the needle in her vein hooked to a bag of liquid. The vision still pained him. They were going to operate on her spinal cord, for pity's sake! What had possessed him to let his fragile wife endure such a thing? What?

He straightened a bit, regaining control of himself. It was his role to be strong for his children, grown though they were. He was their rock, second only to the Lord—the Rock of Ages. Again he relinquished the results of Emma's surgery to almighty God in prayer. Even so, he was a man with a heart full of love . . . and worries. And fear was setting in.

"Dat, do you want to get something to drink . . . or a snack, maybe?" Mose leaned over and asked.

"Ain't hungry." Sol shook his head.

"Nothin' at all?"

"Couldn't think of eating."

Sighing, Mose reached behind his head and rubbed his neck, apparently needing something to eat or drink himself. Or some fresh air.

"Go ahead, if you want." Sol eyed his other sons—tall, strapping fellows.

Mose shook his head. "Nee—no. Denki."

Joshua got up and headed for the snack area. Then the younger boys, Eli and David, followed. *They're anxious,* Sol decided, closing his eyes to rest them for a time.

He let his mind wander back to last night, when he'd held frail Emma close before they'd fallen asleep. Emma had been the brave one, he recalled. Brave and stoic, saying he mustn't fret. *"Remember what the doctor told us."* He'd needed to hear it from her. No one could reassure him like his wife.

She'd said something else, too—wanted him to let Beth Browning know how the surgery went. Sol had promised her he'd stop by tomorrow morning. It was the least he could do.

Looking now at Brandon, whose right arm was mending in its cast, Sol noticed Hen sitting closer to him than usual. Sol hadn't witnessed much affection or even companionship between them before. But today was different—or was Hen just feeling awful needy right now? No, the more he regarded them, the more he sensed the intangible spark between a man and the woman who loves him. Had something changed?

He let his eyes drift over the whole lot of them, these dear ones who cared so much for Emma and for him. How thankful Sol was to God for each life represented here. *I'm a blessed man.*

High over the main window, the sun shone through a decorative transom, making for an eye-catching design. He stared, drawn to the radiance, scarcely able to keep his eyes from it.

Then, as he watched, the light reflected through a prism of sorts and resulted in a miniature rainbow. Colorful rays danced before him like a heavenly promise. He embraced it as a sign that all would be well.

But when yet another hour came and went, Sol's former fear came back even stronger and camped at the door to his heart.

Hen's gaze skittered around the attractive room. There were so many people crammed into the space, she thought unexpectedly of Preaching service. How very crowded it always was there, too. She shifted where she sat—she needed to get up and move around but didn't want to leave and miss hearing the surgeon's report. There had been times when she fully understood the expression "climbing the walls." This was such a time.

Her attention focused on Brandon. His eyes were closed again, but earlier he'd seemed to enjoy conversing with Dad and her brothers. If she had known the surgery would last this long, she might've suggested her husband remain at home after all, resting as his doctor had so strongly advised.

She recalled the many prayers she and her family had offered up for him. What was God's will for her husband? She felt torn between her concern for Brandon and her mother.

Leaning back into the sofa, Hen remembered how healthy and full of life Mom had always been before her accident. Hen regretted how she'd essentially abandoned her frail mother for Brandon, fully expecting Rose and Mammi Sylvia to pick up the slack. Oh, she regretted so many of her choices through the years.

Had she always been so self-centered? Why was it so hard to empty herself of her tenacious will? Her selfishness? To reach out wide to embrace family, friends, and others? Hen felt as if the choices she had made had turned her inward, her way of seeing the world as murky as Brandon's own weeks of darkness.

Her mother had written to Hen after Mattie Sue's birth, thrilled to welcome another grandchild into the family. Yet despite the kindly letter, Hen had withheld her baby from her parents, not visiting them at the farm, expecting them to see her on her own terms—at her modern house in town. Wincing at the thought, Hen turned to look at her father. *They deserved so much better from me.*

Hen's breath caught as she observed her dad wipe his eyes with his blue kerchief, his hair looking too neat for this time of day. His lower lip quivered as he slowly bowed his head, and she wished she was sitting over there next to him. *Lord, give Dad strength for this difficult day,* she pleaded. *And guide the surgeon's hand, I pray.*

CHAPTER 16

*S*ome time later, the long-expected surgeon pushed through the doors, still wearing his green scrubs. He removed his white cap and explained the reason for the extended time in some indecipherable remarks, focusing his attention mainly on Dat. Rose was nevertheless heartened when he stated that the surgery had been as successful as could be hoped for. Now they'd have to wait and see if Mamm would be free of pain, once her body healed from the operation.

Dat and Joshua rose and shook the man's hand, thanking him. They were told that once Mamm was settled in the ICU, Dat would be permitted to see her. "And anyone else who is family." The surgeon's face cracked a rare smile when Dat informed him that they were nearly all family. *Bishop Aaron and Barbara almost are, of course,* Rose thought.

Just knowing her mother could start to mend now, Rose began to feel somewhat lighter. She headed for the snack area to purchase a package of peanut butter crackers to share with Suzy or Hen. On the way back to the waiting area, she stopped at the water fountain to relieve her thirst.

Forty more minutes passed before they were encouraged to relocate to yet another waiting area. And goodness, the gawks they received as they moved through the hospital corridors! Rose assumed they were a spectacle, because these hospital folks were far enough removed from Plain communities that they didn't often encounter Amish. One English visitor looked like her hazel eyes might pop right out of her head as she stared.

The new waiting area was even smaller than the first, and Rose stood for a while near a window, thankful to see the sky again.

After Dat and Joshua had visited with Mamm briefly, Dat asked Hen if she'd like to go in next. Observing this rotation, Rose decided it was best that she not go in after her sister, even though she wanted to with all of her heart. She just felt so queasy and light-headed at the thought of the drainage tubes and IV and other equipment attached to her mother. Her oldest brother had looked ashen when he returned to the waiting room. He'd had to lean forward for a time, his head in his hands.

"Tell Mamm I love her," Rose whispered to Hen, who clasped her hand. She seemed to understand without Rose saying more and tiptoed away to Mamm's room.

Brandon was up pacing the floor, running his hand along the wall to steady himself. It struck Rose that he might like to go in, as well. She slipped over to Dat and whispered her suggestion.

Dat rose quickly and fell in step with Brandon, placing a hand on his shoulder. Brandon brightened, obviously grateful for the unexpected invitation.

When Hen emerged from the room, Brandon was ready and eager to visit Mamm. When he leaned near and told her what he wanted to do, Hen nodded and accompanied him into the room. The door closed behind them.

Tears sprang to Rose's eyes and she looked away, trying to conceal her emotions. She was so struck by whatever good and lovely thing was happening between Hen and her husband.

He's truly part of the family.

Hen was pleased at Brandon's request to

see her mother. She stood next to him beside the slightly elevated hospital bed. Carefully, she folded the sheet down and straightened it near her mother's chin, aware of the sounds of various machines and monitors. Leaning over, she lightly kissed Mom's forehead, then smoothed her hair at the part, seeing that the bun was still pretty well intact. As she straightened, she noticed Brandon appeared to be smiling down at Mom, as if he could actually see her.

Hen patted her mother's hand, her heart pounding at the possibility that Brandon's sight might be clearing some.

"Thank you for sharing your courage with me, Emma," Brandon said. "The pain you've endured . . ." Brandon paused a moment, seemingly searching for the right words. "I want you to know you've been a great help to me, and I appreciate it."

Mom tried to nod her head. "That's all right, son. Thank the dear Lord we're this far, ain't?"

Son. There it was again.

"We don't want to tire you out." Hen squeezed her mother's hand. "You rest now, all right?"

A slight smile spread across her lips. "You both take care, ya hear?"

"You too," Brandon was quick to say.

"I'll visit you again." Hen threw a kiss toward her mother as they made their way to the door.

"Don't worry one little speck, Hen, dear."

Hen couldn't promise that, but she would do her best to trust for healing. "She's going to need lots of rest," Hen remarked to Brandon in the hallway. "I'm surprised the doctor allowed us to see her so soon after the surgery."

"I'm glad he did," Brandon said, his eyes blank now. "You can be glad she came through it so well."

Hen agreed, wishing she might find strength in her husband's embrace, needing the support. But she drew a deep breath and guided him back to the waiting area, wondering if his time of dependence upon her was coming to a close.

~

Sol thought primarily of Emma during the ride back to Quarryville . . . and to Salem Road. Thankfully, the driver was not a talkative chap, and Sol leaned against the headrest, his eyes closed for a good part of the drive home. His heart was with his precious wife, lying alone in the hospital bed. He had wanted to stay right with her all the night long, as he always did at home. He could sleep while sitting in a chair, couldn't he?

Yet here he was, riding home at Joshua's insistence. *"You need your rest, Dat . . . she'll be well cared for."* Hen had agreed and encouraged him to return to the farm for the night, as well. Even so, it had been hard for him to leave the ICU. *Leaving Emma behind.*

If he remembered correctly, his wife would remain in the intensive care unit for three days, then be moved to the recovery area on another floor, in a semiprivate room. After that, an ambulance would transport her to a nearby rehabilitation facility for about three weeks, assuming all went well. Once she could return home, she would need up to nine months of rehab treatments, two to three times a week.

Will all of this make a difference for Emma, Lord? he prayed. If it did, then the day's trauma to her body would be worthwhile in the long run.

As for Sol, he would visit her nearly every day. Already his sons had lined up with others to help with his barn and field chores. Being it was winter, though, he had less to think about . . . till early spring, when the plowing and planting would begin.

"You all right, Dad?" Hen asked from the seat behind him.

He nodded with a slight sigh.

"Just checking."

He didn't feel up to saying much, but he knew Hen cared for him deeply. Rose, too, dear flower that she was. He didn't blame her for not being able to spend a few minutes with Emma. It was hard on all of them, seeing her like that.

But now, Brandon . . . of all things! He'd noticed him make eye contact with Hen several times today. If Sol wasn't mistaken, Brandon's sight had returned somewhat, albeit briefly, while they were waiting. Sol was too weary to ponder the implications of this, yet he hoped Aaron's visits had softened Brandon's heart toward the things of God . . . and ultimately toward Hen, as well.

~

That evening, after Mattie Sue was tucked into bed, Hen returned downstairs to the kitchen and found Brandon sitting at the table, hands folded as if in prayer.

"Brandon?" she said. "Are you all right?"

He raised his head, and she saw the unwavering gaze on his handsome face.

She felt the weight of his silence.

At last he spoke. "Hen, I can see clearly right now."

"Oh, this is such good news!"

He smiled fleetingly. "All day long, my

sight's been on and off. I didn't want to say anything . . . didn't want to detract from the surgery."

"I thought perhaps you could see Mom when we were in her room." She went to his side and they embraced. "This is just wonderful," she said, pulling out her chair and sitting near him.

He reached for her hands and leaned forward at the table. "I keep waiting for the shades to fall again . . . like before. But so far, so good." He looked around the kitchen, his gaze lingering on Mattie Sue's coloring pages arranged neatly on the gas-run refrigerator. Then, turning, he looked past the cookstove, toward the small front room, where he'd spent many hours snuggled with Mattie Sue and Wiggles. Once again, his gaze found hers. "I was beginning to think this day might never come."

"I'm so happy for you." *An answer to prayer!*

"Like I said the other night, Hen . . . I appreciate what you've done for me all these weeks." His eyes searched her face, her hair, as if marveling at what he saw.

She stiffened, shielding her heart from what more he might say. "Mattie Sue and I were glad to help you during your recovery," she said softly. "We were happy to be here for you."

Here ... She wondered if she should've said it differently.

"Well, I can take care of myself now. I don't want to put you out any longer, Hen. It's obvious you love this life."

Not without you. She could not speak for fear of crying.

Neither of them spoke for a time. It was painful sitting there, feeling suddenly disconnected from him when they should be rejoicing. Yet Brandon remained attentive, his eyes drawing hers.

"Mattie Sue will be so thrilled tomorrow when she realizes you can see," Hen said at last.

"I can't wait to take a look at her," he said. "She's sleeping, right?" He moved away from the table.

"Go on upstairs ... you won't wake her." Hen smiled. "You'll be surprised how much she's grown in the past few weeks." *We all have, in one way or another....*

CHAPTER 17

Hen found Brandon peering into the open refrigerator early the next morning, already dressed for the office. His five-o'clock shadow was quite unmistakable; even though he could see, he'd opted not to shave yet again. Had he decided to grow a beard?

"Good morning," she said, still wearing her bathrobe and slippers. "You're up early."

"Need to get caught up with some things at the office, now that I can see again." He closed the refrigerator door.

It was true that he'd missed much at work during his recovery. Even with Bruce's assistance, there would be a lot to tackle. "Will you need a ride?"

"Bruce is coming by for me—I gave him a call from the hospital yesterday. But thanks for asking."

She recalled the tiffs they'd had over her balking at driving him. So why did she mind that he wasn't asking today? "What would you like for breakfast?"

His eyes twinkled. "Well, what if I cooked for a change?"

"You seriously think you can use a cook-stove?"

He grinned and glanced at the old stove. "You know me too well. If it's going to be edible, I guess you'll have to cook." He went to the cupboard and pulled out three plates, still eyeing her mischievously. "Pancakes or waffles would be great, thanks."

"I'll put the order right in," she said. It did her heart good to see him get around on his own. Surprised, she watched him set the plates around. Never before had he offered to help in the kitchen, let alone do something like this spontaneously.

Soon Mattie Sue came wandering downstairs in her cotton nightgown, her hair disheveled, eyes bright. When she spotted her daddy setting the table, she frowned for a split second. Next thing, she was flying to him, hugging his knees, laughing, then crying. "Daddy . . . you're all better!" He reached down and picked her up with his good arm, laughing with her. She cupped his face in her small hands, her nose nearly touching his. "You can see me, can't ya, Daddy?"

"I sure can."

"That's like God answering Beth's prayers for Mammi Emma. It's just the same!"

Brandon smiled. "I stared at you for the longest time while you were sleeping last night." His eyes filled with tears and he kissed Mattie Sue's cheek. "This is the best day of my life."

"Me too, Daddy." Mattie Sue kissed his cheek over and over until she began to giggle. "You can see the calvies now," she said. "And Dawdi and Mammi and . . . pretty Mommy."

"Sweetie, let's get washed up for breakfast," Hen said, embarrassed.

Mattie got down and hurried over to Hen, who was flipping a pancake. "We should have a party, ain't so?"

"Honey, Daddy has to go to work soon."

Brandon intervened, motioning for Mattie to go and wash her hands. "We'll have a breakfast party, how's that?" he said, hurrying her along.

After breakfast, Hen and Mattie Sue washed up and dressed for the day. Hen looked at her green work dress and hesitated before putting it on. Thoughts of Brandon filled her mind as she picked up her room and helped Mattie do the same before heading back downstairs to bake an angel food cake, knowing that Bruce would have stopped by to pick Brandon up some time ago.

The teakettle hummed steadily while she placed the cake in the oven, then wiped the counters clean. At the far end of the kitchen, over near the back door, she saw a note and picked it up. *Thanks again for everything, Hen.* *—Brandon*

"What's it mean?" she whispered, looking around.

Trembling, she ran upstairs and discovered that his things were gone from his room. Did he mean to return later, after he collected some fresh clothes? But if so, why not say as much? Oh, she didn't know what to think!

Based on their conversation last evening—and the fact that he'd chosen to sleep again in the guest room—her fears began to compound. It was just as likely he'd moved back to town permanently and planned to push forward with the divorce.

As Hen left his temporary room, she noticed her open Bible on the table beside the bed. Apparently he had been reading it since his sight was restored. She wondered if his sudden interest was an outgrowth of having talked to her mother or to Bishop Aaron. Whatever it was, she was grateful. God was surely at work in his heart, just as Rose had said recently. *And yet . . .*

Hen wasn't sure what, if anything, to tell Mattie Sue. "O Lord, help me know your wisdom," she prayed before looking in on her daughter, playing quietly in her room. Not saying a word, she made her way slowly downstairs to check on her cake, realizing the depth of misery she'd put Brandon through back in October. That miserable day four months ago when she'd packed up and left him.

I understand now the terrible pain he felt.

She shuddered as she grasped the gulf that separated her from her husband, in spite of their love. It was of her making, after all.

Only a few days ago Brandon had voiced his concern. *"What has changed?"* he'd asked her rather pointedly.

What, indeed?

~

Solomon's sleep had been fitful last night, so he'd put his time to good use, praying for Emma as he often did in the wee hours. This far removed from the hospital, he simply had to entrust her to God's care. Feeling all in today, he was relieved not to be in charge of driving horse and carriage as he put on his coat and hat, then reached for his woolen scarf.

At that moment, Hen called to him and stepped inside.

"How was your night, Dad?"

"Oh, as *gut* as one might expect."

Her expression toward him was tender. "I worried you might rest poorly." Then she sighed and abruptly turned to look out the window, not making an effort to remove her heavy shawl. "Dad . . ." Her voice broke. "Brandon's things are missing. I think he's moved out."

"I saw him earlier. Noticed he was getting around all right—must be seein' fairly well, jah?" Sol had pondered Brandon's departure but wouldn't tell his daughter he'd seemed in a rush to get going. "Didn't quite expect it to happen this way."

"Expect what?" she said, frowning. "Do you know whether Brandon's going back to town to live?"

"Well, he had a duffel bag and some other things tucked under his good arm," Sol admitted.

"Did he talk to you before he left?"

"Just to poke his head into my woodshop and say thanks."

"That's what I came to find out." She turned to go and paused to look back at him thoughtfully. "I'm so sorry for all the pain this has caused you and Mom. The whole family, really."

Sol nodded, but he would spare her what he was thinking—Brandon's suggestion that Hen return home to get her obsession with Plain life out of her system had backfired terribly.

"I wanted to go along with you to see Mom." Hen sighed. "But I doubt I would be much support for her."

"Oh, she'll understand."

"Will you tell her Brandon's moving home?"

He shook his head. "Not yet, but I'll let her know his sight's returned—she'll be mighty glad 'bout that."

A sweet yet sad smile flitted across Hen's face and she waved good-bye.

Sol slipped on his gloves and headed out to the driveway to await his driver, his heart heavy.

~

As they pulled into Gilbert Browning's lane, Sol could see the progress the other Amishmen had made just since the day before yesterday, when Sol and Aaron had helped to finish framing in the extra room. "It'll be done in no time," he remarked to the driver before getting out.

Gilbert was outdoors, walking briskly about the perimeter of the addition. He wore a thick black overcoat and black earmuffs, and there was a spring in his step. Sol told him the good news regarding the surgery and asked him to relay it to Beth. "For Emma's sake."

"I certainly will," Gilbert said, nodding. "Beth was up praying in her room awhile yesterday, so I know she'll be glad to hear this."

"Let her know we appreciate her prayers, won't ya?"

Gilbert's smile deepened and he said he would. "I know she'll spend a good part of the day thanking the Lord now."

"We can all learn from that, jah?"

Gilbert shook his hand heartily. "Thanks for stopping by, Solomon. Beth will be thrilled."

With that, Sol wandered over to talk with the bishop, saying he'd try to get back to help some this afternoon. "If there's sun left." But Aaron was adamant that he not rush away from the hospital. Even so, Sol had given his word to pitch in and help.

~

When Sol entered the door leading to the ICU, he wished he'd brought Rose along. The girls were so good with their mother, especially when she was ailing so. He thought of

all the years Rose had sat by Emma's bed-
side, so long she'd nearly sacrificed her chance
at marriage. Now, though, he guessed from
the few asides Mose had given him that she
had been introduced to someone, although
he knew very little about the new prospect
from Bart. *A fair distance away,* he thought
with some regret.

When Sol arrived at his wife's room, he
found Emma in a far worse state than prior
to the surgery. Her face was blotchy red, like
she'd suffered an allergic reaction. Her bun
had come undone in the night, and he leaned
over to kiss her tear-streaked face. The doctor had warned them that postsurgery pain
was unavoidable, but Sol hadn't expected this
level of distress. He asked if she'd been given
anything to ease the pain.

"Jah, morphine," she whispered. "It's
made me really nauseous." She added she
didn't know which was worse, the excruciat-
ing pain or the wrenching stomach and vom-
iting, enough to worry the nurses about her
stitches.

"Ach, Emma," he said, his heart breaking
as he noted the angry rash on her face also
covered her neck and forearms.

"The doctor's orderin' something without
a narcotic for me. And something to soothe
my stomach."

They'd taken great care to warn the hospital before the surgery about Emma's past problems with pain medication, but Sol realized communication sometimes broke down in the shuffle between doctors. Still, he didn't like it one bit.

She's replaced one pain with another.

Praying silently, he asked God to intervene. Then Sol tried to occupy Emma's mind by reading the Bible aloud. When the nurse came to administer the new medication and after Emma seemed calmer again, he told her Brandon's good news.

Her face lit right up. "Brandon can see? Oh, thank the dear Lord!"

Sol only smiled, not sharing about their son-in-law's departure, or that it appeared he and Hen were right back to where they'd started last fall. No need to burden Emma with all that today.

~

Rose Ann had seen Brandon outdoors earlier, wearing his tan overcoat—one sleeve hanging limp—and dress shoes when Bruce parked in front of Hen's Dawdi Haus. Brandon had walked right to the car, placing his duffel bag in the backseat just as any sighted person would, to the obvious amazement of his partner, who'd gotten out to assist him only to discover that Brandon needed no help.

Guess he doesn't need Hen's help any longer, either, Rose thought sadly as she pitched hay to the field mules with Mose and Josh, working in Dat's stead. All the while she breathed a prayer for Hen and Brandon . . . and for Mamm.

Rose had just returned to the house when she spotted Barbara Petersheim through the window, arriving by horse and carriage. Feeling mighty blue, she removed her work boots and welcomed her mother's friend with open arms and gratefully accepted the chicken casserole and a side dish of succotash. Aunt Malinda Blank, Mamm's older Maidel sister, had also stopped by with a pot of chili right after Dat left with the van driver, so they were well fixed for supper.

"Denki!" Rose kissed Barbara's cheek and put the casserole on top of the cookstove, covering it with dish towels.

"It oughta stay *gut* and hot right there, ready to eat." Barbara's cheeks were redder than Rose had seen them.

"Mighty cold out, ain't?"

Barbara patted her plump hands together as she moved closer to the stove. "I'll say."

Rose invited her to sit and warm herself. "I should've gone to see Mamm today," Rose said, her voice husky. "I hope I didn't hurt her feelings yesterday."

"Well, how's that?"

"Because I didn't go in to see her after she was out of recovery. Oh, Barbara, I just couldn't!"

Barbara reached for her. "Dear girl, listen to me. Your Mamma surely understands; I just know she does." Barbara stroked her hair like Mamm had when Rose was a little girl. "We must give your mother into the Lord's care. Can ya do that, Rosie?"

Rose nodded, but she missed Mamm something awful and told Barbara so. "It's goin' to be weeks till she's home again."

"Well, sure. But think how wonderful it'll be for her to live without pain . . . if the Lord God wills it."

"Oh, I pray it's so."

"Your Dat's with her today, I s'pose."

Rose said he was. "Hen wanted to go, but she's stayin' with Mattie Sue." She didn't say Hen's husband apparently had returned to the world. Barbara would find out soon enough about Brandon's leaving.

"You'll visit once she's out of the ICU, jah?" Barbara asked.

"I surely will."

Barbara rose out of the rocker with considerable effort. "Do you need any other help today, Rose Ann? Cleaning or whatnot?" Barbara looked her over, then her gaze drifted to the work boots in the utility room. "You're helpin' out in the barn, I 'spect?"

"Jah, till I got so cold I thought I might just turn purple." Rose laughed softly. "Good thing Dat's not here to see, 'cause he'd tease me for sure."

"Let your brothers do the outdoor work." Barbara patted Rose's cheek. "You take care of yourself, hear?"

"I'm tryin'."

"Well, if you're sure you'll be all right, I'll head over to Gilbert Browning's with food for the men building the addition."

"No need to fret over me," Rose said, following her to the back door. The cold seeped in through the cracks. "I hope you have your lap robes for the carriage."

"Jah, ain't but a short ride though."

Rose watched till Barbara was safely inside the carriage. Shivering again, she closed the door, hoping her brothers wouldn't think she was avoiding her barn chores. The minute she got herself warmed all through, she would go back out and finish up. Then later, Rose would check on Hen to see how she was faring, pained as she surely must be. Rose determined to do her best to console her sister. What else could she do?

CHAPTER 18

By Saturday afternoon, Hen felt practically sick with grief. Mattie Sue had sobbed when Brandon hadn't returned last night for supper. Hen had held her darling close, letting her cry as Wiggles tilted his furry head, observing them, his tail as still as a twig.

Hen had tried to conceal her emotions from Mattie Sue thus far. She was thankful for Rose's help and listening ear. Such a precious sister! Hen hoped she hadn't put a damper on her sister's joy—later today was to be the first real date between Rose and her prospective beau.

Presently, Hen kept busy mending socks for her father. As she worked, she thought of her mother. Hen and her father had talked at length that morning before he left for York. He seemed to have high hopes for getting Mamm into a rehabilitation facility in Lancaster and was working toward that end—much more convenient for the family, too. Hen longed to see her mother again, not for her own consolation, but to offer comfort.

It is in giving that we receive. She thought of the prayer she'd found tucked into her mother's Bible years ago.

Hen's mind turned back to Brandon. *If only I'd given more.* It seemed like days since Brandon left, but alas, only yesterday he'd packed his things and left his short note. She'd never known such misery . . . such painful uncertainty. It was all she could do just to go through the motions of a normal day.

With both Brandon and Mom gone, the world was strangely empty. Hen stared out the kitchen window at the drive, hoping to see Brandon pulling up to the house.

He'd felt trapped in his blindness, he had told her.

"Well, he's free of that now," she said. The realization made her both happy for him and sad for herself.

~

Despite Mamm's hospitalization and Brandon's leaving, Rose could not quell her excitement for the upcoming evening as she dressed for her date with Isaac. She looked forward to seeing him again and refused to let herself feel guilty about it.

She checked in her hand mirror to see if her part was nice and straight and the rest of her looked presentable. She wondered if she should call Isaac by his nickname or his given name. She said "Ike" softly, trying it out, though there was something equally appealing about the name Isaac. Of course, she didn't have to decide right at first. She would let the evening play out. After all, tonight was the result of a blind date of sorts, so she shouldn't hope for too much, even though she had enjoyed his company last Sunday.

Going downstairs, it was easy to slip out of the house unnoticed, since Dat was still in York with Mamm, and Hen and Mattie Sue were over in their little house. She'd gone to see Hen again earlier this afternoon, taking some mending along. Rose had tried to steer the conversation away from Brandon as they worked while Mattie napped. Hen, however, kept bringing the conversation back to her husband. *"He wants his modern life, and there's no changing that."*

"You of all people should be able to sympathize," Rose had said.

Hen stared back at her as if she'd said something wrong, and Rose had felt she best be going. She'd left the basket of worn socks there, mighty perplexed as she walked back to the main house. Was her sister really so unable to see past her own nose?

Now Rose was glad she'd worn her boots and mittens and warmest woolen coat and scarf as she made her way up Salem Road to where Isaac had said he'd meet her at dusk. It was certainly about that time, and she wished she'd brought along a flashlight.

Within seconds a horse came trotting toward her—she heard the clip-clopping better than she could see the horse. But she knew without a doubt it was Isaac as he called "Whoa, boy!" His voice was firm and confident as he gave the command.

Like Dat's. She smiled to herself.

The night was very cold. But as long as the wind didn't come up, they'd be all right for a little while. She did feel sorry for Isaac, who would have to drive a full forty minutes or so back to his home in Bart in his open buggy. *He'll be an ice cube, for sure.*

Isaac held a flashlight, guiding her way toward him. As she stepped into the brilliant circle of light on the ground, he said, "Hullo, Rose. Nice to see ya again."

"You too, Isaac."

He helped her into the carriage. "It's a nice night, jah?"

She agreed.

"Good thing it's not too cold yet."

She nodded, wondering if his face and ears might already be too numb for him to know just how cold it really was. "It's s'posed to be cloudy tonight, so that's *gut*."

"Jah, my *Daed* always says it's colder when it's clear out."

"My Dawdi Jeremiah likes to say the clouds make blankets over the earth."

"Well, he's right."

They went on like this for a bit, talking about the weather and this and that, just the way she liked it. *Getting acquainted nice and slow-like.*

"Do ya play much Ping-Pong?" he asked.

"No, but I think it's fun. Do you?"

"Several times a week . . . at my employer's house. They've got a big room in the basement with a Ping-Pong table."

"This is the English farmer you work for?"

"Best thing I ever did, getting hired on by Ed Morton."

Rose was a little surprised at that.

"I was unbeatable at the game last year," he said. "Not to boast."

She chuckled. "You're mighty sure of yourself, ain't?"

"Maybe so—if you're talking Ping-Pong. Jake recently stole the championship from me."

"And you want it back."

"I'm workin' on it!" He laughed, obviously enjoying himself.

After a time, he asked if she'd ever heard of the groundhog that went to a garage sale, a story he'd heard from a cousin in Missouri. "This here chubby critter got into a bag of clothing set aside for a yard sale," he told her. "Somehow or other it managed to get from the bag into a hole in the garage."

Rose listened, picturing the dilemma.

"Seems the family heard a lot of racket beneath the floor—the frightened critter dug himself clear into the kitchen of the old farm-house. When one of the preachers came over, he found the hole in the garage where the animal had slipped in, and guess what he did?"

"What?"

"Stuck a hose in there and flushed him right out!"

"Poor thing must have been terrified," Rose said, adding, "Sounds like something one of my brothers might do."

"Mose, maybe?"

"Well, not so much him, but maybe one of the others."

"Mose must be one nice brother."

"He's also a wonderful-*gut* father . . . and husband."

She wasn't sure, but she thought Isaac winked at her just then.

He talked of his many Amish and English friends over in Bart. She kept waiting for him to mention his twin brother, Jacob, but he didn't.

Soon, he was telling about some New Order Amish teenagers in Ohio who weren't allowed to date or court till *after* church baptism. "Never heard of that before," she said.

"It's one way to get you in the church before ya realize what you're doin', seems to me."

She was surprised he'd say that. "I don't know. Might be a *gut* idea for some."

He turned toward her. "Are ya baptized already, Rose?"

"Joined church when I was fifteen."

"Really, now? I don't know too many who join so early."

She explained it was partly because of her mother's ill health. "Mamm was afraid she might not live long enough to witness my vow to God." She waited, wondering if he might point out that it certainly wasn't the best reason for entering into the holy ordinance. But when he said no more on the subject, she had to ask. "Are you baptized, Isaac?"

"Not just yet."

She wondered why not but didn't know

him well enough to inquire. "My father always says it's important to be ready first. 'Tis a mighty big step."

He agreed. "Ain't something to enter into lightly."

She didn't reply to that, still curious about why he hadn't followed the Lord in holy baptism yet.

"I'll make my vow sooner or later."

She nodded, relieved. Plenty of young men put off baptism for as long as they could.

"Who's your bishop?" she asked, wondering if it was the one appointed to them temporarily for the next six months.

When he named Bishop Simon, she realized it was indeed one and the same. "So he oversees our church and two other districts, jah?"

"He's a busy man—a stickler like Old Ezekiel. Everyone knows that about him." Isaac kept his hands on the reins, never once making Rose think he might reach for hers. "Three churches to tend to is more than a full-time job." He asked what had happened to their former bishop. "Is he ill?"

"No." Rose realized then that because Isaac wasn't a church member, he was not privy to what had happened to cause Aaron Petersheim's ousting. It wasn't her place to bring it up. She changed the subject, thinking about the stories he'd told earlier. "You must have relatives in Ohio and Missouri."

"My mom has Plain friends from there. They write circle letters every other week," he explained.

"I thought maybe you had cousins out there, too."

"Not that I know of, but they do seem to turn up where you least expect—lots of my relatives will even hire drivers and come in from out of state to attend husking bees and whatnot."

She'd heard the same thing from her cousin Esther Glick, who'd married on Thanksgiving Day. "When was your last husking bee?"

"Oh, maybe a year or so ago."

"Did ya have apple pie after the big meal?"

He nodded. "That and German chocolate sauerkraut cake—my favorite dessert. But the best part was the line dancing, with a fiddle, guitars, even a mandolin or two."

Rose's eyes grew wide. "Goodness' sake, we don't have gatherings like that round here."

"The big ol' bass fiddle is the most fun."

"And there's dancin', ya say?"

"Well, amongst some of the buddy groups, jah. But the gatherings are mostly for pairin' up."

Rose supposed that if she asked around, she could probably find out where there were various progressive groups doing such dancing in her own area, too. She'd just never considered that particular crowd.

Isaac talked about the music and the hilarity at these gatherings, and his description of the sights and sounds drew her like a magnet as she visualized every word . . . every phrase. She was so entertained, she couldn't imagine being with anyone else under the blanketed cloud cover overhead—not on this very happy night.

Breathing in the brisk air, she leaned back in the seat as she listened to Isaac talk about "practice Singings," which certain Amish-Mennonite young folk attended on Wednesday nights. "A minister accompanies them while they sing together in unison. Sometimes they sneak in a harmony line."

"Two or more parts?" she asked.

He nodded, grinning.

"And where's this you're talkin' about?"

"Sugarcreek, Ohio. Some of the Plain women there wear pastel-colored dresses and the men own and drive cars."

She didn't know why Isaac was talking so much about other states and church districts, but because he hadn't settled down yet and joined his own church, he was entitled to "talk out" his own answers, like Dat used to tell

Rose's older brothers to do before they bowed their knees to the church and to almighty God.

The evening sped by, and after a few hours, Isaac brought her back to Salem Road and parked at the end of Dat's driveway. Rose's cheeks were so cold she could hardly move her lips to say good-bye.

He politely helped her down and walked her nearly to the back door. "I hope you didn't get too chilled."

She smiled. "Oh, I'll get warmed up soon enough."

"Well, you take *gut* care, Rose. Hope ya had a nice time."

"I did. Denki."

She didn't turn to watch him run helter-skelter back to his carriage, but she heard his boots crunching against the ground as she slipped quietly into the warm kitchen. She stood beside the cookstove so she could get thawed out right quick. And it was then Rose realized Dat had stoked the fire just for her, guessing she was out this frosty night.

When the feeling returned to her nose and fingertips, Rose pulled off her boots and set them just so near the stove. Then, tired but pleased, she climbed the stairs to her room. For the first time in a good many weeks, she felt like dancing a jig. Just not one accompanied by fiddles and guitars and whatnot. Goodness!

She lit the gas lamp in her room and dressed for bed. Instead of going right to sleep, Rose found Isaac's letter in the drawer and reread every word, wondering why he hadn't asked her to meet up with him again next week. Wondering, too, if he might write his invitation instead.

CHAPTER 19

$\mathcal{H}$en had such difficulty sleeping Saturday night, she got up and repeatedly walked the upstairs hall. When that didn't tire her, she slipped into the room where Brandon had slept during his stay. *All but one night.* Yet she couldn't let herself dwell on that sweet time with him. She brushed it aside lest the memory hurt her even more.

Eventually, she leaned down to press her face into Brandon's pillow, yearning for his familiar scent. Alas, she'd stripped the bed and washed the sheets and quilts up nice and tidy, just as any Amish hostess would after a guest departed.

A guest . . .

Lying there, she stared at the doorway and into the hall, hearing her little girl moan in her sleep. Her heart broke for Mattie Sue even now as she rose and tiptoed across the way. Gently, she lowered herself onto Mattie's bed and looked into the dear, innocent face.

Hen hadn't told Rose how hard Mattie Sue had cried Friday evening at the table, too distraught to eat a bite, when it was clear her daddy wasn't coming for supper. Nor did she tell her sister how Mattie Sue had taken herself off to bed Saturday afternoon and sobbed so hard she'd slept for two hours. It was during that time Rose had come with Dat's socks and two sets of darning needles. Surely, though, it was an excuse to look in on them. Rose was so kind and caring. Hen wished now she'd treated her better during the years in town. *With Brandon . . .*

Before October, whenever Hen and her husband had a conflict, no matter how bitter, they rolled to the middle of their bed and made up with great affection that very night. Never before had they struggled like this . . . or for this long.

Hen looked lovingly at Mattie Sue, her blond curls gracing her shoulders as she slept. The little white organdy prayer cap hung nearby on the bedpost. *I can't keep her from her daddy. She loves him . . . and he loves her.*

She left Mattie's side and went to her room to light the lantern. Then, carrying it downstairs, she checked the stove and added more logs. Quickly, she located her Bible on the end table in the front room. Placing the lantern close to the page, she read from Genesis, chapter forty, reminded of Joseph's perseverance in the face of many difficulties. He trusted that God was in control. Joseph's great hope didn't come from his own willpower—or from wanting his own way.

Willpower fades ... it doesn't last, she thought. *I must trust God to work in my husband's life. And mine.*

In the quiet, Hen knelt to pray beside the settee where Brandon had sat to play with Mattie Sue and Wiggles. She focused on one thing only. Not on what she wanted or thought she had to have in order to be happy, but on God's love. Was it possible to demonstrate that kind of love to her husband? Was she willing to let go of her own will—give it up to God's sovereignty?

Hen prayed, pouring out her sadness, her sorrow . . . and her words of repentance. Wiping away her tears, she rose, picked up the lantern, and carried it back up the stairs. It was time for rest now as the peace of God filled her heart. And then and there she knew what she must do to mend her marriage. Sure as her husband could see once again, she knew.

After Preaching tomorrow, Hen told herself, pulling another quilt over her precious girl.

~

Rose typically did not daydream during the sermons at Preaching. But this Lord's Day her mind was still caught up with Isaac Ebersol and their first date. In fact, she'd thought of little else since she snuffed out the gas lantern in her room late last night.

Goodness, had she ever known such a unique fellow? Even more fun-loving than Silas Good, and not as conservative. The fact that Isaac seemed to delight in going to the barn dances he'd described didn't bother her too much, not when she'd never actually heard they were forbidden by her church. Yet somewhere inside her, Rose knew it was best not to tell Hen nor any of her sisters-in-law about them. Nor Dat, either. It wasn't as if she'd ever find herself going to such a line dance. After all, Isaac hadn't even asked to see her again.

And that was the main reason Rose sat in church pondering the young man from Bart. Oh, she certainly did hope he'd ask her on another date, and soon. He was very different from any of the young men who'd casually taken her riding. She thought briefly of Hank Zook. But no, Isaac wasn't like anyone she'd ever known. *Not even like Nick . . .*

Then and there, Rose planned to surprise Isaac and bake his favorite cake for his twenty-first birthday in August: German chocolate sauerkraut cake. *If we're still seeing each other by then!*

~

It was well after the shared meal following Preaching when Hen left Mattie Sue with Rose Ann and drove to Quarryville . . . to Brandon's street. She pulled up in front of the house and parked, staring at the yard, the porch. Had she truly lived here once?

Hen hadn't expected to feel such a gamut of emotions, especially sadness. Her hands were clammy, clenched in her lap. She'd worn her woolen shawl over her Amish dress and apron, and she felt worse than merely out of place.

Gathering her wits, she stepped out of the car to knock on the front door.

Brandon answered, wearing blue sweats and a shocked look. "Hen. This is a surprise."

"May I come in?"

He opened the door wider and stepped aside. "Nice to see you."

"Thanks." She reminded herself to be sure to speak only English this visit. There in the small entryway, she took in the familiar sights, remembering how she'd felt living here, bringing their baby home from the hospital. . . .

Brandon motioned for her to sit on the sectional in the living room. He sat nearby, although not next to her. For the first time, he did not ask immediately about Mattie Sue, or even inquire after her whereabouts.

Finally she ventured, "How's your sight today?"

"Shadowy now and then, but becoming more dependable each day," he said with enthusiasm.

"That's wonderful to hear."

He nodded, the moment somewhat awkward. "So, tell me, how's your mother's doing? Any word?"

Hen made herself breathe before answering . . . still staring at Brandon. He seemed so friendly.

She recounted her mother's progress so far. "She'll be out of the ICU tomorrow, Dad said."

"Terrific . . ." He smiled. "And how's Bishop Aaron?" he asked. "Have you seen him lately?"

"Well . . . at Preaching today, though I didn't get a chance to speak to him. I visited some with Barbara, though." Hen wasn't sure what to say, but they continued making small talk until an even more uncomfortable lull developed. Hen's gaze fell to the coffee table, and she was dismayed to see a real estate brochure and a business card there. Sighing, she forged ahead. "I guess you're wondering why I'm here."

"Not to see me?" He smiled again.

She motioned toward the real estate brochure. "I just hope I'm not too late."

"Late?"

"I take it you really do want to sell the house."

"Oh, that. I meant to talk to you, but—well, it's not easy getting in touch with you."

She could hardly swallow. "So you're moving ahead with the divorce?" She stared down at her folded hands. This was going terribly. Hen wished she hadn't come.

"I didn't mean to give you the wrong impression, but—"

"No, no. I understand. Like you've said before, nothing has changed."

"Hen, please, hear me out."

"You live in your world, and I live in mine."

"That's where you're wrong. *Everything* has changed . . . at least for me."

She searched his face. "I don't understand."

Brandon leaned forward. "Going blind, even temporarily, helped me see what I've been missing, what I was too imperceptive to realize before . . . too unwilling to grasp."

He spoke so earnestly and with such care that it gave her the courage she needed.

"Brandon, I came to tell you I want to come home. That is, if you're still willing to have me."

"What?" He frowned . . . then brightened.

"I'm leaving the Amish life behind for you. For us." She thought of their elopement. "And this time I mean it."

"Hen, I can't let you do that."

"No, you've misunderstood. I *want* to come home, Brandon."

He leaned back on the sofa, his eyes intent on her. "I've known for a while that I was a fool to require you to wear modern clothes and pretend to be English when you're clearly Amish through and through."

"But—"

"I won't let you give up something that makes you so obviously content. That would be cruel."

She wanted to please him, wanted to erase this serious frown on his handsome face.

"When I was blind, I couldn't see your Plain clothes, but I saw *you*, Hen . . . who you are, fully and completely. It took being without my physical sight to realize how terribly blind I was, that my wife is beautiful in every way, no matter what Amish dress she's wearing."

Hen blushed and looked toward the window. The room was resplendent with sunlight, just as she'd always remembered. This lovely room . . .

"I was surprised how you took care of me," he continued, "even though I'd talked repeatedly about divorce."

She breathed in everything he was saying, hoping for more.

"Your entire family accepted me despite everything, as if I belonged—not the outsider I've been determined to be."

"So then, why do you want to sell . . ." She couldn't go on or she might cry.

"The house?" He chuckled thoughtfully and rubbed his hands together. "I want to look for a place closer to your family, somewhere in the country."

She was stunned. "You're telling me you want to move . . . *closer?*"

"Honestly, Hen, I never thought I'd say this, but I miss the country. You know, the sound of barn swallows chattering in the distance."

"The way the haze hangs low on the fields first thing in the morning," she said, knowing he'd seen it only once—the day he'd left.

"And all that fresh air." He laughed. "Do I sound like a poet?"

She shook her head. "I can't believe this."

"I've been considering the idea for the

past week. Maybe a house near Salem Road.
What do you think?"

"I . . ." She was overcome with joy. "Oh,
Brandon, I don't know what to say."

He ran a hand through his thick shock of
hair. "Well, I figured if my wife and daughter
weren't going to budge, then I might as well
go to them." He moved over next to her on
the sofa. "Would that be all right with you,
my love?"

She had to be dreaming. Brandon never
talked like this—not even when they were dating.

"I have to admit it," he said with a trace of
embarrassment. "There's something about
the Plain mindset—and their values, too."

"Brandon, I never thought I'd—"

"Listen to me." He slipped his good arm
around her. "There's something about *you*,"
he said, smiling into her eyes. "I want us to be
a family again . . . you, me, and Mattie Sue."

She longed for that, too.

"We can have the best of both worlds—
your Plain life intermingled with my English
one. I know we can make it work."

"But how?"

"Well, with God's help."

She let it slip. "Jah," she whispered.

"Maybe we could attend the little country

church near Salem Road, or sometimes go to the Amish Preaching service."

Now she knew she must be dreaming!

Brandon held her near. "After learning to live without TV, I'd give that up in a heartbeat in exchange for telling stories and reading to Mattie Sue after supper."

"And in the blink of an eye, she'll be doing math homework and want you to double-check it," she added, laughing softly.

He suggested there were many other things he enjoyed doing with their daughter. Things that would not cause a rift, like before.

She heard the sincerity in his voice. He wasn't kidding. Her husband was willing to sacrifice for her, just as she was for him. *Like Dad suggested months ago.* "Brandon, listen . . . I don't have to wear Amish clothes, I really don't."

"I'm cool with it—do as you wish." He paused and reached for her hand. "I really am."

She smiled up at him. "I've come to realize that I can wear pretty dresses and skirts and not feel like I'm sinning. More important, I don't have to dress Plain to be accepted by God."

"But I thought you wanted to join your parents' church?" he asked.

"I did, but my faith and my relationship

with you are more important than the trap-
pings of Amish life." She paused, blinking
back tears. "Don't you see? I'd do most anything to be with you."

He pressed his face against hers. "Hen,
honey . . ."

"I'm sorry for being so selfish." Hen
reached up and removed her Kapp and took
the pins out to let down her long hair. "Can
you forgive me?"

Brandon did not answer with words. His
eyes lingered over her hair, her eyes, and
slowly, yet with resolve, he leaned near and
his lips found hers. She surrendered gladly,
nestling ever closer into his ardent embrace,
joyfully returning his kisses.

CHAPTER 20

Not a sound was to be heard in the snowy field where Solomon had gone walking after church. He craved some time alone and a jaunt through his fields. Emma's hospitalization caused him great concern, as had the dogmatic second sermon today, preached by Bishop Simon, the overseeing bishop from Bart. *Nothing at all like Aaron's preaching.* Sol had tried not to allow any speck of resentment to raise its ugly head as he listened. Still, it was awful hard to see Aaron Petersheim sitting two rows in front of him and not feel pangs of sorrow for his neighbor. The clock was ticking toward the end of Aaron's ministry.

The People had stayed around longer than usual during today's shared meal, perhaps because it was so cold no one was in a hurry to hitch up and head home. And, too, the fellowship brought its own sense of warmth on such a frigid day.

Sol had noticed Hen and Rose sitting close together at a table during the second serving when the younger adults ate. Both looked rather solemn and he wondered what was going through their minds.

Then, right after they arrived home from church, Hen left Mattie Sue with Rose and got in her car and rushed out of the driveway and up the road. Though she didn't say, Sol presumed his daughter was hurrying off to see Brandon. And, oh, did he ever hope so!

Earlier, while the men waited outdoors for the women to lay out the cold cuts and pie, Aaron had confided that Brandon had asked him to read from the Bible about God's sovereignty the last time they'd talked. Sol wondered why he'd waited this long to say something, but he didn't question the man of God—which was how he still viewed Aaron Petersheim and always would.

When Sol asked about Brandon's reaction to the Scripture reading, a slow, lingering smile came to Aaron's ruddy face. *"Well, he was all ears, that I can tell ya."*

Sol had felt like he might burst right there. And thinking about it now, he still did. So he walked, letting all of this soak in.

~

Instead of letting her leave for the farm alone, Hen was pleased when Brandon suggested riding along so they could tell Mattie Sue of their plan to move to the country. Brandon also thought the three of them might like to spend one more night together in the Dawdi Haus.

On the way, they discussed replacing his car, which had been totaled in the accident, but Brandon didn't exhibit any real urgency about it. He actually wondered aloud if it might be possible for them to get by with only one vehicle, even suggesting she might want to drive horse and buggy once in a while.

"You mean it, Brandon?" She eyed him suspiciously as she drove the back roads.

"Well, it would mean having to feed a horse. Guess we'd need a small barn, too."

She smiled. "I don't think you're serious."

"Think what you want . . . but I didn't mention this idea merely to tease you."

"Mattie Sue *would* love having a horse, even if we don't buy a buggy."

They talked about other ideas he had, such as having electricity but also gas lamps for occasional use.

"For atmosphere, you mean?" She chuckled.

"Well, why not?" He was flirting with her.

"If it's all right with you, then it's fine with me."

"We'll give Mattie Sue some of each of our worlds—how's that?"

Again, Hen was amazed—and delighted—at his eagerness to accommodate her. And all these thoughts had come to Brandon even before he'd known what *she* was willing to give up for him! God had found a way to bring them together, and it was truly for the best. Oh, wouldn't her family be surprised!

~

Back in the cozy Dawdi Haus late that afternoon, Mattie Sue was overjoyed. She snuggled with her daddy as they sat on the settee. "Are we goin' to live close to Dawdi and Mammi?" She beamed at the news of Brandon's search for a country house.

"We'll see what's for sale, honey."

Mattie Sue pressed her face against his good arm.

"You can come along with Mommy and me when we go looking, how's that?"

Hen had to purse her lips to keep them from quivering at the happiness of it all.

This was like a scene from one of her sister's many books. Thinking of that, Hen realized Rose didn't know what Brandon and she were considering—her sister had been quick to shoo Mattie Sue home when she spotted Hen's car in the drive, keeping herself out of the way. But, first things first, Hen must slow down and let things play out. She leaned back in the chair while Brandon answered Mattie Sue's many questions, their daughter reminding Hen very much of herself.

"Yes, I'll stay with you and Mommy tonight—it's our last night here, so we'll celebrate." Brandon kissed her rosy cheek. "Okay?"

"And then we'll pack up tomorrow, ain't?"

He looked at Hen. "There's not much to pack, right, hon?"

"I'm leaving my Amish clothes here, so not much, no."

"Can *I* wear my Amish dresses back at home, Daddy? Perty please?"

Brandon shook his head. "Hmm . . . you said you want to dress like Mommy, right?" He winked at Hen.

Mattie Sue's eyes grew wide, her hand resting on his cast. Then a slow smile broke across her cute face. "Ach, I think you're pullin' my leg. Aren't ya?"

He kept a straight face for a moment. Then his eyebrows rose as he fessed up. "You—and Mommy—can wear whatever you'd like. Well, within reason."

Mattie Sue burst into giggles, clapping her hands. "I knew you were kidding!"

Brandon said he'd return to pick them up after work tomorrow. "I'll load up the car . . . and take both of you home with me."

"And then we'll move to the new house in the country?" Mattie Sue asked.

"We have to find it first, honey. We'll trust the Lord for that," Hen replied, hoping she wasn't speaking out of turn.

Brandon reached his arms around their little girl and nuzzled her cheek with his chin.

Hen was riveted by the two of them. Brandon really was a devoted father. How could she ever have doubted it?

~

Rose Ann rolled up on one elbow and looked at Hen from her spot on the old bed. They'd come upstairs to talk privately in Rose's room while Mattie Sue and Brandon helped Dat in the barn, putting feed in the animals' troughs. Rose studied her sister's face and reached for a pillow, pushing it securely behind her. "This all happened so fast, ain't?"

Hen nodded her head. "God is surely working in us."

"Ach, and quicker than I ever dreamed possible."

Hen sighed. "I have a lot to make up for,

insisting on my own way for so many months . . . about working at the fabric shop, for one thing."

"Are ya quitting, then?"

Hen blinked and looked down at her hands. "Brandon and I haven't talked about that, but I'm willing to give it up."

"Do ya think he'll put his foot down, like before?"

"I doubt it. He seems more relaxed. He's changed . . . we both have."

Rose's heart was warmed by the fact Hen had taken her into her confidence. Oh, to think her sister and husband were going to be together once more, their love renewed! And, with God's help, maybe now they'd find true happiness, one that wasn't tainted by selfish whims. It was as Rose had always hoped, in spite of the possibility that she might not see Hen as often again. And in that moment Rose realized that she, too, wanted something more than mere pretending and daydreaming about a lifelong love. She wanted to live in the here and now, not through her books.

"Is there anything I can help you with tonight?" asked Rose.

"You're helping right now, just by being here." Hen pulled her to her feet and gave her a sisterly hug. "And your prayers . . . you'll keep us close that way, jah?"

Rose promised. "Mamm will be overjoyed at this."

"Brandon and I'll go see her soon and tell her ourselves. You have no idea how fond he's become of Dad and Mom—all the family, really."

Rose opened her door and followed her sister downstairs, thinking how things would be from here on out and missing Hen already.

When they stopped at the back door, Rose asked if she could come over tomorrow to help pack.

"There's very little to do, mostly Mattie Sue's bedding and books and toys."

"We can make short work of that."

Hen smiled and kissed her cheek. "Mattie Sue would love having you come, if you'd like."

"I'll let yous be tonight. Unless you want to have supper here. It will be just Dat and me."

Hen set her chin. "Denki, but I'm looking forward to spending our last evening just the three of us. I hope you understand."

Love makes people beautiful, Rose thought, gazing at her sister. Everything about her seemed to radiate joy. "No worry. Have a wonderful-*gut* evening together."

Smiling sweetly, Hen waved, saying, "Oh, we will" over her shoulder.

Hen's meaning had not been lost on her—tonight they wanted to embrace their own little family. Rose watched her sister step across the walkway to the Dawdi Haus one last time and wondered how she'd ever managed all the years Hen had lived in town. To think Hen and her family might live neighbors to them soon!

Rose fairly danced back into the kitchen, hoping with all of her heart that nothing would change Brandon's or Hen's mind.

What a wonderful new beginning, she thought.

CHAPTER 21

Washday dawned, and before Hen packed, she and Rose hung out the week's washing for their grandparents, as well as for Dat. Hen had also laundered her Amish dresses and aprons, which she planned to leave behind, thinking Mammi Sylvia could offer them to one of the young women in the church. Rose suggested they didn't have to concern themselves with that just yet—there was time to decide.

Hen's face shone as they worked. Of course, it might've been the brisk breeze that put a bright red cherry on each of Hen's cheeks. Rose couldn't imagine a better outcome for the three of them. *The entire family.* She thought of Mamm, recalling how much stronger she was last evening, when Rose went along with her father to visit after supper. She and Dat had been hard-pressed not to reveal Hen's happy news, but they would leave that to her and Brandon, who planned to stop by the hospital later today. The very notion made Rose feel light with joy.

~

Rose hurried out to the mailbox Tuesday, wondering if there might be mail from Isaac. Not only was there a letter from him, but there were two from Mamm, one for her and one for Dat. Her heart beat fast as she thought of Isaac's letter, but she read the short one from Mamm first, comforted by the familiar handwriting. Mamm was quite sentimental, saying how much she missed everyone, just as she'd said Sunday evening when Rose visited her at the hospital. Mamm was eager to return home, and Rose could hardly wait for that day, as well.

It'd be awful nice if you could tell Barbara I'm grateful for her prayers and her love. Will you give her my greeting, Rose, dear? When I'm stronger, I'll write to her, too.

Rose brushed away her tears, hoping to visit Mamm again soon with Dat. Things were so quiet around here with Hen and Mattie Sue gone. Rose hoped Mamm's days of rehabilitation—she was scheduled to be moved to a center in Lancaster later this week—would speed by.

After rising to stoke the fire, Rose read Isaac's letter. What had he written this time? Curious, she tore open the envelope.

Dear Rose,

How are you? I hope you and your family—your Mamm especially—are doing well.

We had a no-Preaching day on Sunday, so there was plenty of visiting going on. Some of my cousins told me about a gathering nearby, this coming Saturday evening. Would you like to go? I'd come pick you up in a car driven by one of my Mennonite cousins. Likely it will be too cold for you to ride both ways in my open buggy, and I can't ask for the family carriage. My parents will be using it to visit Bishop Simon and his wife for supper that night.

If you'd want to go, just drop me a note. I'll have it in a day or so.

Until I hear from you,
Isaac

She smiled at his enthusiasm and wondered if it might be a Ping-Pong tournament with several other couples. He'd mentioned on their first date how he enjoyed playing.

Lots of fellows she knew liked to play and were nearly impossible to beat.

There was no question in her mind that she wanted to accept Isaac's invitation, even though he'd mentioned going by car—a cousin's, no less! How odd that was! Still, it would be a good chance to find out more about this young man who was related to her own sister-in-law.

Rose folded the letter and pushed it neatly back into the envelope, then took it upstairs to slip into her drawer. Hurrying downstairs again, she hoped to contain her anticipation, or Dat might notice and wonder what was up.

~

Solomon knew better than anyone how to make Emma smile. He had spent more than eleven years encouraging her while she was wheelchair-ridden. And since her surgery, he'd taken her a card every few days, brought from Rose's greeting card box. He liked the idea of filling up every inch of the corkboard across from her bed with greetings from dozens of relatives and friends, including Aaron and Barbara. He'd make sure the cards decorated her new room at the Lancaster Osteopathic Hospital, too, where she would be receiving specialized rehabilitation therapy. There, the whole family could rally around her, taking turns cheering her on through what would be a long and grueling rehab process.

Emma would be spending her birthday there at the rehab center, as well. Sol would urge all of them to visit her on that particular day—coming up in nine days now. Perhaps Sylvia or Rose could bake a nice two-layer cake.

He'd thought of bringing something for Emma's sweet tooth, too, but decided it might be better to wait till after she was transported to Lancaster and was settled in. As it was, she had a surprisingly good appetite, eating the generous food portions on her tray. Never once had she complained about the hospital fare as some folk did.

Emma's postsurgery pain had improved dramatically with the aid of ice applications and electrical devices. The orderlies came in frequently and moved her into various positions to ease the pressure on her spine, as well.

Sol's driver turned onto Salem Road. The woodsmoke pouring from his neighbors' chimneys cheered Sol, and he noticed Deacon Esh's gas lamps lit downstairs in his house, his wife and daughters no doubt cooking supper. Sol knew this stretch of road like the back of his hand; even as a boy, he'd walked it to the fishing hole come Pentecost Monday, and to the old one-room schoolhouse.

How good it'll be for Emma to see home again—weeks away yet.

Passing the Petersheims' place now, Sol recalled Aaron's sympathetic smile yesterday. Evidently Brandon and Hen, with Mattie Sue, had stopped in to see Aaron and Barbara on their drive back to their place in town. *"They came to thank me for visiting Brandon while he was recovering in the Dawdi Haus,"* Aaron had said, obviously surprised. Solomon was pretty tickled when he considered it. Not just a little had changed between the bishop and Brandon Orringer since their first meeting.

The accident altered something in Brandon's heart, Sol realized anew, just as the frightening experience had changed Hen.

Sol wouldn't permit himself to think how his daughter might be doing today—as a young widow—had the worst happened to Brandon last Christmas. No, it was like the two of them had been given a second go at their marriage . . . and at life. Mattie Sue would have both her parents living under the same roof. The thought made him misty eyed.

He could hardly wait to see them again. And soon he would give Mattie Sue her first riding lesson. It would be fun to teach such a lively youngster to ride. Sol hoped it would strengthen their special grandfather-grand-daughter bond.

When they pulled into his lane, Sol paid the driver and asked to be driven to York again in the morning. "Could we leave right after breakfast, say around seven-thirty?" He would return to Gilbert Browning's sometime past noon to work on the addition.

"Sure, that'll be fine." The driver thanked him and waved good-bye.

Sol got out and walked toward the house, where the welcoming lights of home beckoned. He could see Rose Ann moving about inside, preparing their meal. What he wouldn't give to know if she was being courted by a God-fearing Amish fellow. He hadn't heard anything more from Mose about the introduction they'd set up over there—as was their custom, he really wasn't supposed to know. Still, Sol was curious as a cat and made his way through the back door, calling, "Hullo there, Rosie! What's for supper?"

CHAPTER 22

"Are you getting into the swing of modern life again?" asked Diane Perlis as she and Hen drank coffee together on Wednesday morning. Diane had dropped by on her way to take Karen to her preschool playgroup.

"S'pose I am." Hen offered her some fruit from the bowl in the center of the table where they sat in the breakfast nook.

The sound of Mattie Sue and Karen playing down the hall in Mattie's room brought a smile to both women's faces, as the little girls chirped like happy birds. "They've missed seeing each other," Diane said.

"I think so, too." Hen nodded, uncertain how Diane would take the news about their plan to move to the country.

"You and Brandon should come to dinner sometime—the girls would enjoy that." Diane pushed her long hair over her shoulders. "We all would."

"Sure," Hen said. "We should probably get it on the calendar, since we've decided to sell the house," she added.

"You've listed it?" Diane looked surprised.

"The For Sale sign will go up shortly."

Diane frowned, her dark eyes blinking. "Why, Hen? Is Brandon selling his share in the business, as well?"

"No, we'd just like to find a house out a ways."

"But not too near the Amish, right?"

"Actually . . ." Hen couldn't help but smile. "We want to be *surrounded* by Amish farmland." She didn't divulge the fact that Mattie Sue was probably telling her little friend the same news right now. In fact, if she wasn't mistaken, Mattie was teaching Karen how to talk Deitsch; she could hear the girls laughing together. *Won't Diane just faint?*

"Wow, this is big, Hen."

"I know it."

"And Brandon's in favor?"

"It's his idea."

Diane's mouth dropped open. "No kidding."

Hen explained that the accident and Brandon's slow yet successful recovery at her parents' farm had played a role in his decision. "His priorities have really changed."

"Whatever suits your fancy," Diane muttered, taking another sip of coffee. "Hard to comprehend."

"I'm sure it is," said Hen.

During a lull in the rather awkward conversation, Hen mentioned that Mattie Sue would still be able to play with Karen as long as the dolls were dressed modestly. "No Barbies. We want the toys to reflect our values."

"Good luck enforcing any of that at this age."

Hen was aghast. "But, Diane, if you can't have a say in your child's life during her preschool years, how can you expect to influence her to make wise choices when she's a teenager? And if she doesn't know where you draw the line, how will she ever learn to share your beliefs?"

Diane shrugged. "You're talking about toys, Hen—don't you think you're making too much out of this?"

"Brandon and I can't afford to wait till the right moment comes along to teach Mattie Sue about what's important. If we don't talk about kindness or patience and compassion in our daily life, we might miss our chance. Values like that can't be pulled out of thin air."

Diane inhaled loudly.

"How we live reflects what we love most. It's about faith."

Diane's eyes squinted nearly shut. "That's such a loaded word."

Hen was feeling exasperated, but she wouldn't let her English friend get under her skin. "All right, then . . . it's about the Lord."

"Listen, Hen. Faith for you might be about God, but I believe in myself."

The last thing Hen wanted was to argue. It was clear why they didn't see eye to eye. "You know, confidence is one thing," she replied. "God also gives us that. I was talking about living a life to glorify Him."

Diane looked over her shoulder. "Karen, honey, we need to go." Her expression was pinched and her voice too loud. She called to her daughter several more times before marching off to find her and then getting her wrapped up to head out. Her good-bye was brief.

Did I say the right thing? Hen wondered later. She poured milk for Mattie Sue, somewhat amused by Mattie's desire to keep wearing her Amish dress. Her daughter had mimicked Hen and not worn her organdy prayer Kapp since they arrived home, however.

Thinking again of Diane Perlis and Karen, Hen knew she might have very little time left to spend with them, especially if all went well with the house search. She felt she'd failed in her attempt to be a thoughtful friend today. *Please help me be more patient with her, Lord.*

"I miss playin' with the bishop's grandkids," Mattie Sue said, her mouth all white from the milk. "And Beth, too."

I miss a lot of things, Hen thought. She peeled a banana and gave Mattie Sue half. "Let's think about the good things we have right here—count our blessings. All right?"

"Okay, Mommy. What's the first one?"

"Well . . . at the top of the list is that Daddy can see again and is getting stronger every day. And soon, he'll have his cast off."

Mattie looked up at her, nodding. "Being home with both Daddy and you is the best to me!"

Hen smiled down at her darling girl. "Oh, honey, I love you so much!"

Mattie Sue set down her glass of milk and stood on tiptoes to kiss Hen. "I love *you*, Mommy." With that, she wiped her face with the back of her hand and dashed back to her room to play.

Hen cleared the table and picked up the kitchen, then set about organizing the things she wanted to take in the move. It was going to be a challenge to keep this house nice and tidy for potential buyers—for the unexpected call from a real estate agent eager to show it at the drop of a hat. Mattie Sue helped some by arranging her own toys on the shelves in her room.

Hen whispered a prayer of gratitude. They were a family once again. And Brandon had kept his word and unplugged the TV, spending his free time with her and Mattie Sue. He'd also let it slip that he'd visited a small country church where Bruce and his wife had recently started attending—one not far from Hen's parents' house. So, at least one of the Sundays while he was staying at the Dawdi Haus, Brandon had attended church when Hen had assumed he and Bruce had gone to the office to work. Her husband was certainly full of surprises!

~

As always, Rose enjoyed going to the Thursday morning quilting bee. And the next day, she spent time working side by side with Mammi Sylvia to hand-dip dozens of candles. Since keeping extra busy helped pass the time, Rose baked several loaves of bread, taking some to Barbara, as well as to Annie Mast. Annie seemed quite pleased she'd stopped by, which gave Rose a good opportunity to see the twin babies, Mary and Anna, already nearly two and a half months old. Rebekah Bontrager had stepped away from the stove, where she was preparing supper, to visit a bit with Rose, as well. Rose enjoyed the pleasant time of conversation with both women. Rarely did she see Annie at Preaching anymore, since the weather was simply too cold to risk bringing the babies.

By Saturday afternoon, Rose had also visited Mamm twice in her new location, enjoying the fact it was just a hop, skip, and a jump to see her now. Rose had even made a family visiting chart so they wouldn't cluster up and wear Mamm out. That way, there were certain days for each of them to visit, which gave Mamm something to look forward to. Dat seemed equally pleased with her idea and pronounced her "an especially thoughtful daughter."

Her father didn't comment, however, on Rose's best blue dress that she was wearing this Saturday evening. Although he looked mighty curious as he sat in the rocking chair near the stove, reading his Bible. "Have yourself a nice time, Rose Ann" was all he said when she walked past him after waiting and waiting for him to take his leave of the kitchen.

She hoped to goodness Isaac's cousin knew better than to pull his car into the driveway. That would not go over well with Dat—much too brazen. And while it was fine to hire a driver to travel the busy highways, it was another thing altogether to go courting with a fellow whose cousin owned a car. Akin to grafting a maple branch onto an oak tree.

But Rose needn't have concerned herself—Isaac's cousin crept a healthy distance up the road, just far enough away that she had no fear of Dat's or Bishop Aaron's spying her getting into the sedan.

She was happy to see Isaac again. After they greeted each other and heard about each other's week, Rose inquired about Leah Miller. "Is she still seeing your twin brother, maybe?"

"Oh jah, Jacob's taking her to a youth gathering tonight," he said.

This made her rather curious to know where Isaac had in mind to take *her*. Rose didn't press, though, telling herself to be patient. It felt peculiar that his Mennonite cousin was merely the driver and didn't have a girlfriend sitting with him while Isaac and Rose sat on either side of the backseat. *Like we have a hired driver.*

When they pulled into the long lane of the farmhouse, Rose wondered if Isaac might at last reveal where they were going. But he said nothing, instead getting out and going around to open her car door. "Is it a Singing, then?" she asked as she heard the lively sounds of a guitar and a fiddle drifting out from the upper level of the barn. The fast music was altogether foreign to her but exciting none-theless.

"There'll be more dancin' than singing tonight," he replied quietly.

Rose fell in step with her new fellow, torn between anticipation and her own hesitancy. Surely Mose and Ruthann were not aware of Isaac's more progressive leanings. *Ach, surely not!*

The thought of Nick crossed her mind then, startling her. Would her old friend enjoy such a barn dance? Would he even know how to line dance? Dismissing the image of dark-haired Nick, she smiled back at her date, who slid open the barn door and let her in first, courteous as always. Immediately upon entering, he was recognized by a number of youth who waved and called, "Ike!"

Already there were so many teenagers crammed into the upper level of the barn, Rose felt almost too warm, despite the cold outside. During the first dance, Rose hung back, just watching. But Isaac was eager to teach her the different steps, showing her how to move forward in the line, do-si-do, and other easy maneuvers once he managed to get her on the floor. *Is this really so wrong?* she wondered, moving her feet ever so slowly to the rhythm of the guitar.

She was plumb out of breath by the fourth

line dance, though not so much from physical exertion as from her own conscience. Was she pushing past the boundaries set by her baptism?

What would Dat and Mamm think?

But as the night progressed and the toe-tapping sound of the jamboree-style music became more familiar to her ears, Rose set aside her worries. Isaac's flirtatious winks and infectious laughter nearly made her forget herself—and her guilt! She was actually sorry when the musicians ceased their playing and packed up their instruments for home, the evening at an end.

Outside, while they waited near the road for his cousin to meet them with his car, Isaac reached for her gloved hand. She was quite convinced he thought of her as his own special girl. And Rose rejected her earlier reluctance brought on by the line dancing and rambunctious music. No, she wouldn't change anything about this wonderful-good night. Not a single thing.

CHAPTER 23

*D*ays later, on a cold February evening, Rose Ann served a spicy pumpkin roll for dessert, with hot coffee. Sol and Rose were sitting at the table when they heard a car pull up outside. A few minutes later, Sol was surprised to hear Hen knock at the back door, calling before she let herself in. "Oh, you're still eating," she said, her face rosy from the cold.

"Kumme have dessert with us," Rose offered, patting the bench beside her.

"Smells yummy!" Hen slid in next to Rose and reached for the knife to cut an ample slice. "Dad, Rosie . . . I'm so excited. We've found a wonderful farmhouse not far from here. I told Brandon I just had to drive over and tell you."

Sol felt his pulse quicken. When Brandon

and Hen had first mentioned wanting to move to the country, he'd hardly believed it. "Where is the place?"

"Just around the corner—barely a stone's throw away. Brandon says if we don't sell the house in town soon, we can simply rent it out. That way, we can move more quickly. And . . . we want you and Rose to see it sometime before we close the deal."

Rose practically fidgeted next to her sister. "Oh, can we, Dat?"

"Why, sure." Then, looking at Hen, he said, "Yous really want to live near Amish farmland?"

"Well, the two of us took your suggestion to heart and made some compromises for the sake of our marriage." Her eyes twinkled. "This just happens to be Brandon's."

Sol's heart swelled at the joy he saw in his daughter's eyes—the pain of recent months but a mere memory. "Well, that's a big compromise, I'll say," he replied. "Wait'll your mother hears this."

"Brandon and I plan to tell her together."

Sol reached for a second piece of pumpkin roll, shaking his head in amazement. "Such a mighty bighearted gesture on Brandon's part."

Hen smiled and nodded. "He says it's the least he can do for Mattie Sue and me." She leaned in conspiratorially. "Plus, he says he kind of misses being near Plain folk—you and Mamm especially."

Sol noticed Rose brush away happy tears.

"Well, *gut* news, indeed," he said, his heart filled with gladness.

~

February's final days faltered as frost-bound soil gave way to fog and rain and early bulbs. Meanwhile, Solomon continued to cross off the days on the kitchen calendar, anxious for Emma's homecoming.

At last, March came in earnest, along with mud and the annual farm sales associated with it. And then, just one day shy of three weeks at the local rehab center, Emma was finally to be released into Sol's care. Overjoyed at the prospect of her return, Sylvia, Hen, and Rose Ann planned a surprise gathering in her honor. A special feast, complete with the three women's best recipes, including the standard main dish served at weddings—roast with tender, shredded chicken and a rich gravy. Delicious!

Feeling downright giddy, Sol had gone around inviting their boys and families the day before, then went over to Brandon and Hen's new place, and last to Petersheims'. He and Brandon set up the extra folding tables and chairs, which spilled into the front room, before Sol stopped to clean up a bit, change clothes, and head off to Lancaster with the driver.

Emma's coming home. Praise be!

∼

Never before had Sol seen such joy on his daughters' faces as when he carried Emma up the walkway and into the house. Tears rolled down Rose Ann's face when she spotted them, and Hen came right over and kissed her mother's cheek, smiling. Brandon stood beside her with Mattie Sue perched high on his shoulder. Even Beth Browning was present, observing quietly.

"It's wonderful to see all of you," Emma said, eyes glistening. "But ya really didn't need to go to all this trouble."

"Oh, we *wanted* to!" Hen and Rose Ann declared in unison, which brought a wave of laughter all around.

Barbara Petersheim waited till all seven sons had greeted their mother before inching forward to pat Emma's hand, their eyes locking for a second in a sweet way as only best friends do. Brandon had seen to it that Emma was comfortable there in the padded rocking chair, where she was managing quite well. Sol was grateful for the strength she'd gained from daily therapy sessions these past weeks.

The younger grandchildren, including Mattie Sue, had brought simple handmade items as tokens of their love, including cards and artwork. And Rose surprised Mamm with the set of teacups and saucers hand painted with Rose's namesake, saying they were once Yost Kauffman's. Emma's face glowed as she lovingly thanked Rose . . . and each one about her. Her delight at being home and with her family again was clear to all.

Emma was flushed by the time they gathered at the various tables—the children in the kitchen and the rest of them scattered across the front room. Her posture looked straighter, and she seemed more alert and energetic than before. Best of all, she was completely pain free.

When Sol bowed his head for the table blessing, he had to deliberately swallow twice. Best to keep his emotions in check, lest the whole bunch of them commence to weeping for joy. And before he ever raised his head, he felt his wife's small, cool hand on his and thanked the dear Lord in heaven for this most remarkable day of days.

PART TWO

My friend, judge not me,

Thou seest I judge not thee.

Betwixt the stirrup and the ground

Mercy I asked, and mercy found.

—WILLIAM CAMDEN

CHAPTER 24

On the last day of June, around nine o'clock in the morning, Rose decided to surprise Barbara Petersheim with a basket of freshly baked sticky buns. The sun was making its slow climb through the trees as she weaved her way through the barnyard and out toward the short-cut. The path was well worn from all the years of neighborly visits. Tall trees lined the way, providing a sanctuary from the sun.

She was halfway to Petersheims' when a yellow taxicab stopped at the end of their lane. A tall, dark-haired Englischer in tan slacks and a mint-green short-sleeved shirt climbed out and paid the driver. He walked with purpose toward the farmhouse.

Suddenly, Barbara rushed out of the house, the hem of her skirt fluttering behind her. Rose stopped in her tracks, staring as Barbara threw her arms around the man. "Can it be?" Rose whispered, her heart pounding in her ears.

Yet Barbara's cries of delight at the unexpected reunion left Rose Ann with no question in her mind. *Nick's back!*

She felt stunned seeing him there, walking with Barbara around the side of the house and up the back porch steps. He had not even a speck of luggage, so Rose assumed he was visiting only briefly.

"This is unbelievable," she whispered, nearly beside herself as she sat on an old tree stump, not certain what to do with the still-warm cinnamon rolls in the basket. If she returned home without taking them to Barbara, Mamm and Mammi Sylvia would surely ask questions, and Rose would have no choice but to reveal why she hadn't made the delivery. As intuitive as her grandmother and mother were, they might read between the lines and suspect Rose was still carrying a torch for her old friend.

I must guard my heart, she thought, remembering Isaac.

Glancing toward the neighbors', she decided to leave the basket of buns on the back porch in hope that Barbara or Nick might find them.

～

Sol had heard through the grapevine that Nick Franco might possibly be in the area, but he'd not told a soul—not even Aaron. Supposedly, the wayward young man had been seen in English clothing inquiring about a house to rent near Quarryville.

That Monday morning, Aaron came in the door to Sol's woodshop, his face ashen. "Got a minute, Sol?"

He pulled up a stool for his friend. "*Was is letz?*—What's wrong?"

"Nick's back. He's over at the house right now, sitting with his feet under our table, talkin' a blue streak."

Sol hardly knew how to respond.

"Says he's come to apologize—to ask for forgiveness and confess his part in Christian's death."

Sol's heart sank at this confirmation of his fears. So Nick *had* played a role in his foster brother's death! "Now, *this* is a surprise."

"That's what I thought at first . . . and now I really don't know what to think. He also insists he wants to join church. But if ya saw him, well, you'd realize he's anything but Plain anymore, Sol."

"What's he say to that?"

"Just that he feels called to be Amish . . . and that he wants to make things right."

Sol was speechless.

"I mean with the membership . . . with everyone." Aaron stopped to mop his brow with his kerchief. "Nick wants to bow his knee before the Lord God and the brethren—and wants to talk things over with Bishop Simon in Bart, too."

"What changed his mind, I wonder?" Sol was baffled.

"All I know is he wants forgiveness . . . so he says."

"Well, has he asked it from you and Barbara?"

"First thing out of his mouth when he arrived a bit ago. And he asked for it as humbly as anybody could wish."

This was so hard to believe, Sol couldn't trust his ears—or Nick. What was he really thinking? "You don't think he's come back for Rosie, do ya?"

"Hard to say."

Sol shuddered. From what Mose had told him, Rose had been seeing Ruthann's cousin from Bart for months now. Who could know, but they might even be engaged. "Guess time will tell why Nick's really here and whether or not he came back for the right reason."

Aaron continued. "I'll admit it was awful hard lookin' him in the face."

"Did he give you any more to go on

. . . 'bout Christian's accident?" Sol almost dreaded asking.

"No." Aaron rubbed his forehead with the back of his arm. "And his contrite words just don't match his English getup."

"So will he stay with you or what?"

"That I don't know, either." Aaron shook his head and took off his straw hat. "I almost asked him how he expects to fit in at Preachin' with his fancy clothes and that English haircut."

"Well, sure . . . why don't ya?"

"Haven't gotten that far. Had to get out for some fresh air . . . prob'ly shouldn't have left Barbara over there alone like that."

A tremor went through Sol.

Aaron glanced toward the door. "I *could* use some extra help with fieldwork," he said.

"Couldn't we all?" But Sol wasn't about to offer Nick any type of work . . . or give him the time of day, for that matter. He sighed, feeling bad about his skepticism. "Just how far does forgiveness go in this case, Aaron?"

"I wonder the same." Aaron rose from the stool to leave. "The timing is awful surprisin', given the brethren will make their final ruling, the start of next month. Even so, Nick seems mighty sincere."

Has someone set Nick up to return on the eve of all of this? Sol worried.

Planting his hat square on his head, Aaron made his way outside. Sol stood watching him walk through the verdant meadow between their houses. He squinted at the sky, bright with the morning sun. There were many hours of work ahead today; he could not let this news rattle him.

Glancing at his house, Sol dreaded going inside for even a drink of cold water, let alone his typical midmorning sticky buns and coffee. He certainly was *not* going to be the one to break the news to Emma and Rose Ann. In fact, if he could somehow back up and begin the day all over again, that would be just fine by him.

Sol turned back to the woodshop, going to sit on the stool where Aaron had been just minutes before. He groaned loudly, reliving the words from his neighbor and friend. *"Nick's back."*

This was the very last thing he'd expected to hear from Aaron this summertime morning. Now or ever.

CHAPTER 25

*R*ose went around opening all the windows at home, coaxing in wafts of cool air. *Everything seems the same, yet so very different.* Her friend Nick had returned and she felt so *ferhoodled*. Hearing his voice inside the Petersheims' house when she left the basket of sticky buns on their porch had made Rose's stomach do flip-flops.

Is this just a visit, or has he come back to stay?

It was already quite warm indoors and she recalled how hot and muggy yesterday had been, without the benefit of a breeze. The smell of fresh dough lingered in the kitchen. She had brushed it lavishly with melted butter and given it a good sprinkling of brown sugar and cinnamon. She'd even added two-thirds of a cup of raisins to the mixture. *Barbara will love it . . . so will Nick.* She laughed a little, realizing his first taste of Amish baked goods upon his return might be of her very own!

She stared out at the sky—a brilliant blue with nary a cloud. Across the sweeping meadow, the ancient trees along the well-worn path swayed gently, their branches intertwined at the crowns. She spotted Aaron Petersheim hurrying along the dirt path toward his house, nearly running. What a true and loyal friend their former bishop had been to her father and vice versa—seeing each other through some difficult times. Aaron had been a good friend to Hen's husband, as well, guiding him spiritually during his recovery. Her sister's reunion with Brandon last winter had been such a blessing . . . and Mattie Sue also seemed happier than ever. *Wouldn't Mattie be thrilled about Nick's return if she knew?*

Rose heard Mamm come from the sitting room, wheeling herself into the kitchen on her own, her upper body much stronger now. Her Bible lay open on her lap as she settled near the window, the sun spilling in all around her. "I like being near you, Rosie, while you cook and whatnot."

The weeks away from home had made her mother more grateful for company. "I like havin' you near, too, Mamm."

Then, turning her attention to making the noon meal, Rose set about frying the thawed hamburger she'd set out on the counter. After just a few minutes, a new aroma began to fill the kitchen.

"The smell of hamburger cooking always brings back memories of you and Hen growin' up, right here . . . at my feet." Mamm smiled.

"Such a happy childhood you gave Hen and me, Mamma. Denki for that."

"Well, that's what mothers do, jah?"

Rose hoped to do the same for her own children in due time. And she was fairly sure Isaac was getting close to asking her to marry him. Of course, he'd have to join the Bart church pretty soon in order to do so this wedding season. And she'd have to transfer her membership to his church district, as well. "The dinner in a dish will be ready in short order," she said.

"Sounds mighty *gut*," Mamm replied, and Rose continued her cooking.

Meanwhile, her mother read aloud from the Psalms. Rose enjoyed hearing each uplifting phrase. " 'O give thanks unto the Lord; for he is good: because his mercy endureth forever. . . .' "

God's mercy.

She wondered how long Nick planned to stay around. Oh, she could hardly wait to talk to him, yet she wanted to be discreet about how she approached him. Or should she at all?

As her mother continued reading, Rose put the casserole in the oven and swept the kitchen floor. That done, she went out and checked on the first line of clothes, which were dry, so she brought in a big basketful.

Later, when the main dish had finished baking, she reached for the potholders to remove it from the belly of the cookstove. The bread crumbs were perfectly browned on top of the layers of lean ground beef, corn, onion, green peppers, and sliced tomatoes. "Here we are," she said, carrying it over to let Mamm drink in the tantalizing scent. "Looks mighty nice, jah?"

"Smells *gut,* too."

"I'll say."

"Your father will want his nice and hot," Mamm instructed.

"I'll ring the dinner bell, all right?" Rose went out and gave the rope a single swift pull. The bell rang loudly, echoing over the cornfields and beyond.

Upon Rose's return to the kitchen, Mamm looked over at her, eyes so clear and sweet, free of pain. She had been through the fire and back and survived. The Lord had been her fortress through that difficult time, and she'd made sure to tell that to everyone who would listen at both the York hospital and the local osteopathic hospital. One of the Lancaster therapists also had a Plain upbringing, so she and Mamm had knit a special friendship. They still wrote letters every few weeks.

Rose set a pitcher of homemade root beer on the table, then glasses at each place setting. The hot dish would be cooled enough to move from the stove top to the table in short order. Oh, that first taste was always pure heaven!

"What's keepin' your father, I wonder?" Mamm said.

"I'll just go out there and let him know we're ready, jah?"

Mamm nodded, a smile on her face.

Dawdi and Mammi arrived just then and said they'd be glad to join in on the noon meal. "Oh jah, Rosie made plenty for everyone," Mamm said as Rose headed outdoors to find Dat.

But her father wasn't to be found in his usual place in the woodshop. And when Rose looked inside the barn, he wasn't there, either. "Guess he'll come in when he's ready," she decided, walking back to the house.

All of them went ahead without Dat, a rare thing for sure. A man of habits, failing to show up for dinner was certainly not one of them.

Afterward, Rose cleaned up the dishes and put away the leftovers, setting the casserole dish on the back of the stove for Dat. When the table was wiped and dried off, Rose sat and talked briefly with Mamm, who suggested they invite Barbara and her married daughters—Verna, Anna, and Susanna—to put up a nice big batch of beans—string, snap, and can them.

"We'll have us a work frolic."

"Jah, and I'll get to see Anna's new little one again," Rose said, thinking of Anna's April baby, named Barbianne after Barbara, who was very pleased about having a namesake.

Mamm loved the idea of seeing her friend's new grandbaby, especially now that she was expecting another grandchild of her own. Hen and Brandon had been delighted to tell them of the baby due this fall, but no one seemed more excited about the news than the big-sister-to-be.

"I'd like to have Hen and Mattie Sue come, too," Mamm added. "And Brandon, as well, if he can spare the time."

"Shouldn't be a problem," Rose said. "Hen says Brandon spends far fewer hours at the office now."

Together, they settled on next Friday as the day for the frolic. Rose then suggested that Hen and Mattie Sue might also help her weed the vegetable garden out back. How she loved watching Mattie Sue talk to the worms she found in the rich soil, getting her fingernails dirty and pressing her little hands deep into the dirt.

Rose headed out to check on the next line of clothes while Mamm responded to her circle letters. Rose had wrapped her hair in a quick coil of a bun after dressing this morning, and already the loose strands were tickling her neck. Given that Nick was in the area, she wished she'd done a neater job. From a distance, he certainly had looked better-groomed than she'd ever seen him. And with that thought, she let go a soft laugh.

Glancing over at the woodworking shop, she wondered where Dat had gone. Something must've come up with one of her brothers, maybe—or a farming neighbor. She hadn't looked for the family carriage or the market wagon, neither one.

Rose was so deep in thought, she was startled nearly out of her wits when Nick appeared from behind the potting shed.

"Ach!" She stepped back, her heart racing. "I didn't see you there." She scrutinized him.

"Didn't mean to startle you, Rosie," he said, still very worldly looking in his English clothes. The green of his short-sleeve shirt highlighted his strong, tanned arms. "It's great to see you."

She tried to say something nice in reply like "You too, Nick," but the words were stuck.

He chuckled, his dark eyes shining. "You haven't changed a bit."

She eyed him curiously—his English haircut, his crisp, clean shirt and pressed trousers in light colors, no less. "No, but you certainly have!"

He smiled his old mischievous smile . . . the one he'd reserved only for her, out in the stable, or when they'd taken Pepper and George riding. *All those years.* "Want to take the horses for a run?" he said, as if sensing the direction of her musing.

Their eyes met and her heart skipped a beat. "Just like that, Nick? Do ya really think we can pick up where we left off?" Her head spun all of a sudden.

"Well, we have much to catch up on," he replied. "It may be hard to believe, but I've come to set things right."

She studied him, noted the way he formed his words. "You sound different. College must've done that to ya."

"You heard about that?"

"Jah. Dat and the bishop went lookin' for ya in Philly. Mrs. Schaeffer told them you were going to a community college somewhere nearby."

"Yes, but it wasn't for me."

She wasn't sure what he meant. "Then you're done with higher education?"

"We should talk about that." He stepped closer. "There's so much I want to tell you, Rosie. So very much."

She looked away, composing herself. It was much easier talking to him when his English getup wasn't distracting her—like all the times she'd talked to the wind and pretended he was there listening. Like the night she'd taken Pepper out for a gallop, crying her eyes out . . . missing him.

"I've had my fill of the world, Rosie. I want you to hear this from me, so there's no mistaking why I've come home." He paused a moment. "That is, if my parents will have me."

My parents . . .

"Your leaving has been so hard for them, considering everything," she cautioned.

He nodded and she saw understanding in his eyes.

"I'm deeply sorry for all the pain I caused them." His eyes searched hers. "And you, too, Rosie."

He motioned for them to walk and she left the clothes on the line, falling into the rhythm of his step. Like old times, they walked toward the barnyard and out to the meadow, to the treed pathway.

"I read your letter," he said.

She stopped walking. "Which one?"

"The one you left in the tin box last December."

She could scarcely breathe. "*You* took it?" Her face burned with embarrassment at the words she'd written: *I love a man I can never marry. I miss you, Nick.*

"Our secret mailbox . . . ain't?" He smiled quickly.

She shook her head, refusing to look at him now. Not this handsome college upstart. Nick Franco, who had been, in many ways, with her in the stable every day since he left—every minute in the barn a reminder that they'd worked there together all those years. Then, just like that, he was gone from her. Out of reach . . . lost to the world.

And here he was, walking with her . . . back from the "edge," as he'd called the boundary between the Plain and modern worlds.

They slowed their pace beneath the dappled sunlight in the leafy cove. "When I read what you wrote about the bishop . . . my father . . . I wanted to return immediately, like you suggested." He shrugged. "But I just wasn't ready."

"What do ya mean?" she asked.

"I needed time." He glanced at her. "Time

to get my heart right with God. I realized He only seems to be silent."

She looked up at him, surprised at his honesty, and attempted to erase the unfamiliar aspects of him—the way he expressed himself, the way he looked—and focus only on his face, his sincere eyes. "God is always there," she said. "We learn that when we give up our will for His."

"And that's not easy."

She agreed. "You throw everything on the mercy, on His purpose for your life. Trusting that He knows best is the hardest part of all."

"I had to wrestle with so much, Rosie...." He looked away, his words trailing off. "Years of self-pity ... and living with a brother who made my life miserable at every turn."

The allusion to Christian caused her to bow her head. Half afraid to hear what Nick might admit to next, Rose changed the subject.

"I can't believe you read my letter." She was still stunned at this.

"Well, you wrote it to *me*." He smiled broadly. "And I must say it sounded convincing enough."

"I wrote it during a very hard time, Nick." She attempted to laugh it off. "Ach, I was prob'ly *ab im Kopp*—crazy in the head—that day."

"Over half a year ago." Nick glanced toward the tops of the trees. He was quiet for a moment, the call of birds the only sound. "Are you still seeing Silas Good?"

She shook her head.

The air seemed to go out of him.

"We parted ways a while back." She sighed, not sure how much she wanted to share. "I released him from our engagement last Christmas."

"You did?"

"He loved someone else more." She paused to lean against a nearby tree.

Nick tilted his head and folded his hands, his fingernails trimmed and neat. "What else have I missed, Rosie?" He seemed to look right into her heart.

"So much." She told of Hen and Brandon's reconciliation and their purchasing a renovated farmhouse around the corner. He was also surprised at Mamm's surgery.

"She's still immobile from the waist down, but she has no pain and is able to take part in life again. She especially enjoys the gatherings with the womenfolk she missed out on for so long."

His eyes softened. "Are you still working for Gilbert Browning?"

She said she was and mentioned that three generations of Brownings were now living under one roof, counting Beth's grandmother. "In fact, my father—and yours—built on a large room where Grandma Browning can live out her sunset years."

"Wish I'd known," Nick said. "I would've offered to help."

Rose smiled.

"Also, the bishop over in Bart has been overseeing our church district for months—appointed by Old Ezekiel."

Nick cringed at the name of the highly revered bishop; the man's reputation wasn't easily forgotten. "What can be done?"

"That lies in your hands, Nick."

He nodded thoughtfully and glanced skyward. His gaze returned to rest on her, his eyes warm with affection.

Instinctively, Rose stepped back, wrapping her arms around her middle. "There's something else you should know." She sat on a rock nearby. "I'm nearly engaged to someone new. I . . . I think ya'd like him."

"*Engaged?*"

"Nearly."

"But in your letter . . ."

She shrugged. "I never meant for you to see it. Honestly."

"Well, you know what I think?" He perched himself on the old tree stump and leaned forward, his clasped hands almost touching hers. "I think you secretly hoped I would."

She shook her head modestly. "I know it had your name on it, but truly it was meant only for God's eyes." Suddenly Rose felt drained of energy.

She looked back toward the house and her family's clothes waving on the line. "I should get back to work," she said softly. "It's really a shock seein' you again."

"I haven't forgotten the last time we were together . . . in Philly." His voice was almost reverent. "It was hard to let you go."

She remembered how tenderly he'd held her, and how guilty she'd felt because she belonged to Silas . . . or so she'd thought. But now, regarding him there in front of her, she was reminded that she'd prayed he might return—especially for Aaron's sake. She offered a smile and added quickly, "Maybe now the bishop's unjust silencing can be lifted at last."

"That's what I'm hoping," he assured her.

"So you came back for that—to help reinstate his ministerial duties?"

"Among other things." His eyes held hers.

Her heart fluttered, which seemed inappropriate, given that Isaac was courting her. And in fine fashion, too, with more dances and Singings and buggy rides in the moonlight.

He wasn't one bit shy about telling her how much he cared for her, both in person and in the letters that were quickly piling up in her dresser drawer.

Nick's voice brought her back. "I'll be helping my father with fieldwork. Hope to see you again, Rosie."

She turned to leave but looked back at him.

"What is it?" he asked softly.

For a split second, she almost wished he'd come home months ago, before she met Isaac. But, shaking her head, Rose said no more and hurried back up the path, leaving Nick sitting there on the old stump in his too-fancy clothes.

CHAPTER 26

After the encounter with Nick, Rose returned to fold more clothes from the line, relishing the scent of sun and air on the dry clothing. Once that pleasant chore was accomplished, she spent a half hour picking strawberries, her bare feet pressing into the mulched soil as she went.

Later, Rose was delighted when Barbara Petersheim dropped by to thank her for the cinnamon rolls. Mamm suggested Rose offer their neighbor some fresh strawberries and cream and also some toast with butter and a mixture of brown sugar and cinnamon, as well as tea served in Mamm's pretty rose teacups. A real treat for Rose, Mamm, and Barbara so late in the afternoon.

All the while they listened as Barbara told of Nick's return. The sunlight poured into the kitchen, and for this moment it almost seemed like nothing dreadful had ever happened to the Petersheim family.

Barbara spoke kindheartedly of her foster son, exhibiting loving acceptance in word and deed. "I'm anxious to sew for him. He needs some Plain work clothes right quick," she said, her fleshy cheeks quite pink.

"He'll need church clothes, too, since Preaching's comin' up again here before long," Rose observed with a glance at Mamm.

Mamm, however, looked ferhoodled, like she scarcely knew what to say. That Barbara had never ceased caring about her foster child was unmistakable, and truth be known, those two words were merely legal jargon. Anyone listening now would say Barbara had never thought of Nick Franco as anything but her very own.

"Are ya sure he's staying long enough for you to bother sewin'?" Rose asked.

"Oh, I'm mighty sure."

Yet how can she possibly know?

"I'm rejoicing at this lost one come home," Barbara said.

"Will he want dreary-colored shirts again?" Rose asked, remembering the dark colors Nick had always favored.

"Hasn't said."

Rose wondered if the light colors of his

modern clothes meant Nick had changed in that regard. For sure and for certain, he'd seemed altogether different earlier today— except in the way he had looked at her.

"More than anything, I hope he can help the bishop keep his ordination," Mamm interjected, and Rose was glad for the distraction.

Barbara's smile was sweet as she pulled a hankie from her sleeve and dabbed at her neck. "Seems the Lord sent him back just in time. We'll have to wait and see what Bishop Simon and Old Ezekiel decide."

Rose listened as Barbara explained that the powers that be would be most interested in Nick's willingness to prove himself and eventually join church. "*Awwer Gott is immer gedreilich*—But God is ever faithful." Barbara's blue eyes shone with such trust.

"Nick wants to become a church member?" Mamm asked, eyes wide.

"He certainly does," Barbara said. "I have no doubt whatsoever he'll soon be an upstanding Amishman, just as Aaron and I have always prayed."

"Bless your heart, Barbara. If anyone will follow the Lord in this, it's you." Mamm lowered her head in gratitude to God.

Rose walked with Barbara to the back door when Barbara was ready to leave. She thanked them for the treat.

"I hope all goes well for Nick . . . and Aaron," Rose said softly. "It'd be so wonderful if our bishop is reinstated."

Barbara nodded, her eyes shining with tears. "Wouldn't it, though?"

Rose watched her go, her heart buoyed by Barbara's faith.

Returning to the kitchen, Rose felt her mother needed to be assured that Nick's proving was a good idea. "I truly believe God means for him to do this."

Mamm raised her eyes to meet Rose's. "You seem mighty sure of yourself."

Their eyes locked and it was Rose who looked away first. She could've said right then that Mamm needn't worry, that Isaac Ebersol was her beau, but she honored the Old Ways and kept that to herself.

"What if Nick came back for *you,* Rose Ann? What then?" Mamm studied her hard. "He was awful fond of you. Barbara herself told me so some time back."

Rose wouldn't admit to any of that. It would only add fuel to the fire, and there was no need. "I'm not interested in Nick Franco," she stated outright. *Not anymore.*

Mamm sighed and laced her fingers on her lap. "Well, I'm relieved to hear that."

Now it was Rose's turn to ask questions. "You must not believe he's back to stay, then?"

"I won't judge, but it's hard not to think otherwise." Mamm glanced out the window toward the bishop's place. "Time is a truth teller."

Rose nodded and began to set out the supper fixings.

"I hope and pray you have a real nice fella," Mamm said suddenly. "One who loves you dearly."

To this, Rose pressed her lips together so she would not smile and give herself away.

~

At supper that evening, Dat looked peaked and said very little. Rose assumed by that he knew Nick was back. He did look quite relieved when Mose and Josh wandered into the kitchen a few minutes after the table blessing, mentioning he'd gone over to Josh's earlier, "on a lark." The boys planted themselves in their former spots, bowed their heads on their own, and joined in eating and talking. As time went by, it was apparent they didn't know of Nick's return, which surprised Rose. Why hadn't Dat told them, when they had been so outspoken about the death of the bishop's only biological son? *"A needless loss of one of our own,"* Josh had boldly declared last November, the day after the burial service.

Barbara Petersheim's tender words of forgiveness came to mind then and stayed with Rose through the meal. Rose was willing to forgive but hesitant to fully embrace Nick's return. After all, hadn't her heart changed its loyalty from Nick to Isaac?

At meal's end, Dat solemnly announced that Nick had come back to make amends and help reinstate Aaron's position as bishop.

Mose exhaled audibly and Josh's eyes widened.

"Being's we're neighbors and church members, I want us to support Petersheims in whatever they choose to do," Dat continued. "Nick has much to make up for, we all know that."

The flat tone in his voice gave him away, but Rose knew he was trying to do the right thing, under God, in giving Nick the benefit of the doubt. Naturally she and her brothers would comply with their father's request, as was their way.

'Tis best . . . following God's commands.

~

Rose saw nothing of Nick all that week until Friday morning, when she happened to spot him walking through Aaron's barnyard.

She noticed his Plain attire and knew Barbara must have sewn for him. Rose wondered how he felt now, after a few days back home. Did he still believe he was cut out to be Amish?

She forced her eyes away when she heard Barbara's voice yoo-hooing as she came up the back walkway for the green bean frolic. Going to the back door, Rose held it open for Barbara and two of her married daughters, Verna and Anna, and Anna's cute baby girl. *"Willkumm, Freind!"* she greeted them.

The Petersheim women had brought several large pails of string beans. Combined with those Rose had gathered from the family garden, they had quite the pile. Hen and Arie Zook came to help, as well, bringing their children. Hen was the only one without beans in hand, but Rose intended to share plenty with her, since Hen was offering her help.

The talk quickly turned to Nick, although Rose tried to steer the conversation to other things. Barbara beamed as she worked. "Our son's ever so changed," she said, which made Hen glance at Rose.

Mamm sat with a bowl of fresh beans on her lap, her fingers stringing away. Mattie Sue and Becky Zook chattered near Arie's sleeping baby boy, both of them busily talking, too. The day was hot and muggy, as were most July days, and the pungent smells of the season filled the room, wafting in from the fields. Rose had several large pitchers of homemade lemonade placed on the table, hoping to keep the womenfolk refreshed and happy.

Rose was glad when Hen said she'd like to have a barbeque over at their new house the last Saturday in July. "And all of you are invited . . . and your families."

Mamm's eyes sparkled. "We'll bring the potato salad," she said. "I just love a good picnic with barbecued chicken."

Arie agreed, her pretty brown eyes shining as she looked over at Hen, who was snapping beans as fast as ever. Arie's freckled face bunched up in a grin as she turned to peek at Mattie Sue and Becky playing with several of Rose's faceless dolls and jabbering in Dutchified English.

"I wanted you to know that I quit my job at the fabric shop recently," Hen told Arie quietly, but Rose heard all the same.

"Goodness, that's surprising," Arie replied.

"Brandon thought so, too."

Rose observed her sister with her best friend and wondered what Arie might say to that. But Arie remained still.

"Honestly, I'm just so busy making curtains and the crib skirt for the nursery, and I'll have more to do come November," Hen told her. "But I'll miss working around the Amish ladies—I know I will."

"You'll have plenty to do with two little ones, believe me." Arie smiled, looking at her own children, over near Mattie Sue.

"Well, I'm ready to be a stay-at-home mom again," Hen said. Her glossy hair was pulled back in a low ponytail to keep her cool. "Spending time around your adorable little Levi and some of the other babies in the community really stirred up a longing in me. I can't wait to have another child."

Rose knew exactly what Hen meant: She, too, had felt besotted with mother-love after holding Anna's infant daughter, Barbianne. She could hardly wait to hold her own wee one some precious day. Of course this wasn't anything she and Isaac had ever dared to discuss; it was too soon. But she *did* know of one courting couple who liked to talk about how many children the Good Lord might give them once married: Leah Miller and Jake Ebersol, who were already engaged, or so Leah had confided in Rose after the last Preaching. Rose had to smile at the thought she and her dear friend, Christian's former sweetheart, might very well be sisters-in-law one day. Leah had endured so much pain and grief, Rose couldn't be happier for her.

Later, during the meal Rose served,

Barbara announced that Nick would be at the next Preaching. "All of you can see him there," she said with confidence.

Rose wondered if Nick would confess openly to the members his part in Christian's death. She shivered as she remembered that horrifying day.

"We'll stand with ya through this," Mamm offered.

Looking serious, Arie Zook nodded her head, as well, and Rose assented as she recalled Dat's counsel the day Nick returned. Everyone here was in one accord. Except for Hen, perhaps, but she was really only on the outside looking in. Like the Petersheims, they would welcome Nick back with open arms . . . yet it remained to be seen how the ministerial brethren would receive him.

CHAPTER 27

$\mathscr{A}$ wood thrush in the undergrowth along the road sang momentarily, then quieted as Rose Ann walked past at twilight on Saturday. The darkness crept up so much later now than when she and Isaac had first started seeing each other last winter. It made for a shorter amount of time to spend together before the wee hours. Of course Rose had never cared to be out much past midnight, which Dat and Mamm appreciated. Rose was mindful that her parents were inclined to lie awake till she arrived home.

As she walked, she breathed in the freshness of the evening hour. The neighbors' cows had long since wandered into the barn in their usual lone line. And just beyond the crest of the hill, where Deacon Esh and his family lived, an owl screeched high on a thick bough, calling to another owl down pasture. Rose had thought of the deacon and the two preachers plenty of times since Nick's arrival. But she had no idea what the Bart bishop thought of the whole prickly situation. She wasn't about to ask Isaac, because he most likely wouldn't know anyway.

Isaac greeted her warmly and helped her into his shiny open buggy. She still couldn't believe he traveled five miles to come and see her, especially last winter in the cold and wind. Only once had he asked his Mennonite cousin to drive him by car to get Rose.

Each weekend, she anticipated their dates. There were always interesting things to talk about, or new and compelling stories to tell, many of them humorous. Tonight was no exception as Isaac was nearly on the edge of his seat about an upcoming trip to Ocean City, New Jersey, that would encompass next weekend. His English employer, Ed Morton, had invited him to go along on their family vacation, of all things, and because Isaac had never been to the ocean, he'd readily accepted. "Just think of seeing those big beaches, and the wind on the waves. I'm even going to try my hand—well, feet—at surfing."

She enjoyed his enthusiasm but knew she'd miss him.

"I hope you won't feel I'm neglecting ya, Rose."

She shook her head. "How's that possible?"

He drew her near. "You're a peach, ya know that? And I'm the happiest man alive."

Snuggling in, she enjoyed the nearness of him, even on such a warm evening, but wondered why her heart didn't beat as fast as when she and Nick had embraced. Quickly, she dismissed the thought, knowing Isaac would make her a mighty fine husband, handsome and attentive as he was.

Isaac talked of his fieldwork during the past week, how Ed had him doing all sorts of interesting things. She enjoyed the cadence of his words, the way he expressed himself. And she felt so included in his life, although she'd never met Ed Morton or his family. She knew beyond a shadow of a doubt Isaac loved her—her and no one else.

~

Isaac said his good-byes to Rose after walking with her halfway up the lane. She called her own farewell, then hastened toward the house, the air still warm around her.

A shadowy figure wearing a hat waited near the back door of the house, sitting on the stoop. *What the world?*

"Rosie . . ." a low voice said as the man rose—*Nick!*

"What're ya doin' here?" The idea he would be so brazen, well, she couldn't fathom what he was up to.

"Thought we could go walking." He looked up at the sky, bright with moonlight.

"I've already been out for hours."

"With your beau?"

Rose didn't feel she should have to acknowledge that. "I'm goin' inside."

"Can you spare a few minutes?"

"Dat will wonder where—"

"Aw, he's asleep, Rosie."

She looked at Nick, frowning now. It was unthinkable to go from being with Isaac to spending time with another fellow on the self-same night. "Lots of parents lie awake till their daughters are home," she replied.

"Give me ten minutes. That's all."

"What for?"

"We're friends. We could always talk to each other . . . about everything."

She hesitated before saying it. "Don't you think those days are gone?"

"Do they have to be?"

She felt terribly strange talking to him so privately like this.

"There are many things you don't know,

and I'd like a chance to set the record straight," he said.

She felt a sudden breeze and shuddered, thinking of the afternoon Christian and Nick had gone riding together. She'd seen the aftermath—Christian all laid out and bleeding on the table in Barbara's kitchen, dying. Turning away, she shook her head. "I'd rather not," she whispered. "I don't mean to hurt ya, Nick."

He brushed her elbow, his touch gentle. "But I hurt *you*. I read it in your letter."

The letter. Oh, how she wished she'd never written it! "Don't say any more, Nick. Please."

"Just listen—I need to say this." His gaze was solemn. "I'm truly sorry, Rosie. I wish I could make it up to you."

"To *me*?" Her lip trembled as she thought of poor, dead Christian. "What about Barbara . . . and the bishop? What about them?"

"I know, believe me, I do." He raised his hands, palms up. "There aren't any easy answers."

She shook her head. "That's true." *Yet Barbara had welcomed him home.*

"Rosie . . . please."

"I couldn't be more pleased that you've come to make things right for the bishop. But it might be best if we don't go walking tonight. Or any night, really."

He stepped back slowly. "I understand."

It was so unlike Nick to let her be without any teasing that Rose was momentarily silent. Then her voice returned. "Denki now . . . and good night."

He turned and left quickly, heading for the shortcut beneath the trees that fairly glistened in the moonlight.

She remembered how delighted Barbara had been the day Nick returned . . . and at the work frolic, too. Nick's foster mother had encouraged everyone present to open their arms to receive him back.

Rose sighed as she watched her old friend hurry toward the grazing land, his head bowed. *I've been unnecessarily harsh.*

She should've gone right into the house, then and there. With all of her heart, she knew she should just step inside the safety of Dat's house, put on her cotton gown, and dream sweet dreams of Isaac. Her wonderful-*gut* father would warn her against spending even a speck of time with the likes of Aaron's prodigal, if he were awake and lying in bed next to Mamm, wondering why on earth his Rosie-girl was out so late.

Rose should never have followed Nick into the shelter of the canopy of trees to hear whatever was on his heart. But a true friend didn't shun another. And it was the place of the People to show mercy and offer forgiveness . . . like the Lord required of them.

Sol held his breath where he stood at the open hallway window. He'd heard voices, although hushed at first. Sol hadn't meant to eavesdrop, but it was impossible not to hear what was being said—Nick's urgent plea to explain something to his daughter. And Rose's unswerving resistance.

Till now.

His heart fell when he saw her hurrying toward the dirt path between the farms, and he leaned on the window frame to steady himself. *Did I influence her wrongly?*

He'd ofttimes regretted the day Nick had come to live next door, and now was one of those times. He observed Rose Ann catch up with Nick just before the trees. Nick turned quickly when he heard her call—turning with great surprise, no doubt. Sol couldn't see his face, but he remembered all too well how a young fellow feels when in love with a beautiful girl, and he was mighty sure Nick's pulse was racing with more than gladness this very moment.

CHAPTER 28

For hours now, Hen had been lying awake, rising to check on her feverish little girl. Concerned, Hen prayed that Mattie's fever would break by morning. The sleepless night was one of many to come, she knew, as she would soon be caring for a newborn. To think she'd come so close to never having another baby.

Sitting up in bed now, Hen looked over at her sleeping husband, thankful they'd reconciled their differences. *A blessing in every way.*

They'd had plenty to hammer out, no question about that. But she had stepped lightly where Plain tradition was concerned, surprising herself that she didn't mind driving a car when the need arose, or using electric appliances. No longer did she go without makeup; she put a small amount of mascara and lip gloss on when she went out with Brandon—the natural look. And she wore her hair swept up in a comb in back, other times in a loose ponytail, or even bouncy and free, with relaxed curls. She also preferred fashionable skirts and dresses to the cape dresses and aprons she'd favored last fall.

The same was not true for Mattie Sue, who continued to childishly cling to the Amish way of dressing and doing her hair. Hen assumed, given enough time, Mattie Sue would abandon the traditional Plain garb and hair bun, just as she had the Kapp. For now, both Hen and Brandon were fine with it.

Getting up again, she pushed her bare feet into soft slippers and headed to Mattie Sue's room. Filtered light from the moon shone through the blinds, making a vertical design on the pastel yellow bedsheet. She felt Mattie's forehead and cheek. *Still very warm.* Sitting on the edge of the bed, Hen reached for Mattie's feverish hand and prayed.

After a time, she went to get a wet washcloth and dabbed it against her daughter's face. Mattie stirred in her sleep as Hen placed the washcloth against her forehead. Her temperature reading had indicated a low-grade fever hours earlier, when Hen tucked Mattie Sue in for the night. But the fever had spiked in the past two hours. She wondered if Mattie Sue had picked up a flu bug from Becky Zook at the work frolic yesterday; even considering the day's heat, her friend's daughter had looked rather flushed. It seemed strange, though, for Mattie to come down with something so quickly. She thought of waking her again to give her more ice chips to keep her hydrated.

Hen decided to wait awhile, letting Mattie sleep. She padded down the hall, enjoying the comforts of this lovely old house, completely renovated by the former owners. They were truly the happy recipients of some very meticulous hard work.

Going to look out the dormer window in Brandon's upstairs office, Hen raised the blinds and surveyed the road and fields showered in moonlight. Rose was possibly still out with her beau tonight.

Even though she knew her sister continued to see someone, Hen was unnerved at Nick Franco's return. She could not forget how close the two of them had been, nor the look of affection she'd seen in Nick's eyes the day he'd carried her sister into the house after she'd injured her leg. With Nick so close by, Hen worried they might resume their old friendship, which was anything but a good idea.

Still, I'm not one to object.

She closed the blinds and went back to

look in on Mattie Sue. This time she talked to her quietly, raising her enough to slip several pieces of chipped ice into her mouth. "This'll cool you some, sweetie," she whispered before kissing her damp forehead. It appeared the fever was beginning to break.

When Hen was satisfied that Mattie Sue was peacefully asleep once again, she made her way back to her own bed, where she found Brandon wide awake and propped up on his pillow.

She went to the pine chest at the foot of the bed and pulled out an extra pillow, then curled up next to him.

"How's Mattie Sue feeling?" he asked.

"Better."

"Oh good." He lowered his head to look at her. "I can't say I've slept very much."

"Like a worried Mamma, perhaps?"

"Like *you*, Hen." The tenderness in his tone warmed her heart.

"Well, she's going to be all right."

He laced his fingers through hers and was quiet for a while. Then he said softly, "How would you like to visit the little country church again sometime?"

They'd visited several other congregations, but none had seemed quite right. "I'd like that," she said, "but Mattie Sue won't be well enough tomorrow."

He agreed, then said thoughtfully, "You haven't asked to attend your parents' church."

"No," she said. "The service is given in high German, so you wouldn't get much out of it."

He poked her playfully. "Who *are* you . . . and what have you done with my wife?"

"Don't be silly." She chuckled, yet she did wonder where they'd end up finding a church home for their growing family.

"We could sit with Bruce and his wife and little girl next Sunday, perhaps?" He reminded her that there had even been two Plain couples in attendance last time they'd gone. "Remember?"

The latter was meant to be the selling point, of course. Brandon was the ultimate negotiator. How else had he persuaded her to marry an Englischer?

"Mattie Sue won't stick out so much then, jah?"

"She's only five. Who cares what people might think?"

If only she could be more like Brandon in that regard. "So you really like this church best out of the several we've visited?"

"Well, the sermon last time really got me thinking."

She listened attentively, so thankful for the transformation in her husband.

"The minister talked about a young man in the Old Testament who was terribly wronged, yet persevered in his faith in the midst of persecution. The pastor said that his fortitude came from his faith—that God was in control no matter what was happening around him."

"Was it Joseph?"

"Yes." He rolled over and kissed her. "Joseph with his amazing technicolor dreamcoat. Only this was *after* the coat was taken by his brothers and they'd sold him to strangers. Imagine that?"

Hen was enjoying this. The country preacher had managed to grab Brandon's attention, just as Aaron Petersheim had. Who could ever doubt that God was the ultimate lover, the great pursuer? Last year at this time, her husband would never have talked like this—and in the middle of the night, no less!

"Yes, I'd like to go with you to that church again," she murmured before falling asleep in his arms.

~

Surprise registered on Nick's face as he turned to see Rose there on the dirt path. "I'm sorry," she said, wringing her hands. "I didn't mean to be rude before."

He smiled in the dim moonlight beneath

the dense trees. "I'm glad you changed your mind."

She nodded hesitantly, still not sure she'd made the right decision. "We were friends for a *gut* long time." She began to walk alongside him. "And I want to hear what you have to say."

"I had my own version of *Rumschpringe,* Rosie. And during that time I came to realize who I am."

"Jah?"

"I'm Aaron Petersheim's son." Nick paused and looked at the bishop's barn in the near distance. "And I'm Amish. I couldn't leave this life, hard as I tried. What the bishop taught me actually took. I just didn't know it."

"Till now?"

"Yes, until recently." He glanced at her. "I wanted to finish out the spring semester— needed to let things play out. I had to see how I might fit in as a modern man first."

"Beyond the edge, ya mean?"

He nodded.

"So . . . it wasn't all you thought it would be?"

"Not even close. The world didn't make me happy. I missed Amish life, missed everything about it."

She shook her head. "I keep thinkin' I'll wake up and find this is all a dream."

"Good or a bad one?"

Rose shrugged and looked away, so intent was his gaze. "Seems like you've been gone forever . . . and yet—"

He inhaled thoughtfully. "What?"

"Ach, it's like you never left."

"Being with you here, like this . . . walking and talking like we used to, I think I know what you mean."

She was silent—she needed to resist the yearning, the feelings that had once been so strong. She feared the embers were still alive, waiting to be fanned into flame.

"We should go riding sometime. I know I suggested it before, but how do you feel about it?"

Give him an inch and he wants a mile, she thought. *Just as before . . .*

"Nick, we need to remain just friends." She remembered how he'd pushed things past friendship in the ravine—the earnest tone in his voice as he'd told her he loved her.

He sighed. "Sure, we'll keep things friendly . . . since you're nearly engaged."

She was relieved . . . and oddly, a little disappointed, too.

They moved to the part of the path deepest in the trees. Here only glimmers of moonlight pierced through the thick canopy of leaves, but Rose knew the moon was now in the west. It was much too late; she should return home.

"What do you say we go see Pepper. Want to?"

"At this hour?"

"It's nice and quiet in the stable."

"I must go back, Nick. You don't know my Dat, if ya honestly think he's asleep." She glanced back at the house. "Even Mamm might be awake."

"All right," he said reluctantly. "But first let me tell you that I'm going to start baptismal instruction and join church with the rest of the baptismal candidates in September."

"Does Bishop Simon know?"

"My dad and I are going to talk with him tomorrow. We didn't want to wait till next Preaching, so we're heading over to Bart to see him."

My dad ... Before his return, he'd never referred to Aaron that way.

"I really hope Bishop Simon lifts the silencing," she said. "It never should've happened."

Nick sighed and put his hands in his pockets. "I'm to blame for that. I have so much work to do to offer atonement."

She was nearly stricken by his remark. "The Lord will forgive ya, Nick. Only He can atone for our wrongdoing."

"I believe that. Mrs. Schaeffer taught me to anchor my heart to the Cross—something I never understood before. You know the woman I'm talking about?"

"The director at the shelter, jah."

"She helped my mother understand how to receive the Lord before she died." He paused to gather himself. "She taught me to pray from my heart . . . like I'm talking with a close friend."

Rose had never heard him speak about God like this. "Such wonderful news!" she said with a jubilant heart.

Nick laughed softly, the sound ringing through the shadows.

They began to walk slowly again, and Rose wondered if there was more he wanted to say. "I'm curious. Are ya goin' to grow your hair out like the rest of the menfolk?" She was testing him.

"I certainly will."

She stopped walking. "I hope things go well for you with Bishop Simon tomorrow."

"Denki, I'll let you know . . . if that's all right?"

"Sure," she said. "But I'd best be goin' now."

"Rosie . . ."

The way he said her name sent a charge through her. She couldn't let them fall back into their romantic ways. She'd promised herself she wouldn't—for both Isaac's and her sake.

"We'll talk again, jah?" She gave Nick that much before turning to hurry through the tunnel of trees toward home.

CHAPTER 29

$\mathcal{D}$at carried Mamm carefully through the summer kitchen and out the back door to the family carriage Sunday afternoon. He'd chosen Alfalfa, their most docile horse, for the fifteen-minute ride over to Mose and Ruthann's.

Rose climbed in next to Mamm, making sure the special seat padding and pillow were situated behind her. Rose was anxious to see Mose and his family again, especially young Jonas, Barbara Ann, and little Sally.

"Such a lovely day. I feel so cheered—better than I have in years." Mamm smiled at her.

"The sunshine's surely been *gut* for ya," Dat added. "And all the therapy you've been havin' . . ."

Rose had to agree. "Maybe seein' Hen and Brandon so happy makes a difference, as well.

And knowin' their new baby is comin' soon."
Rose, too, was relieved her sister had settled
down for good. Hen had even shared some
time ago that she and Brandon were looking
for a church!

The carriage rolled along at a comfortable
clip. On either side, rows of corn were aligned
right up to the ditches, where bushy spikes of
foxtail grass grew. The rich, dark earth flashed
between the rows, but it was nothing like the
blur of scenery she'd witnessed the times she'd
traveled by van.

Presently, Rose watched a flock of robins
fly out of the highest bough of a cottonwood
tree as the horse and carriage passed. She felt
considerably more relaxed today, after last
night's talk with Nick.

"I heard from Barbara that Nick's workin'
long days for Aaron," Mamm said suddenly.

Rose wondered why she would mention
this and waited to see if Dat would say anything. But there was complete silence on the
right side of the buggy, so she assumed Dat
was hoping for the best with Nick but inwardly
skeptical. *As many still are . . .*

She glanced at Petersheims' farmhouse as
they rode past; she didn't want to be caught
gawking. Bad enough that she'd followed Nick
on the canopied path last night. She understood his wanting her friendship again, but

much had changed since last fall, when he'd run off. *So very much* . . .

~

At Mose and Ruthann's, Rose immediately spotted her nephew and nieces outside playing "horsey." Jonas made neighing sounds and bobbed his head, a knotted rope tied to his waist as he pulled his younger sisters, Barbara Ann and Sally, in a makeshift cart.

"Well, lookee there." Dat got such a kick out of his grandchildren. "Mose used to play horsey like that with his own brothers back when he was Jonas's age."

"All Amish children do at one time or 'nother," Mamm added.

Rose was also reminded of Beth's thrill at riding in the pony cart.

"Kumme play with us, Aendi Rose," Jonas called as he trotted over to Mose and Ruthann, who sat on lawn chairs trying to keep cool.

"You make a better horse than I do," Rose said, laughing.

"Jah, she's too old for that," Mose said, a merry glint in his eyes.

"Oh, now, you!" Rose waggled her finger at her brother. Then she went to greet Ruthann, who gripped her hand instead of getting up.

Dat carried Mamm up to the porch and set her in one of the vacant chairs, then shook Mose's hand in greeting.

Rose pictured herself sitting on a porch with Isaac, years from now, drinking home-made root beer, watching their children play on a manicured lawn. She imagined them swinging on a long rope in the hayloft, squealing with glee as they took turns.

It was fun to think of Mattie Sue soon having a baby brother or sister. She wondered if Hen secretly had a preference—maybe a son this time, for Brandon's sake.

"We have oodles of raspberries comin' on awful fast," Ruthann was saying. "I've been out picking but can't keep up. I've sold more pints than I can count at our roadside stand." She mentioned the neighbor girl was coming over tomorrow again to help pick, after the washing was out.

"You want us to come make some jam?" Rose offered with a glance at Mamm.

"Oh, would ya?" Ruthann said. "That'd be such a help. And fun, too!"

Mamm said she'd join in if Dat would bring her, and Rose suggested also inviting Mammi Sylvia and Barbara Petersheim. Ruthann brightened. "Mammi might keep an eye on little Sally while we work. She's getting into everything these days."

Ruthann returned her attention to Rose. "So, how're things over in Bart?" she asked rather sheepishly.

Rose gave her sister-in-law a quick frown, hoping to discourage any further talk of Isaac, but not before her mother gave Rose an appraising look. *Ach, so surprising Ruthann would ask such a thing!*

Rose thought about Isaac, wondering if he might ask her to marry him soon . . . and if they'd use his preacher or hers for their vows. Isaac's in Bart might be inconvenient, living that far away from her parents' house, where the wedding service would take place.

But Rose shouldn't fret just yet. She knew better. *Worry leads to gray hair,* Mamm had always said, pointing to her own.

The afternoon was hot and humid, and Rose offered to go in and pour some cold root beer for everyone. Gratefully, they all accepted, and Rose went into the kitchen. As she set the glasses on a tray, she saw a pattern for crocheted booties on the table. Later, when she returned outside, Rose noticed the way Ruthann protectively folded her hands against her stomach. She handed the glass to her, thinking happily that yet another Kauffman grandbaby was on the way. Oh, to have one of her own someday!

~

After supper Tuesday evening, Brandon and Hen dropped by with Mattie Sue to visit. Hen was in the process of gathering family recipes and began to jot down several while Mamm recited ingredients and instructions from memory.

Mattie stayed around only a short time before asking Dawdi Sol if they could go see the calves. Rose went with them to the back door just as Nick wandered over to say hello to Mattie Sue in the yard.

He gave a nod to Dat before saying to Mattie, "I saw your family's car pull up and thought I'd come by."

Mattie Sue ran over to him and asked if he'd like to join them in the barn.

"Sure," Nick said, his eyes on Dat, "but only if it's okay with your Dawdi."

Dat gave his assent and excused himself for a minute at Mamm's call, leaving Nick with Mattie Sue.

In short order, Nick picked up Mattie and set her high on his shoulders, Mattie's melodious laughter ringing out in the muggy air. Soon she was saying how much she missed him.

"Where've ya been all this time?" Mattie asked.

Rose smiled as she watched them head to the barn. Nick ducked comically in the open doorway, and Mattie Sue giggled again and patted his straw hat as they disappeared inside. Rose moved away from the screen door, going back to visit with Mamm and Hen as Dat made his way outdoors. Why did it sometimes seem as though time had stood still while Nick was gone? *As if nothing much had happened.*

~

Saturday night arrived—the evening Rose usually spent with Isaac for their weekly date. Instead of sitting home while he was in New Jersey at the ocean, Rose decided after redding up the kitchen to visit Hen.

She told her parents where she was going and left the house, making a beeline for the stable door. The barn was still warm and humid from the hot day as she slipped into her favorite horse's stall. Months had passed since she'd last gone horseback riding, but since she didn't feel like taking the time to hitch George up to the buggy on this muggy night, she would simply ride horseback to Hen's.

George chuffed about, uncooperative at first. She talked quietly, calming him as only she knew how. "You're hot, too, aren't ya, sweet boy?"

The horse nuzzled her chin.

"And you're rarin' to go." She stroked his neck and offered a sugar cube. "We'll have us a nice ride." Glancing out the window, she hoped Nick wouldn't see her and think she wanted him to join her. Now that she thought of that possibility, she wondered if she ought to be taking George at all. But George raised his head, eager as always. She didn't want to disappoint him.

"All right, we'll go," she said, leaning her face close to his nose. "You ready?"

George's glossy eyes followed her as Rose approached him to mount on the left. Then they were off, taking Salem Road up to the first crossroad and over north to Brandon and Hen's pretty farmhouse.

~

Upstairs at Hen's, Rose enjoyed seeing the pastel yellow and green baby things her sister was making for the nursery. The cozy room was as large as Rose's own bedroom, with a sturdy oak rocker Brandon had asked Dat to make. The crib was already in place, as well as an antique bureau and dressing table with a cushy yellow pad.

Hen also showed her a new wall hanging she was making—still in many pieces. "It's similar to Mattie Sue's," her sister explained.

"You're ready for either a boy or a girl, jah?"

Hen touched the patchwork pieces she would soon quilt. "Between us, Rose, it doesn't matter to me. Having another little girl would be such fun for Mattie Sue, but a boy would be nice for Brandon. I'm sure he wouldn't be too keen on taking a girl out hunting, you know?"

"Well, a girl could go fishin'."

Hen's hazel eyes twinkled as she glanced toward the window facing George, tied up outdoors. "And a girl could go horseback riding with Aendi Rose."

This made Rose laugh softly.

"Does Dat care that you ride George?" asked Hen more quietly.

Rose pressed her lips together. "I really don't ride much anymore. Hardly ever."

"So it's all right as long as you don't go often?"

Hen had her but good—her sister knew that the brethren frowned on grown folk riding. Horses were for pulling carriages and fieldwork. "Well, once I'm married, I prob'ly won't."

"You *probably* won't?"

Rose giggled.

"So, dare I ask if the wedding will be this autumn?"

Rose tried not to smile and looked away.

"Seems you're not going to tell me." Hen nodded knowingly and led her to Mattie Sue's room, showing off two new frilly white pillows she'd recently made. They sat on the neatly made bed as Hen told Rose her idea to sell baked goods out on the back screened porch to bring in extra "pin money" for baby clothes and other nursery items. "Arie Zook is doing the same thing this summer," Hen said.

"I like the idea."

"And Brandon's fine with it since I'm not working at the fabric shop anymore."

Rose touched her hand. "Do ya miss it, sister?"

"Some days, but all in all, not so much."

"You seem very happy," Rose said.

Hen reached to hug her. "The Lord's been so good to me and Brandon . . . mending our hearts. Our marriage has never been stronger."

Rose squeezed her tight. "So *gut* to hear."

When they returned downstairs, Rose found Brandon and Mattie Sue doing a paint-by-number page at the kitchen table. Rose wandered over to watch, and Mattie Sue quickly explained that it was from a Bible story.

"Baby Moses in his basket," Mattie Sue told her.

Hen found her recipe notebook and went with Rose to the front room. The flick of a switch brought a flood of light.

"Do you miss usin' gas lamps?" Rose was curious to know.

"Oh, sometimes." Hen had a faraway look. "But modern conveniences are best for our life together, and that's what matters." She opened her notebook. "Some of these recipes have been around for generations but have never been in print. I want to make a book for each family in the church district," Hen said. "As a little thank-you for the months Mattie Sue and I lived at Salem Road."

Rose nodded and blinked back tears. "It was a learning time."

"Oh, goodness, more than you know."

They perused through the recipes, and when Hen asked Rose to write one or two of her favorites, Rose decided on hot water sponge cake and Amish meat loaf.

Later, Hen remarked how very sultry the nights were. "We've talked about installing air-conditioning, but I'm not so sure we really need it, and Brandon's leaving it to me to decide what I'm comfortable with."

"What about fans?"

"Oh, we have them going, believe me." Hen laughed. "But they just push the hot air around."

Rose looked about, taking in all the beautiful things Hen had on display—the china cups and saucers she'd collected through the years, and the satiny throw pillows in tans and brown scattered across the upholstered sofa. Some of the furniture in this room was new, as were two framed prints. One had the look of an old painting—a shepherd girl in a lovely meadow with a lamb in the crook of her arm.

Hen's voice grew softer. "Have you heard that Nick's session in Bart with Bishop Simon ran amok? Arie's husband, Elam, told her so."

"What on earth?! No . . . I hadn't heard. What'll happen now?"

"Bishop Simon wants a longer proving time for Nick than is typical. According to Elam, Bishop Simon and Old Ezekiel are going to discuss it soon."

"Why's that?"

"They want to see if Nick actually follows through and attends baptismal instruction and whatnot. Everything he does is being scrutinized."

"Is part of it that he confessed his role in Christian's death?"

"Evidently he did, but Bishop Simon seemed to think Nick's story had too many holes."

"Well, for pity's sake." And here Rose had hoped Nick's return might benefit his foster father. "I hope Nick's coming back won't be for naught."

"It just might be. Bishop Simon's nearly as traditional and strict as Old Ezekiel, and he's peeved that Aaron didn't manage to get Nick into the church years ago. And now with folks still suspecting he's had a hand in Christian's death . . ."

Rose didn't know what to think, but she knew she didn't like hearing things third- or fourth-hand. Surely Dat would know more directly from Aaron. Oh, her heart ached for their wonderful neighbor-bishop. To think Nick might not be able to make a difference after all!

CHAPTER 30

On the Lord's Day, Mamm got ready to attend Preaching service for the first time since her surgery. She was feeling better as each week passed and eager for church.

Rose watched as her father took the wheelchair out of the back of the buggy and carried it into the temporary house of worship. Soon he returned to carry Mamm into the big farmhouse, where he placed her gently in the padded wheelchair near the back of the gathering room.

Rose waited with Mamm in the large, empty room while Dat went outdoors to line up with the men and boys, prior to the start of the service. "Are ya feelin' all right, Mamm?" Rose asked.

"My dear girl, I've been yearnin' for this

day since returning home." Mamm folded her hands and smiled with expectation.

They heard the ordained brethren entering the house, and as they filed into the room, Rose was relieved to see Aaron Petersheim still included with the group of ministers, though she couldn't help but recall Hen's discouraging news.

How long before he's completely cast aside?

The day was already stifling, and Rose wished they'd held the meeting in the barn like they often did during July and August. They were all stuffed indoors because strong winds were forecast for later in the morning. Mamm, bless her heart, might need to be wheeled out to the porch early to get some air.

Once again, Rose missed seeing Hen and Mattie Sue here, on Mamm's special day of return. It was comforting, however, to know that Hen and her little family were also attending church somewhere today. Soon the older men, including Dawdi Jeremiah, entered, followed by the next generation—her Dat and other menfolk in his age group. And then the unmarried fellows walked in, arranged by age—the older ones followed by the younger.

Nick Franco came in with the other courting-age young men, including Hank Zook and Ezra Lapp and dozens of others. If this was a normal year, more than half of them would be married come wedding season.

Nick went to sit on the second row of benches with Aaron's sons-in-law, including Verna's husband, Levi, who had made repeated attempts to befriend Nick through the years. All of them sat with heads bowed in an attitude of prayer.

When everyone was gathered inside, Mamm reached for Rose's hand and clasped it gently. During the first hymn, her eyes shone with joyful tears. *O Lord, bless my mother with your loving-kindness this day,* Rose prayed silently.

The preacher then gave his customary welcome to the membership and youth there. *"Gnade sei mit euch und Freide von Gott unser Vater.* Grace be with you and peace from God, our Father."

Fleetingly, Rose let her mind drift back to the times she'd sat with her mother in church, with the other women. She had been at Mamm's side other times, too—at market as a little girl, where she helped set up the display table of embroidered items and all the jars of jams and jellies. It wasn't till after Mamm's accident that she'd begun to make and sell the boy and girl cloth dolls, all faceless—except for the one with the downturned mouth and sad eyes. She knew she ought to pull out the stitching on that one so her nieces wouldn't see it. It was her responsibility to provide them with a devout example in life, just as so many had done for her.

Rose's focus had only just returned to the orderly service when a howling wind and driving rain came up suddenly, gusting in through the open windows. Nick was one of the young men who leaped to his feet to help close them.

What's become of the boy who wanted nothing to do with church? She observed him with not only curiosity but wonder.

∼

After the rainstorm blew over, Rose and Leah Miller ran into each other outside during the first seating of the shared meal. While the ministerial brethren and visitors ate, Rose stood under the shade of a big maple tree, trying to escape the noontime heat as she waited for the youth to be called in for their seating. Leah smiled brightly as they greeted each other.

They made small talk while they fanned their perspiring faces with the hems of their white aprons; then Leah mentioned Rose's younger cousin Sarah. "She was mighty surprised to see Nick at the first instructional class early this morning. Before church, over at the preacher's house."

Rose had expected to hear this, based on what Nick had told her. Even so, she was glad to hear he had actually gone.

Leah continued. "Sarah says he seems real different. Like he's livin' in the same skin as before but with a new heart."

Did Bishop Simon sense any of this? Rose mused. Alas, the Bart bishop had only just met Nick. How would he know how much the young man had changed?

Someone rang the dinner bell, and Rose and Leah and the other young people made their way toward the house. Several of the fellows lagged behind, discreetly eyeing the girls.

Please, Lord, give the overseeing bishops your wisdom alone, Rose prayed as she headed indoors.

~

An hour after Dat and Mamm left, Rose was still helping redd up after the common meal. She hadn't wanted to leave too quickly, hoping to talk more with Leah Miller. The pair were now walking toward home together, being careful not to step in the many mud puddles on the road. They walked companionably awhile without saying much amidst the sound of crickets and a few rowdy crows over yonder near Millers' big spread. The heavy rains had turned the fields into a shimmering green mantle.

Leah paused in her stride. "Well, I wasn't goin' to say anything," she began, her voice faltering, "but from what Jake has indicated, he's more traditional than his twin brother. But maybe you know this already."

"Know what?"

"That Isaac's pushin' the *Ordnung* a bit."

Rose knew he enjoyed the line dances and whatnot, but she hadn't thought he was in danger of crossing any serious boundaries.

"Does Isaac ever talk of his Englischer employer?" asked Leah.

"A little." Rose wished for the paper fan she'd left back at the house. "What do you know that I don't?"

"Just that he's spending a lot of time with them."

"Like this weekend's trip to the ocean?"

"There's some concern surrounding that, jah."

Rose took this in. "Well, Isaac knows I'm baptized Amish. Why would he court me unless he plans to join church himself?"

Leah shrugged. "Sorry—not sure I should've said anything."

Rose touched Leah's arm. "What more are ya tryin' to say?"

Leah glanced about, as if concerned someone other than Rose might hear. "Jake worries the farmer's family will rent bikes on the boardwalk . . . and that Isaac will, too."

Rose shook her head. "I really doubt Isaac would do that. Besides, he's not baptized yet."

"Guess I stuck my foot in my mouth," Leah said with a sidelong glance. "Don't mean to sound like a gossipy hen."

"Oh, I don't mind you tellin' me. But Jake doesn't have anything to worry about," she assured Leah.

They walked to the end of the lane and parted ways. Several buggies passed Rose as she headed toward Salem Road, kicking up mud as they went. Silas Good rumbled by and waved, an unmarried sister on either side of him, looking mighty uncomfortable all jammed together in a buggy meant for two.

Rose waved to Silas and his sisters, glad she'd removed her dark hose and shoes in the outhouse after Preaching so they wouldn't be ruined. Even though her toes squished into the mire on the road, she didn't mind going without shoes.

She thought of Isaac running barefoot on the wet sand at the beach, hoping his time at the shore was as innocent as she'd dared to claim.

CHAPTER 31

*S*olomon had witnessed firsthand Aaron's benevolence toward Nick, offering him a job, as well as two vacant bedrooms to use upstairs, including Christian's old room. Whenever Sol thought of it, these gestures struck him as almost inconceivable.

But when he voiced this to Emma as they settled on the porch following Sunday afternoon barn chores, Emma reminded him that he, too, had been merciful to a wayward one: their own daughter Hen.

Funny, but he'd never thought of it quite like that. Sol saw his wife's point, though, and patted her hand as they drank the ice-cold lemonade Sylvia had made. He could hear his mother-in-law humming snippets from the *Ausbund* hymnal through the screen door as she puttered around the kitchen, making sandwiches from the eggs she'd hard-boiled yesterday.

"What do you s'pose Aaron's daughters and their husbands think of his extending such generosity to Nick?" asked Emma.

"Well, I know Anna's husband ain't so keen on it. Says we ought to be careful, since Nick was most likely responsible for Christian's death—let his anger get away with him, an' all."

Emma set her glass down on the small table between their wicker chairs. "But isn't that the same as withholding forgiveness?"

"We're human, Emma." He looked at her. "I know what I said . . . yet I just want to be on the safe side when it comes to our family . . . 'specially Rose Ann."

"But the Lord forgives."

"He surely does," Sol said.

"And don't forget what Aaron asked of us."

"I want to honor his request and welcome his son back, but it breaks my heart to think of Nick getting it in his head to pursue our daughter again." Sol couldn't bear the thought of telling Emma he'd seen Rose dash out to the meadow a week ago, calling to Nick as if they were a courting couple. He bit his lip— it was a dangerous thing, the bond that still existed between them.

"So you must think Nick killed his brother, then?"

"Nothing changes the fact they were together when Christian was injured. And they were quarreling viciously before they went riding—I saw them carryin' on." Sol ran his hand over his beard. "Only the Lord knows what happened afterward."

"You must not believe Nick told the truth that day, then."

"Well, neither does Bishop Simon, I'm told."

Emma persisted. "We know for sure Nick helped Christian home after he was hurt."

"Jah, 'tis true."

"Nick could've left him be, ain't? Could've run off right then, but he took the time to bring Christian back, slung over his own horse, leading Christian's horse behind him." She paused, trembling slightly. "I never understood that, and quite frankly, neither does Barbara."

Sol turned. "She told ya this?"

Emma nodded.

Sol hadn't thought about it in this light. His wife had certainly been pondering this plenty, with little to do but read and pray and rest. "Don't fret, whatever ya do," he said. "All right, love?"

" 'Tis a mystery, I'll say."

"And one that might never be solved," said Sol.

They listened to the sounds of deep summer around them as they sipped their drinks— a mule whinnying in the barn and the birds twittering and calling in the backyard trees. An airplane flew over, making a racket, scaring a whole flock of robins out of sheltering branches.

"Just lookee there," he said.

"Who'd ever want to go so fast?" Emma said softly, covering her ears.

"Who indeed?" Sol thought of those who'd left the church over the years. Not many had ever returned—less than a handful. Sometimes he wondered if Nick Franco should've stayed out in the world, too . . . where he belonged.

Sylvia stepped outside and surprised them with a big bowl of cold watermelon cut up in squares. Sol told her it hit the spot, and she sat and had a few bites along with them, remarking on the scorching heat of the day. Sylvia mentioned a circle letter she'd received yesterday. "I read that a church district out in Mount Hope, Ohio, has decided to raise some money for an ailing church member. They're having a haystack supper."

Sol wondered if she might be concerned about Emma's medical bills, but he'd made a very reasonable arrangement with the York hospital, as well as the osteopathic hospital in Lancaster, to make payments over the period of a year. Along with some hefty assistance from the church's benevolence fund, if Sol pinched his pennies, he ought to have a zero balance by next spring. *If the rains keep coming,* Sol thought. They were completely dependent upon the Lord for the corn and hay harvests.

Sylvia mentioned how impressed Jeremiah was that Aaron had welcomed Nick back "in such a fashion" before she wandered back into the house. Sol and Emma's conversation turned to the morning sermons, and eventually, Sol brought up Nick's place at Preaching this morning—sitting clear up near the front. "Just think, Emma. What if he'd already joined church, say, years ago? What might things have been like then?"

His wife dabbed her eyes and brow with her hankie. "Awful sad, really, how things turned out."

Sol agreed. Nick was, after all, only now preparing to make his kneeling vow. Whether or not he followed through remained to be seen. For Aaron's sake—and for the Lord's—Sol could only hope and pray it would be so.

~

After supper, Rose walked across the back lawn, toward the stable, wanting to talk to her father about Nick. But as she approached the barn, she heard a car pull into the driveway. Looking over her shoulder, she saw Mattie Sue's little hand waving out the window at her.

"We've come for dessert," Mattie announced with a grin.

Rose hurried over to greet them. She leaned in Mattie Sue's open window. "You're just in time," Rose told them. Mamm would be ready for sweets, for sure. "Come on in."

Brandon got out and went around the car to open the door for Hen. They walked hand-in-hand toward the house with Mattie skipping ahead, asking if Dawdi Sol was out with the horses. Hen told her to mind her manners and go inside with them to visit Mammi Emma first. And Mattie Sue willingly obeyed.

Mamm was delighted to see the three of them, making over Mattie Sue and smiling blissfully when Brandon leaned down to kiss her cheek. They all chattered at once, starting with talk of the various church services and all the excitement of the rainstorm, and ending with remarks about the coming baby, who was to be named either Andrew or Emmalie, after Emma. The news made Mamm smile brightly.

Dat must've heard the racket, because he came in and sat at the head of the table, where he visited with Brandon to his left. Rose got a kick out of the good-natured banter, and she thought how, just last year, Brandon had been alienated from their family by his choosing. *Well, thank God for his change in heart,* thought Rose as she carried a lemon sponge pie to the table. Then, going back to the counter, she brought over a beautiful white chocolate cake to share, as well.

Dat was telling Brandon the latest from his distant cousin in Wisconsin. Seems he'd written that one of the church districts there had planned a "mystery trip" to another state to tour an old prison that had been in use for a hundred years. "Now, don't that beat all?" Dat said, a twinkle in his eye. "How'd ya like to go an' see a prison for a church outing?"

This brought plenty of laughter to the whole table, including Mamm, who seemed to be enjoying herself as she took it all in. Rose also had to smile at Dat's telling as she handed the cake knife to Hen after first slicing the pie.

"This same cousin told 'bout a little excitement he had when his horse got spooked by a school bus," Dat continued. "The horse ran lickety-split like a house a-fire down the road, chasing after it. Maybe the bright yellow color was to blame. Anyway, when he couldn't get the horse to slow down or stop, my cousin jumped out of the buggy. Poor man, he broke his ankle and a bone in his other leg. But—get this—the horse eventually came to a halt, and my cousin's little white dog somehow managed to stay perched on the buggy seat through it all."

Hen shook her head, amazed, as was Mattie Sue, who asked for yet another story. Merriment prevailed. But Mamm, tittering softly, placed her hand on Dat's arm, as if to say things were getting a bit *yachdich*—noisy—for the Lord's Day.

In a much quieter voice, Dat leaned forward on the table. "How would ya like to learn to ride a pony, honey-girl?" he asked Mattie Sue.

"Ride? Not in the pony cart?" Her eyes sparkled with joy.

"No, smack-dab in the middle of the pony."

She leaped off the bench and ran to him, threw her arms around his neck, and leaned her face against his whiskers. "Ach, Dawdi, this is the bestest surprise ever!"

Dat said not a word as he squeezed the stuffing out of her. Rose smiled. *What a wonderful-gut day this is!* She glanced at Brandon, who wore a big grin . . . his thumbs turned up as if to say *Denki*.

〜

Rose finished reading a psalm before extinguishing the lantern that night. Her eyes were tired and she was ready to fall asleep. When she said her silent prayers, she included Nick, asking God to help him stay on the straight and narrow, knowing what it would do to his parents if he should fall by the wayside again.

She was still curious to know what Nick had said to Bishop Simon last week. Her father had looked awfully tired and headed off to bed with Mamm earlier than usual following Bible reading and evening prayers. So Rose hadn't had the chance to talk to Dat about that—again. Maybe it was all for the best, anyway. After all, she didn't want her interest to give him the wrong impression.

She'd gone to her room and sorted through Isaac's letters, arranging them in chronological order, the very first to the most recent. She tried to imagine what Isaac might be doing right now at the beach. In six short days, she'd see him again, and he'd tell her all about it.

What might she say if Isaac admitted to doing anything rash, as Leah had suggested. Surely her beau had more sense than that, when he meant to join church someday! *Surely* . . .

Yet Leah's remarks lingered long in Rose's mind, and it was all she could do to set them aside, fretting over her beau's supposed strong leanings toward the world.

CHAPTER 32

The following Wednesday morning, Rose helped Beth Browning's grandmother rearrange and organize her dresser drawers and clothes closet. Rose also dusted the furniture and windowsills in the new addition, and washed the windows inside and out.

Later, Beth helped Rose do some cooking. Beth talked happily about her father, saying he was now regularly writing to Jane Keene. "And he calls her sometimes, too—makes him really happy to talk to her."

A few minutes later, the Brownings' neighbor Donna Becker dropped by with some black raspberries, still warm from the sun, enough for Rose to make two pies. Beth wanted to try her hand at baking, so they rolled out the pie dough together while Beth's grandmother sang an old folk hymn from the kitchen table, where she sat sorting through a recipe file. Rose had heard the song several times at the big barn Singings with Isaac: "In the Sweet By and By."

We shall meet on that beautiful shore, thought Rose, wondering what Beth's dear mother was doing in heaven right now. Was she spending time with loved ones gone before? Sitting beneath the Tree of Life?

She looked at Beth, so sweetly trusting and innocent. Yet she'd grown a lot since Rose met her last year, from being nearly afraid to express herself to anyone but her father . . . to feeling totally at ease with Rose and others. Rose felt it was good that her grandmother lived here now. Surely it was a blessing for Beth to have a woman in the house to talk to.

"Grandma sings a lot," Beth said with a crooked smile. "She says she had a really high voice when she was young, but now it's sunk lower."

"People's voices change as they age," Rose said, thinking of her own grandparents.

"She used to sing in a choir when she was my age. In college somewhere . . . I forget."

Rose wondered if Beth wished she could attend college, too. She seemed bright in some ways but struggled greatly in others.

When it was time, they each slid a glass

pie plate into the oven. "One's for you to take home, Rosie."

"Denki." Rose didn't have the heart to say they had black raspberries coming out their ears. But she thought of Hen and Brandon and knew they'd welcome the scrumptious pie. *Especially if there's whipped cream to top it off!*

~

After quickly dropping off the still-warm pie at Hen's, Rose noticed a homemade sign on one of the English neighbor's fence posts, not far up from Brandon and Hen's. *Nickers 'n' Neighs—Horse Boarding.*

How clever. Could Nick do something like this to earn extra money at Petersheims'? He and Aaron might have to add on to the stable, but as fast as they were with building projects, it wouldn't take long.

From what she could tell, Aaron was giving Nick plenty of work to do. But knowing Nick as she did, Rose wondered how long before he'd want his own place. *Though that's not my concern.*

It was her job to focus on the household items she still needed to fill out her hope chest, for whenever Isaac proposed marriage. Just where they'd live she didn't know. Of course no matter where he decided, she would follow. A girl was to let her husband make such important choices, even though Rose knew without a doubt she'd miss her childhood home.

Wherever Isaac is, that'll be home for me. She made the turn into her father's drive and saw Dat, Mose, Josh, and several other men making hay out in the fields. A nice hot day for it.

She pulled in close to the stable to unhitch, thankful for the shade of the barn. Back inside the house, Rose could hear Mammi Sylvia talking to Mamm, their voices drifting this way in the slow breeze.

Glancing over toward the bishop's field, Rose saw Aaron and his sons-in-law and Nick haying, as well. She wondered if Nick had missed the feeling of community while he was gone. Amish farmers did everything together—working, worshiping, and living their lives in accordance with God's ways. It was hard to imagine Nick lasting as long as he had alone in the bustling city of Philadelphia.

She noticed that, from this distance, he blended in perfectly with the other men. Never had he looked as alarmingly English as the day he'd returned home. She guessed it would take some time for his cropped hair to grow out into the traditional style for men, trimmed beneath the ears, with bangs. Just as it would take time to convince Bishop Simon and Old Ezekiel that his interest in God and the church was steadfast.

She finished unhitching the mare and led Upsy-Daisy into the stable for more water, which she also had been mindful to give over at Brownings'. In the barn, Rose noticed Dawdi Jeremiah, a piece of straw dangling lazily from his mouth. "Hullo," she called. "If you're lookin' for Dat, he's out makin' hay."

"Nee, just tryin' to get some relief from the heat." He removed his kerchief and wiped his neck beneath his long, untrimmed beard. "Found me a barn kitten to talk to," he said with a grin as he pulled a tiny gray one out of his baggy bib overalls.

"Oh, how adorable!"

"It's three weeks old or so, best as I can tell."

Rose watched Dawdi handle the kitten tenderly. "You'll have to show Mattie, next time she's over."

"Thought I'd let her name it, maybe."

"Won't Dat just love that—namin' all the barn cats?" Her father wasn't so keen on their getting too attached to the mouse chasers.

Dawdi nuzzled the kitten against his beard, the bitty thing purring like a generator. "This here's one of God's creatures. I say it deserves a name. Don't you?"

"What would you name it?"

"Tillie comes to mind." Dawdi put the cat nose to nose with him. "She looks like a Tillie to me."

"We should see if Mattie Sue thinks so."

He shrugged. "Jah, 'tis *gut* to let the little ones name 'em."

She listened as his talk turned to Hen's coming wee babe.

"Thank the Good Lord for all the young ones in the family," he said reverently, his brown eyes raised to the ceiling for a moment. "Your Mammi Sylvia and I are awful glad things worked out so nicely for Hen."

Rose agreed. "She's very happy."

"Well, so's her feller . . . you can just see it all over his face. Knowin' the Lord's worked a mighty change in him." Dawdi teased the kitten with the straw in his mouth. "Ain't so?"

Rose smiled, enjoying the rare moment with her grandfather.

"Did ya see Samuel Esh's rickety ol' wheelbarrow's for sale?" he asked suddenly, a light in his eyes.

"Can't say I did."

"Well, you walked home from Preachin' last Sunday, ain't?"

"Jah . . . why?"

"You would've walked right past it, then. Don't see how you could've missed it.

Deacon's got it setting out front on the lawn, near the road."

She didn't recall. Of course, she had been deep in thought about Leah's—and Jake's—concern over Isaac at the shore. "Is there a For Sale sign on it?"

"Ach no."

"How do ya know Deacon wants it sold, then?"

Dawdi removed his old straw hat and scratched the top of his gray head. "Well, now, just the way it was situated . . . didn't need a sign. You knew it was for sale by the way it was set there. It ain't really advertising itself to the fancy folk who fly up and down the pavement in their cars. It's a-setting out there to attract attention of farmers who think of that road as the way home."

She smiled, understanding what he meant. "I see."

"A body could get it for a little bit of nothin'. Seen better days an' all . . . served its purpose."

"So, then, are you considering buying it?" She knew better, though she wondered why he was talking so about Deacon's wheelbarrow being put out to pasture, so to speak.

He guffawed and the piece of straw went flying. "What would I do with it? Make a planter for flowers out of it, maybe?" With a grunt, Dawdi sat on a milk can and fanned himself with his hat. "You're a real *gut* one, Miss Rosie Ann."

"Not sure I shouldn't take issue with that." She laughed softly, moving closer.

He winked at her. "Aw, you know I'm just pullin' your leg, honey-girl."

"I know you are, Dawdi."

He wiped his face again with the kerchief while the kitten nestled against him, snuggling into the pocket of his overalls. "You best be goin' in now. Your Mamm and Mammi will wonder what's keepin' you."

"All right, then. I'll see ya at dinner."

A curious smile crossed his face, and he shooed her away with his ratty straw hat.

As she made her way out of the barn and toward the house, Dawdi's remarks about the deacon's old wheelbarrow seeped down into her understanding. Dawdi had always been something of a thinker. Even as a little girl, Rose had enjoyed sitting on his knee as he imparted his homespun wisdom, always including a Bible verse here and there. Mamm believed her own hunger for the Good Book came from her father's particular attention to Scripture.

Rose smiled, glad to be blessed with such a rich spiritual heritage.

She was halfway across the back lawn when she heard what sounded like a milk can clatter, then a muffled call for help.

Turning, she ran back to the barn, rushing past Upsy-Daisy's stall. "Dawdi!" she called, heart in her throat. "I'm comin'!"

By the time she found him and knelt beside him on the barn floor, her dear Dawdi had already stepped from this life into the next. He looked so peaceful lying there, a slight smile on his wrinkled face.

"Dyin's like going from one room to another," he'd told her last year after his stroke.

Lips quivering, Rose leaned her head down onto his chest and remembered every joyful moment spent with him. All the fun at the old fishing hole, hours spent swinging on the tree swing while Dawdi tirelessly pushed her—before her little legs were long enough to keep herself going on her own. And, oh, the watermelon seed spitting contests every summer and the sleigh rides to neighbors up and down Salem Road to go caroling. A lifetime of memories played across her mind, and she relished each and every one.

Nothing could be done for Dawdi now. Before she rose to alert her father, Rose kissed his cheek—her best good-bye. And the gray kitten, who must have jumped when Dawdi fell, came over and nuzzled up against the dearest Dawdi ever, unaware and trusting, clinging with her tiny paws to the big pocket of his overalls.

CHAPTER 33

While Dat and Bishop Aaron handled the funeral arrangements, a group of men headed out to the hayfield, filling in for Rose's father and brothers. Dat had called the funeral director who spoke the Amish dialect and was accustomed to their way of preparing the body, which would be ready for viewing later today . . . and burial this Friday. As was their custom, many church families would pitch in to help, so that not a single member of the immediate family had to lift a finger for the next week and beyond.

Rose slipped out of the house, skipping the noon meal. She couldn't possibly have eaten, nor could she have kept her composure while observing her mother's and grandmother's grief, restrained though it was.

She set off to honor Dawdi Jeremiah by

retracing her steps from last Sunday's walk home. *"Don't see how you could've missed it...."* His words echoed in her memory as she ambled down the road to Deacon Samuel's front yard.

The wobbly old wheelbarrow was still sitting near the road on the front lawn, as her grandfather had said. She went inside and purchased it for only a few dollars—its value far diminished from the original price, years ago.

She thanked the deacon, then told of her grandfather's passing and the funeral at nine o'clock on Friday morning. Deacon Esh offered his condolences and said he would be over in short order to assist in whatever way was needed.

Then, without another word, Rose left to get the old wheelbarrow, picking it up by its splintery handles and pushing it up the road toward home.

She set the wheelbarrow near her grandparents' back porch, then filled it nearly to the brim with rich topsoil. Next she dug up some of Dawdi's favorite flowers, transplanting the pretty red, purple, and white pinwheel zinnias from the side yard, where they were nearly out of view. Rose's tears watered the newly planted blooms as she paid her quiet tribute.

Now they'd have their rightful place near the cozy rear porch of the smaller Dawdi Haus.

At last, she stepped back to admire her project, whispering her grandfather's name into the zephyr. "I'll see you again, Dawdi . . . one sweet day."

~

Isaac's weekly letter arrived that afternoon amidst all the preparations for dressing Dawdi Jeremiah in special black funeral attire and laying him out in the pine coffin for the viewing. Rose took her letter out to the shaded area between her father's property line and the bishop's and sat on her favorite tree stump. There she looked at the Ocean City post-card—*Fun in the Sun*—Isaac had enclosed within his letter, which chronicled his time there: swimming, building sand castles . . . and biking on the boardwalk.

Goodness! Her beau freely admitted to not only riding a bike, but taking his turn driving a dune buggy the farmer had rented. Isaac was truthful and honest. But how did he feel comfortable behind the wheel like that? After all, there were forbidden inflatable tires on dune buggies. *Same as bikes.*

She finished reading the letter, making note of his final words: *I miss you, Rose. Looking*

forward to this Saturday evening. You know the
place to meet. With all my love—Isaac

Heading back toward the house, she was thankful for Isaac's steadfast affection and was eager to see him again. But she didn't know how to address the bike and the dune buggy.

Where the row of trees ceased to crowd the path, Rose purposely slowed her pace. More gray carriages were arriving at her father's house. Word would rapidly spread with the help of a *Leicht-ah-sager,* who traveled to invite family to the funeral, including cousins who were the same age as Dawdi Jeremiah. The invitation would be limited to those closest in age to allow enough room for the immediate family at the funeral service.

Eventually, though, everyone in the church district and the neighborhood would come to pay respects. The word would spread faster than any newspaper could bring it.

People would bring food for the next few days, as well as the day of the funeral, when the family and close relatives gathered after the burial service to fellowship over a plentiful feast as a way to once again resume the patterns of life.

Rose was thankful for this caring tradition—sorrow could deplete a person in body and spirit. She and Mamm would be especially mindful of Mammi Sylvia for a good, long time, making sure she was cared for . . . possibly suggesting she move to the other Dawdi Haus in time, where she could live closer to Rose's parents.

Thinking suddenly of the wedding season, Rose wondered if Mamm would be expected to wear her black mourning dress and apron to her youngest daughter's wedding. *Ach no!* Her mother and grandmother would wear the clothes of mourning for a full year, whereas Rose and her sisters-in-law would wear them for six months. But she realized she was putting the carriage before the horse with that, and she hurried back to the house to help greet the many visitors.

~

Solomon wasn't surprised when Aaron and his sons-in-law dropped by later that afternoon to bid farewell to Jeremiah, who'd already been prepared by the funeral director prior to being returned to the family for dressing. But Sol was jolted a bit when Nick came in the back door and removed his straw hat. He eyed him as Nick approached the pine coffin set up in the front room near the two windows facing Salem Road. Nick hadn't been one to make friends with many of the Kauffman family, so it was striking to see him standing there, gazing so seriously into the simple pine coffin.

For the life of him, Sol did not know what had propelled Nick home after leaving here the way he did. Once Amish youth left, they didn't usually return. *Not even for a short time, like Hen did* ... Was it truly because he desired to make peace with this community?

Sol made it a point to observe where Rose was in proximity to Nick. Far as he could tell, she wasn't in the kitchen washing and drying dishes with several of Sylvia's sisters. Most likely she'd gone upstairs to read or pray, which she was known to do at such stressful times. Poor girl, finding her grandfather out there on the floor in the barn! Made him want to weep for her, just thinking about it.

Nick turned and walked solemnly through the sitting room—right past Sol—without speaking. He looked downright dejected, as though reviewing his own life, perhaps. Sol was touched by his humble spirit, and later when he spotted Nick and Aaron talking together, he couldn't help but be impressed by Nick's respectful demeanor toward the man who raised him ... whatever his doubts.

～

For all the rest of the day and long into the evening, the People came to view Dawdi

Jeremiah, a steady stream of compassionate souls. Visitors knew to enter at will through the back door. Many reminisced fondly about Rose's grandfather, remembering numerous good deeds he had done over the course of his seventy-six years.

Aaron and Nick stayed around the entire time, greeting folk and assisting some of the elderly relatives who'd come. Rose could not help noticing Nick's attentiveness. Since when had he ever been so pleasant and willing to help?

About the time her parents usually retired for the night, Rose felt the need for fresh air and left the house. She strolled over to her grandparents' Dawdi Haus and sat on the porch steps in the fading light, looking at the zinnias in the deacon's former wheelbarrow. She smiled through her tears as she recalled her rather impulsive act, but she felt certain Dawdi would approve.

Staring at the sky, she took pleasure in seeing the streaks of pink the vivid sunset left behind. Dawdi would've enjoyed sitting here and watching, as he sometimes did. *With Mammi by his side.*

She heard footsteps and knew it was her father before she actually saw him. She got up from her spot on the step and followed him to the porch chairs.

"Your Dawdi was well loved," he said quietly.

She nodded. "So many have come already."

He kept his hat on as he rocked in Dawdi's hickory rocker.

"You all in?" she asked.

"Pretty near. You?"

She gave a little smile. "Just needed some time alone."

"And here I come, bargin' in."

"No . . . I didn't mean that, Dat."

He sighed long and slow as the darkness crept closer. "Ya know, your Dawdi used to sit out late in the summertime, after your mother and I had been married for a year or so . . . just a-talking 'bout his future grandchildren. He delighted in each new baby as ya came—had a real soft place in his heart for his granddaughters, 'specially."

"I sure saw that in him," Rose admitted. "And there are so many of us, I don't see how we'll all fit on Friday," she remarked.

"We'll have to spill out onto the front porch, maybe. We'll make do somehow."

"Too bad Aaron can't preach one of the sermons, ya know?" Rose felt sadder thinking about that.

"I feel the same way—and Aaron knows Sylvia would've liked that." He paused and pulled on his beard. "Just won't seem the same."

Rose watched the remaining light in the western sky, holding her breath as the sun went down on the day of her grandfather's passing.

"Your Mamm's takin' your grandfather's sudden death awful hard."

"And Mammi Sylvia?"

"Well, ya know, they were married, what, near sixty years? It'd be like cutting off your arm, I s'pect."

Rose pondered that. "Just teenagers when they wed."

They fell silent yet again. The frogs carried on out near the pond behind the barn, and the bats fluttered around near the barn's edge, scaring away the swallows. Dat seemed oblivious, and Rose wondered if he was ready to get back to the main house, although surely the visits would wind down soon.

"Thought I'd say something right quick 'bout Nick," her father said abruptly. "Seems he's set on makin' his vow come September. Ya might already know."

"I heard he attended baptismal classes Sunday."

"Jah." Dat exhaled audibly. "Aaron said Nick told Bishop Simon he's on the path to

Gelassenheit—the Amish way. Intends to reside quietly in Christ."

She soaked this in. Her father must've sensed she needed to hear this. "Based on that, I don't understand why Bishop Simon won't release Aaron from his silencing. Do you, Dat?"

"Well, it's like anything. You just have to wait an' see if a person's bent on doing what he says."

"Doesn't Simon believe Nick will follow through?"

Dat shook his head. "For some reason, he seems not to."

"What 'bout Nick's confession? Does that have anything to do with it? I heard Bishop Simon's not convinced by Nick's account of things."

"Well, a young man is dead . . . and Nick saw him last, was right there with him."

Rose knew it looked awful suspicious. "Just boils down to a lack of witnesses."

"That's exactly it."

To get their minds on something else, she pointed out the old wheelbarrow. "Did ya see what I did?"

"Figured someone hauled Deacon Samuel's cast-off up here, but didn't know just why."

She shared the conversation she'd had

with Dawdi in the barn before he died. Her father took it all in . . . listening and rocking in the chair.

After a time, the moon appeared to the right of the barn, a waxing crescent. Was Isaac sitting out somewhere staring up at it, too? The thought brought Rose momentary joy in the midst of the sad and solemn day. She was tempted to put Dat's mind at ease about Nick, tell him not to fret—that Nick Franco certainly wasn't a worry for him any longer when Isaac Ebersol was the one who loved her most. *A right fine son-in-law to be.*

CHAPTER 34

The day of the funeral was unbearably hot. Numerous handkerchiefs and paper fans, including Rose's own, were already in use that Friday as the clocks in the house struck nine and the first preacher removed his hat. As if on cue, all the men present removed their own hats before the first sermon, which, aside from some respectful but brief remarks about Dawdi Jeremiah's life and character, was nearly identical in content to the introductory one given at a Sunday Preaching service, though shorter. "His strong faith and his conduct point to the kind of man our brother Jeremiah was," the minister said earnestly. "His was a life that pleased the Lord."

Rose felt honored to be seated between Mammi Sylvia and Mamm, who sat in her wheelchair at the end of the row. She hoped her presence would somehow provide a comfort during the hour and a half service.

After the second sermon and the reading of the obituary, the large front room was vacated and reorganized, and the coffin moved to a location more conducive to the line of mourners filing past.

Rose had been to a few funerals for young people, including Christian Petersheim's. At such gatherings, there was sometimes soft weeping, but considering her grandfather's long and fruitful life, the grieving today was largely evident in the somber expressions.

While the nearly three hundred mourners waited outdoors under the tall shade trees, the horses were gathered around a large wagon filled with hay. Buggies neatly lined up in a double row off to the side.

Rose noticed Nick standing with Aaron and his sons-in-law. Earlier, he'd given her a sympathetic look but kept his distance, which she appreciated, and he appeared to be doing the same now.

Rose spotted her first cousin Sarah demurely eyeing Nick as she stood next to her mother. The two of them were here to help with food and table setting later.

Offering a slight smile to both of them, Rose remained with her sisters-in-law and dear Hen. Her sister had sat in the back of the funeral service with other English neighbors and friends.

"I'll miss Dawdi," Hen whispered to Rose.

"We all will." Rose reached for her hand.

~

Solomon had not expected so many neighboring farmers to arrive for the funeral, especially not those who lived miles away. Still, they'd come, Amish and Englischers alike. Among them was Jeb Ulrich, the hermitlike man who lived in the shanty near Bridle Path Lane. The man was dressed in black and, though clean-shaven, fit in quite well with their drab Amish attire. Presently, Jeb was working his way through the crowd to where Sol stood near Aaron, Nick, and Bishop Simon.

Jeb immediately zeroed in on Nick. "Say, aren't you the young man I saw in the ravine last fall?" The old man's voice was loud enough that Sol cringed.

Nick looked momentarily confused as he realized Jeb was talking to him; then his expression grew cautious.

"I'm glad to see you recovered from your accident," Jeb went on, seemingly unaware of the attention he was attracting. "How's the other young man you were with? He looked to be in pretty rough shape after he bloodied his head."

Sol startled at this and glanced quickly at Aaron, and the two of them, as well as Bishop Simon, inched closer to Jeb.

"Who do you mean?" Sol asked, sure Jeb meant Christian. Yet what a thing to bring up on a day like this!

"Always wondered how that all turned out," Jeb said simply.

Sol was embarrassed at Jeb's impropriety. He touched the man's shoulder to lead him away from the crowd. "If you're referring to Christian Petersheim, I'm afraid he succumbed to his injuries," Sol said.

Jeb stepped back, his face drained of color. "He *died*?"

Sol patted Jeb's shoulder again, hoping he'd find another topic of conversation and spare Aaron any further reminder of his terrible loss.

Jeb turned back to Nick and frowned. "Well, then, I bet you're just sick about what happened."

Nick nodded sadly. "I am."

"It just didn't look that bad, you know? I mean, not from where I was standing. I was sure the other fellow—Christian, you say— would be just fine."

Aaron gasped. Sol was taken aback: It sounded as if Jeb was claiming to have *witnessed* the scene. After all, the man did live on the side of the ravine. Sol ventured ahead. "Jeb . . . were you actually *there* when it happened?"

Jeb cleared his throat and stood straighter, as if to add dignity to his response. "Well, yes . . . I was."

"What exactly did you see?" Bishop Simon put in, his eyes intent on the elderly Englischer before him.

"I was outside in my yard when I saw that young man right there. 'Course he had a ponytail then. It was the strangest thing, seeing an Amish fellow looking like that." Jeb gestured toward Nick. "You look clean-cut now, without all the long hair."

Nick stood unmoving, as though shocked by Jeb's admission that he'd seen him with Christian. Or, Sol wondered, was there more to his discomfort?

"You're referring to Nick Franco, the bishop's foster son," Bishop Simon noted.

"Yes, well, this Nick and Christian came riding real fast along the road into the ravine on their horses. Nick started to get off his horse right there on the boulders, which seemed downright foolish—it's so terribly steep there. But Christian reached over and grabbed hold of Nick's ponytail. He started hacking away at it with a knife, of all things!"

Aaron grimaced, and Sol felt his heart

pause in its beating. To think Christian had taken such a dreadful risk!

"Well, Nick was barely able to stay on his horse at that point. He jerked back and shoved Christian's knife away, but Christian lost his balance and fell headfirst into the rocks . . . taking Nick with him—right down on top of him. It looked to me like both of them were out cold, so I started running toward them, but the underbrush caught me good and I slipped and fell, too. And by the time I got myself up and brushed off, Nick had come to and lifted the other guy up, heaving him across his own horse to get him up to the road. Never saw anything like it . . . not between Amish, you know?"

Sol shook his head, aware how pale the others looked even in this heat.

"I had no idea Christian died. That's horrible . . . and here I've been wondering all this time. Guess I should've asked Jeremiah about him." Jeb was quiet for a moment while they all digested the information he'd just spewed.

Jeb turned back to Nick. "I'm real sorry about what happened. I wish I could have been some help."

Nick gave a brief nod of acknowledgment, obviously still too stunned to speak.

Jeb looked again at Sol. "You *do* know it was this here Nick who showed up at my door—just a boy—the day your wife's buggy flipped over."

Sol shook his head. "It couldn't have been him."

"Nick was just a lad . . . ten years old," Aaron added.

Jeb nodded. "Well, that's right, yes—he was about that age, as I recall."

Sol and Aaron exchanged glances again.

"Well, he came wearing English britches and a T-shirt with some kind of logo on it. Maybe you didn't know he went around with his Amish clothes tucked under modern ones—trying to hide them, I guess. He was a curious one, that youngster. I always felt a bit sorry for him. I warned him once he'd get a tongue-lashing from his father if he got caught doing that."

Aaron cleared his throat.

"No, even though I didn't know his name, I'm sure this here Nick was the one who told me about the upturned buggy that day . . . and your wife lying there, needing medical help."

A tremor ran through Sol. "*Nick* found . . . my wife?" He could hardly get the words out.

"That's right. And I called the ambulance." Jeb's eyes glistened. "I suppose you could even say he saved her life. Might've been hours before someone else wandered along and found her."

This news so soon after the other left Sol reeling. Aaron and the bishop seemed to be having equal difficulty comprehending. Yet no one's astonishment could compare to Nick's. The young man's dark eyes were wide, and his mouth gaped.

Bishop Simon motioned for them to move over near the horses and the hay wagon, where he quizzed Jeb about the day of Christian's accident. Jeb answered each question without faltering, recounting everything he'd just said without shifting a single detail.

At last, Simon acknowledged that Jeb's account matched Nick's own, which amazed Sol, who'd never believed Jeb a reliable eyewitness. *All these years I disbelieved him about the English boy.* But now he felt sure Jeb knew what he was talking about. Perhaps Jeb had not been able to articulate things as well at the time of Emma's accident . . . or Sol hadn't been in a state to believe him. Sol just didn't know.

Sol reached to shake Jeb's hand. "Thanks again for getting help for Emma that day. I'm mighty grateful." *Lord God have mercy on me for doubting this poor man!*

Jeb nodded and wiped his brow.

Sol couldn't resist another glance at Bishop Simon, who looked lost in thought, undoubtedly absorbing all he'd heard.

Without another word, Sol stepped inside with the other mourners.

～

Rose walked to the well-kept Amish cemetery with Hen and Mammi Sylvia while two men carried Mamm to the burial site in her wheelchair.

The grave had been already filled halfway, and Rose and Hen held hands as the People gathered in clusters of families, ready for the final words.

She saw Bishop Simon unexpectedly hand the *Ausbund* hymnal to Aaron Petersheim, and Aaron nodded in agreement to something privately spoken between the two men. Rose didn't understand just what had occurred, but she was delighted to see Aaron Petersheim apparently being given a small part in the burial service.

Aaron went to stand near the hand-dug grave and read a hymn. The grave was then filled all the way and mounded before the immediate family turned to head back to the house for a meal with close family and friends. Brandon would bring Mattie Sue and join them by the time the rest of them arrived there.

Heading home, Rose did not know what to make of Aaron's reading at the grave site.

Had Bishop Simon changed his mind? If so, why now? She looked behind her and saw Bishop Simon walking along the road with Nick—most unusual. "What on earth?" Rose said to Hen.

Hen whispered back that Dat, Aaron, and the Bart bishop had been talking during their walk to the cemetery. "Something's up."

"But . . . at Dawdi's burial?"

"Whatever's been discussed, it looks like Aaron might keep his title as bishop."

"Ach, do you really think so?" Hope shivered through Rose—so many varying emotions in one day. Tomorrow presented even more promise with Isaac's and her reunion at twilight. The pleasant thought gave her courage during the big family dinner—and later, when she and her parents were the only ones left at home with Mammi Sylvia.

~

At the supper table, Mamm caught Rose's attention when she commented on how curious it was that Aaron had been permitted to read the hymn at the cemetery.

"It was fitting for Dawdi Jeremiah's burial hymn to be recited by Bishop Aaron, given that he fasted and prayed for the bishop's restraint to be lifted—that divine mercy would win out," Dat responded. "The Lord works in baffling ways at times."

Rose leaned forward in her chair, eager to hear more.

"According to Jeb Ulrich, turns out everything Nick revealed to Aaron and Bishop Simon adds up." And Dat began to explain the details of the day Christian had lost his life. When he finished, the kitchen was hushed.

"So it *was* an accident!" Rose exclaimed.

"Jah, a dreadful thing, but an accident nonetheless."

Mammi Sylvia bowed her head for a time. Then, looking up, she said softly, "Oh, I do pray the silencing will be lifted."

"It certainly would seem so," Dat replied.

And for just that instant, Rose's grandmother looked more like a bride than a widow.

But the good news of their beloved bishop's likely return to ministry—and Jeb's surprising role in that—wasn't the only thing that brought some lightness to the evening's intimate family gathering. Dat relayed the astonishing news that Nick, as a young boy, had helped to save Mamm's life.

"Seems I've misjudged him," Dat admitted, his expression tinged with regret.

Mamm, Rose, and Mammi Sylvia were amazed—and grateful. But the longer Dat talked, the more proud Rose felt, if not a little humbled, too. This proof of her friend's innocence—something she had always hoped for—nearly took her breath away. Now the entire community would soon know that Nick had not directly caused Christian's death, but it was Christian who'd set in motion the very events that led to his own passing. Truly, God had nudged Jeb to Dawdi's funeral today.

Rose considered all of this, including what Jeb had said about Nick's helping Mamm. Why, in time Nick might even be regarded as brave, once word got out that he'd played a large part in saving Mamm when he was a youngster.

What a turnabout! Divine providence had brought something good out of the ashes, making Nick's return count for something at last. More than ever, Rose was glad to have extended her friendship to the bishop's foster son down through the years.

CHAPTER 35

Rose weeded all day Saturday—first the family vegetable garden, then the various flower beds around the main house and over on Mammi Sylvia's side. Cloud cover brought some relief from the intense heat of the past several days, though Rose still checked to be sure Dawdi's zinnias were moist enough in the wooden wheelbarrow.

After she bathed and dressed that evening for her date with Isaac, she sat for a few minutes near the window in her room, looking out toward the road. She was surprised to see Nick heading off in a spanking-new black courting buggy, with Pepper prancing . . . mane flying. Finally he'd gotten what he needed for proper courting—he must have accepted what Bishop Aaron offered to give him years ago.

"It's 'bout time, dear friend," she whispered, wondering if he was heading off to meet Cousin Sarah or another pretty girl in the district. As convinced as Dat was now that Nick would join church in the fall, Rose didn't figure Nick would take any chances with a girl outside the local district. He'd want to continue to prove himself.

Almost three weeks since his return, she thought, realizing that they had not once gone riding. More than a slight twinge touched her heart.

~

Isaac slipped his arm around Rose as soon as they were settled in his fine carriage, holding the reins in his other hand. He was full of beach talk and hinted that he'd like to take her to the ocean sometime. Could it be he was thinking of going after they were married—for their honeymoon, perhaps? Surely he was!

She spoke of her grandfather's passing, how goodhearted a man he was, and how she'd been there with him before he died. She even shared about Tillie, the kitten he'd named the very hour of his death.

"Not many Amish farmers give a care about barn cats, jah?" He smiled down at her.

"That's for sure. Oh, Isaac, I wish you could've met my grandfather!"

He leaned over and kissed her cheek. "I'd like to meet all of your family . . . very soon."

It felt peculiar that he hadn't met them yet, although since he lived outside Rose's district, he naturally wouldn't know her parents or siblings—only Ruthann's family, because they were kin. The other fellows Rose had dated had grown up in her church, so they were well known not just to her relatives but to all the People.

"Where do ya see yourself living and working someday?" she asked, trying not to be too obvious about her real question: *Where will we live after marriage?*

"I've been considering that for the past few months. It'd be awful nice to stay in touch with my family in Bart . . . and keep workin' for Ed Morton. I've worked for him since I was out of school—after eighth grade, ya know."

"He must know you're a hard worker, then," she said.

"Ed and I go way back."

"You know him well?"

"Oh jah." Isaac grew quiet and Rose hoped she hadn't asked something out of turn.

After a good long time had passed and he said no more about it, Rose changed the subject. "My mother's doin' ever so well now. She has no pain at all."

"Must be a relief for your father."

She got a little choked up. "It was an awful big risk, the surgery, but she and Dat are glad it's behind them."

He nodded. "I'm happy for your mother. For all your family. No one should have to suffer such pain."

"And for so many years." Rose thought again of her father's unexpected revelation— that Nick had been the one to alert Jeb the morning of Mamm's accident. She didn't understand why Nick had never told her, as close as they'd been.

As they rode into the July night, Rose began to relax again, dismissing Isaac's wish to live and work near Bart. At some level, hadn't she known that would be the case? Still, she hadn't expected him to keep working for Ed. She chided herself. Wasn't it enough to be so well courted and cherished?

Isaac's one of a kind, Rose thought.

Even so, she missed the camaraderie she and Nick had always enjoyed. Was it Nick's return that had stirred all of this up again? Isaac *was* very different from Nick Franco, she decided as Isaac hummed beside her in the moonlight. *But I'm Isaac's girl now. . . .*

≈

In the days following Dawdi Jeremiah's

passing, Rose helped Mammi Sylvia distribute his personal effects to his younger brothers and two of his oldest sons. She attended canning bees, entertained both Mattie Sue and Beth—with Mamm—at the farm, and enjoyed watching Mattie Sue become comfortable riding their most reliable pony under Dat's care. She also sewed several yellow sleeping gowns for Hen's coming baby and took them along when Hen and Brandon hosted their barbeque.

To occupy her grandmother, Rose took her and Mamm to visit some shut-in relatives, as well as Annie Mast's twin babies—Mary and Anna, who were now nearly eight months old and crawling and babbling. Now and then, Rose caught sight of Nick from afar, at the bishop's or every other Sunday evening as he took his open buggy up Salem Road. On Preaching Sundays, she saw him at church, but he did not seek her out as always before. According to Cousins Sarah and Mary, who were happy to fill her in, Nick faithfully attended Singings in the local district.

August arrived with temperatures as warm as July's, and it was often too hot to sleep. On such evenings, Rose took her flashlight out to the front porch and read her library books there, as many as two or three novels per week. And she took pleasure in answering Isaac's weekly letters as they continued to see each other like clockwork every Saturday night.

When his letter arrived the first Wednesday in August, Rose read it immediately while walking back up the driveway to the house. Goodness, he wanted to take her somewhere "extra nice" for a late supper out. *What do you think about that?*

"Wonderful-*gut*!" she said to the sky, suspecting what he had up his thoughtful sleeve. It would be all she could do to get through the next few days till Isaac came for her in his courting carriage. Or perhaps, depending on where he had in mind to go for their special meal, he would come in a hired van?

"Are ya talkin' to yourself, Rosie?"

She looked up and saw Nick carrying a sack of feed on his shoulder.

"Well, now, I guess I am." She smiled. "Where are ya goin' with all that feed?"

"Taking it to your father." He looked so different, with his bangs growing out in time for his baptism next month. "Got a second?" he asked her.

"Sure, what's on your mind?"

He glanced toward the field where the trees marked the path. Then his gaze returned to her. "I asked ya before and you didn't seem much interested."

"What's that?"

"The grapevine nearly has you married, ya know."

"I suspect the grapevine's right," she admitted, knowing he would see the truth on her face anyway.

He hesitated for a moment, then shrugged. "I think we should go ridin' one last time, Rosie."

The way he said it struck her. Had he found someone? Was he on the verge of asking Sarah or Mary to go for steady, maybe?

"Just once more?" she asked.

He looked momentarily sad but brightened just as quickly. "I thought it'd be fun. One last run for old time's sake. Besides, the nights are nice."

"Where were ya thinkin' of?"

He looked toward the east. "Doesn't matter. Just want to ride with you, my old friend."

"So now I'm *old*?"

They laughed and it felt good. It had been too long. Rose knew what her answer would be.

"Sure, I'll go . . . as long as we each take a horse."

He chuckled. "Fair enough. Meet me up the road . . . you know where."

She had to smile. "After dusk or before?"

"Why not while the sun's still up? We have nothing to hide," he said.

Rose felt strangely relieved. This ride was merely for friendship's sake.

He gave her a cordial smile and they parted ways. As she headed toward the house, Isaac's letter still in hand, she knew it was perfect timing, since she was soon to be engaged. Who knew but Nick might also settle down real soon?

Our last farewell, she decided. *All for the best . . .*

CHAPTER 36

The sun was a red ball, tumbling fast as Rose met Nick just up from the bishop's house to take George and Pepper out for a canter. They rode east a ways, then turned north on Ridge Road, past the Kings' place and up over the hill to Shady Road. The vistas at the rise were spectacular as they halted the horses to watch the sunset, the sky filled with crimson and gold streaks.

"Ever see one so perty?" Rose said.

"Not this summer."

"Here's the best spot to see it."

"I think you're right," Nick agreed. Pepper whinnied. "Silly old boy," he said, giving him a reassuring pat.

Rose laughed a little. There they were, just starting out on their jaunt, and already it seemed as if all the months Nick was away had dissolved into the twilight. She found herself studying him—she'd never expected to see him again, and now here he was, an upstanding Amishman with no hint of rebellion. His time with Mrs. Schaeffer had altered his life. His dark brown eyes still communicated volumes, but now they were almost gentle.

"What're you thinking about, Rosie?"

She smiled. *He knows me too well.* "Oh, just how very Amish you look now that you're back."

"I *am* Amish. It took a while, but I finally realized where I belong."

She reflected on that as the last of the sun fell out of sight, into the eastern hills. They signaled the horses to move forward.

"Something bothering ya?" he asked as they went.

"No . . . you?"

He chuckled. "Not really, no."

"Well, I'm glad you asked me to ride." Rose paused to quell her emotions. She breathed deeply, then forged ahead. "I've been meaning to ask you something, Nick."

He shrugged. "I'm an open book now."

She decided not to beat around the bush. "My father says you saved Mamm's life when you alerted Jeb Ulrich so long ago."

Until that moment, Nick had been watching her attentively, but he turned away suddenly.

"What's the matter?"

"Nothing."

"But you did save her, right?"

Nick blew out a breath. "I only did what I could."

"Well, the way I heard it, if it hadn't been for you, who knows what might've happened? I'm truly grateful, Nick. Thank you."

In the fading light, he ran one hand along a length of rein as the other held it fast. He sighed. "Even though I might've helped save your Mamm . . ." His voice trailed off and he stared at the sky.

"Nick . . . what?"

He turned toward her again and shook his head. "Rosie . . . don't you see? The accident was my fault."

"What're ya sayin'?"

He was quiet for a time. And when he spoke, his voice sounded hollow and flat. "It's just that . . . there's something you don't know."

She held her breath.

"I'm the one to blame for the buggy flipping over."

"Wha-at?" She felt the blood drain from her head.

"I took Pepper out riding when I knew better. I was too small to ride him, the bishop used to say. Didn't know enough about horses back then."

She listened intently.

"I slid down off Pepper and let him wander about while I played along the road, on the rocks. Then something spooked him and off he went . . . galloping like he was mad, down Bridle Path Lane." Nick's breath caught, as though reliving the terrible moment. "I saw what happened, Rosie. I saw young Pepper crowd your Mamm's horse and carriage. The hill was awful steep on the left—you know the ravine, the way it falls off, nearly straight down on the other side. There was no room for Pepper to pass without pushing the carriage over."

"Ach no . . ."

"When I ran to your Mamma and saw her, bloodied and wounded, I wished it were me lying there on the road." His voice quivered. "Aw, Rosie . . . your dear Mamm.

"For years, I felt somehow cursed because of what I'd done. Then Christian died . . . and I knew I couldn't stay round here any longer. I figured I was no good for anyone."

Her heart went out to him.

"I'm awful sorry, Rosie." He shook his head. "I never meant to hurt your mother . . . or anyone. Not ever."

"Nick, listen to me. Is *that* what's bothered you all these years? It wasn't just Christian's

harsh demands, or your parents' expectations
. . . you thought you were at fault for Mamm's
accident?"

"But I *was*."

"No," she said. "You didn't know what
Pepper was going to do. It could have happened to anyone."

"But it wouldn't have happened if I'd
obeyed and stayed at home, like the bishop
said those first few weeks after I came here."

"You were just a little boy. A troubled one
who needed a home and parents to care for
you and show you what love is." She reached
out a hand, but the horses kept them apart.
"You were not to blame. You didn't kill
Christian, nor were you at fault for Mamm's
accident—neither one. And you were never
cursed. *Never*."

"How can you be so kind to me even now,
Rosie?" Nick sounded incredulous.

"You're my best friend," she said. "And
you always have been, from the moment you
showed up."

Nick sighed heavily.

"Have you told your father any of this?"
she asked.

"The bishop knows everything." He
removed his straw hat and held it against his
chest. "And now, so do you."

Filled with empathy, she followed his

horse when he urged it forward. To think she'd faulted herself for the circumstances leading up to her mother's accident . . . just as Nick had.

They rode without talking for a while longer, enjoying the sweet night air on the mild yet humid night. But the remainder of the outing was colored by this being their final ride together. As they slowed to a trot, Rose was aware that Nick was taking the long way home.

At the end of her lane, they stopped riding and told each other good night. Rose even allowed Nick to reach for her hand. They lingered there like long-lost friends.

"I forgive you, Nick," she said. "Now, please, won't ya forgive yourself?"

He looked at her in the moonlight, their eyes locking. "I think I needed to hear that." He paused. "From everyone, really, but especially from you."

The People expected too much of the little English boy from Philly. Yet Nick had come back to the very folk who had failed to believe in him.

"Take care of yourself, Rosie," he said. "Be happy, all right?"

"You too, Nick. God be with ya." She watched him go, wondering why she still felt nearly breathless in his presence.

~

Sleep eluded Rose. In spite of herself, she kept visualizing the circumstances Nick revealed had led up to Mamm's tragic accident. She shook herself and got out of bed to go and stand at the window. The night was dead, without a smidgen of air. She slipped on her cotton duster and headed downstairs, barefoot, to the back porch and sat there silently.

By the time the moon sat high atop the silo, Rose was weary of the day. Yet she was not tired enough to sleep. So she prayed, "Dear Lord, please help Nick forgive himself, just as you have already forgiven him."

~

For Isaac's twenty-first birthday, Rose made his favorite dessert, German chocolate sauerkraut cake. Their dinner date was tomorrow, but since she wanted to surprise him with it on his actual birthday, she hired a driver to take her to Bart, planning to deliver the cake in person.

Ed Morton's spread of land was much more vast than Rose had ever imagined. She could understand now why he hired so many workers. But out of all of them, Isaac was the only employee who looked Amish, even minus his straw hat.

As her driver parked the van, Isaac walked sprightly through the backyard, toward a nearby tractor. He easily scaled the machine and plunked down into the seat, taking the wheel. Isaac seemed completely at ease with the tractor, despite its huge *inflatable* tires.

Her throat squeezed tight. Was this the type of work Isaac did for Ed Morton? *Does my beau drive a tractor for a living?!*

The van driver came around to help Rose out, distracting her. He reached to get the cake carrier off the seat and handed it to her. "Here you are, miss."

"Denki, I'll be right back," she said and headed for the house. The least she could do was to leave the birthday cake with a note. She would not stay to see how pleased Isaac might be. No, she was too upset to consider talking to him or trying to write much else.

Oh, Isaac, what are you thinking?

At least Rose had the presence of mind to thank Mrs. Morton when the woman offered her something to drink—a chair to wait in, perhaps. "If you like, I can see how long Isaac might be."

Rose refused as graciously as possible. "That's okay. I don't want to bother Isaac just now. I can see he's very busy."

Rose excused herself and made her way toward the van. Surveying the grounds, she was surprised not to see a single buggy any-where. An old beat-up car parked near the barn caught her attention with a bumper sticker that read *Ocean City, New Jersey*. She spied a worn straw hat on the dashboard—*Isaac's* hat.

Immediately, she realized the truth. *That must be Isaac's car!*

This was crazy; her imagination was running away with her. Rose felt as if she'd gone to the other side of the world—definitely the English side, what with all the electric and telephone wires running into the house and the various vehicles parked around the property. And the worst of it was the tractor rumbling through the field with her beau behind the wheel.

Rose felt queasy—she needed to return to the familiar landscape and Amish life of Salem Road. She buckled herself into the van, anxious to get home as soon as possible.

CHAPTER 37

$\mathcal{R}$estless that night, Rose did as her parents had taught her and cast her burdens upon the Lord. She prayed for wisdom and, above all, peace.

The next morning, although tired from lack of sleep, Rose was pleased to hear from Dat at breakfast that their family would be hosting baptismal Sunday, September twenty-first. Such a blessed day! A flurry of cleaning must commence, including scrubbing every wall, window, and floor. Rose would also see to whitewashing the outside fences, as well as tending the flower beds and lawn. Everything must be as neat and clean as was humanly possible.

Today, however, she baked a nice big ham with potatoes for the noon meal. As she puttered in the kitchen, her eyes frequently came to rest on Dawdi's spot at the table, and she had to look away. She missed him so.

Later in the afternoon, she and Mammi made homemade noodles, then cut up pieces of ham left over from dinner earlier. They also cooked up a batch of buttered peas and canned carrots to serve for supper alongside some chowchow and pickled beets, Mammi Sylvia's favorite.

Rose politely excused herself prior to meeting Isaac for their dinner out. This was to be the evening she'd dreamed about for months . . . and now she could hardly think straight due to her concerns. Visions of seeing Isaac driving the tractor—and of that car— could not be blotted from her uneasy mind.

~

Sol had sensed something wrong with Rose at the noon meal. His daughter just wasn't her cheerful self today, and now that he thought of it, neither was Emma.

He wondered if it might be something related to whomever Rose Ann was seeing each and every Saturday evening. *Still the young man from Bart?*

He also knew she'd taken George riding, because he'd seen her leading him from the stable Wednesday evening, before sundown. Sol had assumed Rose's horseback riding had ceased, at least with Nick. Of course, he wasn't sure she'd gone with Nick, especially now that she had a beau. Yet even if she had, Sol wasn't as concerned anymore. Nick was shaping up nicely, becoming as respectable as the bishop had hoped. Aaron had said as much earlier today, when they were shoveling out the manure pit in Sol's barn with Mose and Josh. To think Nick was still on track, studying for his baptism; it appeared he was truly becoming one of them. Not at all *der Lump*—the heretic—they'd understood him to be. *All of us were so wrong about him ... but Rose Ann.*

"So why should Rose—his closest friend—be so blue?" Sol muttered to himself.

~

As soon as Isaac arrived by hired van that evening, he hopped out and opened the door for Rose. "Denki for the surprise birthday cake," he said, kissing her cheek. He smelled fresh and was dressed in his Sunday best.

"Glad ya liked it."

"I admit I didn't share much of it." He grinned as she got in.

"So it's all gone already?"

"Jah, nearly." He chuckled and then turned to her. "Why didn't ya stay around yesterday?

I could've shown you the farm—introduced you to Ed and his family."

She didn't want to say. He must not have any idea she'd seen him driving the tractor—either that or he didn't care. "I needed to get back home to help Mamm. Did ya have a nice birthday, then?"

"Sure did, and the best of it was your cake."

Isaac continued to make lighthearted conversation all the way to the lovely restaurant—a fine dining establishment just north of Strasburg. He must've saved his money a long time for this. In addition to paying the driver extra to wait for them, there were candles and flowers on the table, and an appetizer was presented even before their order was taken. Isaac was working up to something very big, Rose was sure of it.

Isaac handed a pretty little box to her across the white linen draped table. "I bought you something. When you open it, you might not understand. Not at first, anyway."

With everything already going through her mind, she didn't need more to ponder. A box so small seemed certain to contain jewelry—far from being a traditional Amish gift—but she was polite and accepted it.

Inside, she found a delicate gold wristwatch. It was so beautiful, and yet . . .

She looked at him. "This is . . . really lovely, Isaac. But I'm not sure where I'd ever wear it."

"How about when the two of us are together?"

Rose honestly didn't know what to say to this, but at his urging, she put it on to see how it looked on her wrist. "Oh, it's so perty."

He smiled and nodded across the candlelit table. "Thought you might like it."

"I do . . . I truly do." She didn't know what had gotten into her, but she loved being treated like this. The whole evening was so romantic, like something out of the wonderful library books she read and reread.

Halfway through dessert—chocolate mousse and a specialty coffee with a hint of mint and chocolate—Isaac said, "I've been waiting for the perfect setting . . . and the right moment, Rose. I believe this is it."

She held her breath and looked into his handsome blue eyes; they shone with promise.

"Will you marry me, Rose?"

She looked down at the gold wristwatch, the time already set to the correct hour. She'd never, ever dreamed of owning or even wearing something so delicate and pretty. Would she wake up and discover this heartbreakingly beautiful night was a dream? That Isaac was too good to be true?

Ach, but I already know he isn't. This watch was proof of it, and she'd seen him driving a tractor just yesterday. She couldn't just sit there and not inquire about that, or about his church's Ordnung. It was imperative to know where he stood on something so important, as well as his plans for the future. Did he truly mean to embrace the fellowship of the People? How could she give her answer before knowing?

Rose raised her eyes to Isaac as he awaited her answer across the exquisitely set table, his expression clearly one of love and great anticipation.

～

Gentleman that he was, Isaac walked Rose up the driveway to the back door, seeing her safely inside. She waited till he left, standing on the back porch as he climbed back into the van. A mule *hee-haw*ed in the barn, a wheezing, mocking laugh.

The van pulled away. Rose didn't bother to change out of her best clothes before hurrying across the yard to the barn. She carefully climbed up the hayloft ladder and sat there with little Tillie in her lap, the gray kitten Dawdi Jeremiah had named on the day of his Homegoing. Perched in the sweet hay,

Rose began to cry, letting the purring kitten comfort her.

"I believe Isaac truly loves me." She sighed and looked about the dimly lit haymow. "He asked to marry me . . . but I had to say no," she whispered, her tears coming fast now. "I couldn't marry Isaac. I just couldn't."

Torn between the love and marriage she'd wanted so desperately, and what was pleasing to God and the church, Rose felt utterly disillusioned. And wretchedly sad.

Isaac had argued his case, saying it didn't make sense for him to be completely Old Order—he freely admitted to driving the car she'd spotted at the Mortons'. She'd insisted that such things were against her church Ordnung and the way she was raised. But Isaac had said working for Ed Morton was his livelihood—how he planned to support his family and his wife. *"You'd get used to it, Rose. How can you know if you don't give it a try?"*

Give the world a try? That's what she believed he was saying. And in the end she had to be true to her baptism and not let Isaac influence her away from her promise to God. Somehow she'd kept her emotions in check during the rest of their time together.

But now Rose gave in to tears of self-pity, grieving for all the lost years ahead of her— of the love she'd intended to show to Isaac, and of the children she would never bear and nurture.

Exhausted, she leaned back in the hay and whispered, "O Father, I know you want what is best for me." She prayed, "I have to believe this . . . with all of my heart."

A husband with one foot in the world can't possibly be right for me, she thought. *How could such a marriage work?*

She hadn't even thought of Hen and Brandon in making her decision, but Rose realized she'd learned important lessons from the problems their union had faced. She would not make her sister's mistake.

Sometime later, she was startled by a dark silhouette approaching the hay hole across the barn, then suddenly disappearing to the lower level. When she leaned up to look more closely, she wondered if her mind had played tricks. Or had she cried so hard she was mistaken about having seen anything at all? Rose strained her ears, listening . . . and heard muted footsteps fading below.

Ach no! How embarrassing!

But then, what would anyone be doing out here at such a late hour? Surely it was merely her imagination.

She returned to her warm spot in the hay and brought Tillie up close to her heart. As far as Rose knew, the last person to hold Tillie had been her devout Dawdi. She felt strangely comforted by the knowledge and soon fell sound asleep, tears drying on her cheeks.

~

Days passed and the work of digging early potatoes commenced, as did picking and processing an abundance of produce from the family garden. Rose and Mammi Sylvia harvested limas, string beans, corn, tomatoes, squash, cucumbers, and peppers. They joined with Barbara Petersheim and her married daughters, as well as Hen, to can, freeze, and dry all of it, which took up much of their time and energy through the end of August. Rose also managed to help rake hay and sometimes even drove the mules for baling it. She and all the People looked at farming and caring for the land as a spiritual mandate, one of their highest callings. *'Tis a gift to be Plain,* Rose often thought.

But the most revered mandate of all was church baptism. The highly anticipated Sunday was fast approaching, and Rose spent many of her hours and days now on the redding up necessary to host the gathering. Mammi Sylvia assisted, and Mamm wheeled outside to watch them from the porch, sitting in the comfortable custom-made chair Dat had recently purchased for her. The occasional therapy sessions she still attended had been helpful in improving her endurance, and she needed to rest less frequently than before.

Rose kept so busy she scarcely had time anymore for reading. She'd lost all interest in romances, especially now that she was convinced she was past the age for the merriment and matchmaking of the Singings she no longer attended. She confessed to the bishop the dancing she had done with Isaac, resolving to be more true to the Ordnung the brethren had established. And she put her energy into being a blessing to her grandmother, hoping to make Mammi Sylvia's life more pleasant . . . less lonely. The two of them forged an even closer relationship during the many hours spent sewing and going for walks together, two of Rose's delights.

Meanwhile, Leah Miller was more often missing after the shared meal on Sundays, and other times, too. Rose felt sure her friend was slipping away to Bart to spend more time with Jake Ebersol, who was ever observant of the Old Ways. *Unlike his twin.*

Rose had seen the peculiar kind of Amish her former beau wished to be. Closing the door on a future with Isaac had been painful, but it had left her all the wiser.

～

Hen walked over to the farm to help her sister and grandmother wash down the windowsills and sweep the porches in preparation for Preaching services ten days away. While she worked, she noticed Rose's exceptionally quiet demeanor. The spring in her step had vanished, as had the smile on her pretty face.

Has my sister been jilted in love? Hen finished dusting in her parents' former bedroom, now furnished for occasional overnight guests. Remembering how bubbly Rose had been the last time they had a heart-to-heart, it was beyond Hen what had happened. *Much too long ago,* Hen realized sadly. Alas, she'd gotten caught up in her own work as a wife and mother, busying herself with preparations for the new baby.

When the noon meal rolled around, Hen took her old spot at the table, with Mattie Sue across from her. Her father bowed his head and they offered the silent prayer.

As they ate, Dad talked of the upcoming baptismal Sunday. He looked at Mom, then at Hen. "Two of your cousins, Sarah and Mary, are joining church."

"And Nick, too," Mattie Sue piped up, eyes bright.

"How do you know?" Hen asked her little girl.

Mammi Sylvia chuckled at Mattie Sue,

but Rose remained still and uncharacteristically quiet.

"'Cause Nick said so!" Mattie Sue declared. "When he asked me about my Amish clothes. That's when I told him."

Hen leaned forward. "What did you say?"

"When I grow up, I want to join church."

Dad reached over to tug gently on Mattie Sue's ear. "Are ya mighty sure?"

Mattie Sue bobbed her head up and down.

Dad just might get a replacement for the girl he lost to the English, Hen thought, though she realized that much could change between now and when her daughter turned sixteen. *So very much.*

For now, it was sweet to think Mattie was so determined to maintain the Old Ways that she'd worn her little cape dresses and aprons all summer long, even going barefoot and wearing her hair up in a bun. This hadn't annoyed Brandon like Hen thought it might, but it still surprised Hen. Mattie's attire was the last reminder of Hen's own yearning for the Plain life, a yearning that had found its unexpected fulfillment in her marriage and the faith she now shared with her husband.

CHAPTER 38

*A*lthough they'd gathered in various barns for baptismal Sundays other years, Rose's father had decided to meet indoors for this year's baptism Sunday. Rose was glad to be inside on this windy and rainy Lord's Day. She joined her voice with all the People in singing hymns from the *Ausbund* as they awaited the arrival of the nine baptismal candidates.

There was a clap of thunder during the solemn pause after the last hymn, which startled many, Rose included. Then, as if on cue, the applicants slowly filed into the room, taking their designated seats in the center section, near the still-vacant bench set aside for the ministerial brethren.

The congregation, young and old alike, watched respectfully. Rose's own blessed day of baptism came to mind—the day she had turned her back on the world to trust the Lord. Suddenly, she thought of dear Hen, a tear in her eye for her sister who'd chosen against church membership as a teen and later lamented the decision.

Except Nick, who was nearly twenty-two, all of the candidates were in their late teens. Nick's sincere desire to follow the Lord in holy baptism was evident on his countenance even at this moment. Since his return home, he had exhibited the utmost humility and submission to God and the Plain community. He was genuinely transformed.

Presently, he sat with his head bowed with the others, facing the audience but with eyes closed in reverence, undoubtedly rehearsing the things the ministerial brethren had shared with the candidates earlier this morning. The lifetime vow was not to be taken glibly or without great consideration. Once made, it was never to be broken.

Soon the ordained brethren arrived from their quiet meeting upstairs, removing their hats at the back of the room. Slowly they came, moving toward the wooden bench at the front of the room. Rose recognized several visiting ministers, including Bishop Simon from Bart, and sadness rippled through her as she thought of the connection between her own church and Isaac's on this day.

But it was Bishop Aaron who was in charge of the hallowed service. He would have the unique privilege of baptizing his son, Nick.

After the regular sermons, which lasted a couple hours, Bishop Aaron turned his attention to the candidates and gave them special counsel. Deacon Esh then brought in a small container of water and a tin cup. Tears sprang to Aaron's eyes as he gazed upon Nick and reiterated, "The oath is to be made to God, above all." Momentarily his voice broke, but he coughed and managed to recover his poise. "For those of you who are still willing to join the body of Christ as members of this church, and believe this is the right thing to do, you may now kneel."

Nick dropped quickly to his knees, followed by the other eight. Rose heard some sniffling amongst the congregation and felt deeply moved.

As all of the candidates waited for the initial questions from their bishop, the girls removed their head coverings. "Are you prepared to follow Christ and His church and to remain faithful through all the days of your life until your death?"

Rose listened to the words and remembered—to this day she had never known anything more sacred or satisfying than the holy mantle that covered her life at her own baptism.

She noticed Nick's head bowed lower than the rest. It was a struggle to suppress her tears as she rose with the People while the applicants continued to kneel. Bishop Aaron cupped his hands over Nick's head first. Deacon Esh poured water from the small pail into the bishop's hands. A low sigh rose from the People as the water trickled down over Nick's black hair.

Someday will he tell me how he feels at this moment? Rose was unable to stop looking at Nick, kneeling in the remarkably penitent position.

After each baptism, the bishop offered the hand of fellowship, beginning with Nick. "We extend the hand of fellowship, in the name of the Lord and of the Church. Rise up, Nick Petersheim."

Petersheim? Rose could scarcely believe this. Nick had changed his name to honor the bishop!

For an instant it almost appeared that Aaron meant to embrace him. But instead, Nick and the other young men received the customary holy kiss from the bishop, and the pronouncement of peace. Barbara Petersheim in turn greeted and kissed each of the girls as sisters in Christ.

"Now may the most high and almighty God complete the work which He began in each of you, giving divine strength and help through all the days of your lives, until you come to a blessed end through Jesus Christ, God's Son. Amen."

Later, the bishop read from Romans, chapter six. The service concluded with Bishop Aaron instructing the congregation to do whatever they could to assist the new members. "Each one present should continue in faithfulness to God and to the ministry of the church."

The People then knelt for the final prayer. Rose was especially grateful for this time, ready as she was to offer her devout thanks to God for answering her prayers for Nick. *O Lord, you knew all along this day would come, that you would bear much fruit in Nick's life....*

When the benediction was given, the rain stopped and the clouds parted. Sunshine streamed in through the windows like a blessing as the People sang the final hymn, and the former outcast, at long last, was now one of them.

~

Rose's mother and grandmother gently encouraged her to consider going to the

Singing at her great-uncle Daniel Kauffman's in two weeks. Rose listened respectfully, but she felt it would be awkward to return after these long months of being courted by Isaac. And, too, it seemed pointless now.

Besides, it makes me feel sad, she thought.

Then Leah Miller's letter arrived one afternoon. *I don't want to stick my nose in, but I've heard that Nick's no longer seeing your cousin Sarah. I thought you'd want to know . . . especially as Jake tells me you are without a beau yourself.*

Such surprising news! Rose scarcely knew what to think. So she finally asked Dat to take her to the next Singing, curious to see if what Leah had written about Nick was quite true.

As she entered, the upper level of the barn was still warm from the early October day. The sweet smell of stacked alfalfa bales greeted Rose as Rebekah Bontrager spotted her and hurried over.

"I saw you comin' in the lane with your father," Rebekah said, brown eyes sparkling. "I hope ya don't mind . . . but I told Nick you were here."

Rose blushed, terribly embarrassed. Had Silas remembered what good friends Nick and Rose once were and mentioned it to Rebekah? Rose felt like a rutabaga in a watermelon patch. *I should've stayed home.*

Yet Rebekah stayed near, even slipping in next to Rose on the bench, acting like a protective sister once the Singing got under way. Rose appreciated her thoughtfulness, but she really didn't need to be looked after. She'd known these young people all her life . . . nice, upstanding youth who sang wholeheartedly, their heads back, mouths open as they rejoiced. Nick sat all the way at the other end of the table with several other baptized fellows. He seemed very much at home.

When the songs were finished and the fellowshipping and pairing up began, Rose felt downright timid. So many there were so young. Why had she come? Right then she wanted to head home on foot.

But Rebekah would not hear of it. "No . . . no, you're riding back with Silas and me," she insisted.

Rose noticed that Nick was also leaving early, even though Rebekah had supposedly told him Rose was present. Maybe with so many squeezed into the elder Kauffman's barn, he felt uncomfortable seeking her out, even as a friend. Or was he simply respecting her wish that he keep his distance, perhaps not aware she was no longer seeing Isaac? Could that be? As reclusive as Nick had always been, she was half surprised he'd come at all, given he was without a girl now.

If Leah even has it right . . .

Rose felt dreadfully out of place riding home with Silas and Rebekah—till she remembered that she, too, had once done a similar favor for Rebekah.

When she was back in the safe haven of her father's house, Rose sat in bed and opened her Bible in an attempt to push away the memory of the uncomfortable evening. *No more of that, no matter if Mamm and Mammi beg me to go again,* she promised herself.

~

The next morning, after breakfast, Rose confided in her mother that she'd decided against attending future Singings. "I'm just not cut out for them anymore. I hope you understand." She dried her hands on her apron and stood near the sink. "You and Mammi Sylvia mean well." She sighed. *The Lord knows my heart.*

"I just thought—"

"I tried, Mamm; I truly did."

Her mother looked sad.

"All I ever wanted in life was to be a sweet wife and mother." Rose's lip quivered.

"Oh, honey-girl, I know . . . I know." Mamm opened her arms and Rose knelt at her mother's knee and wept.

CHAPTER 39

Rose bumped into Nick two weeks later, as he was coming out of her father's woodshop. He smiled but kept walking, and for the life of her, she wanted to call to him . . . tell him she and Isaac were no longer seeing each other. But that was presumptuous. And anyway, by now surely he knew of her singleness—there wasn't much the grapevine missed when it came to courtship, even though the People tried to keep serious relationships mum.

Rose stood near the door and watched Nick head toward the shortcut to the bishop's land. *Our path,* she thought.

So much had altered in the past year. It was still remarkable to think that Nick had decided to take Bishop Aaron's family name as his own. This was all the talk, especially amongst the older folk. *Nick Petersheim, indeed.*

Rose poked her head in the woodshop door. "Anything I can get ya, Dat?"

"Not that I can think of." His face was dusted with wood particles, like a pan floured for baking.

"I'll be spending the day with Hen and Mattie Sue. Hen could use some help." Her sister was coming up on her delivery date and moved rather slow these days.

"Sounds like a fine idea," he said, "but I'll be needing the family carriage."

"Oh, that's all right," she replied quickly. "It's a *gut* day for walkin'."

"Have yourself a nice time," he said. "Is Sylvia with your mother?"

"Barbara's over visiting," Rose said.

"*Des gut.*" Looking up from his work, Dat frowned as if there was more on his mind. "Say, Rosie, remember that old market tin you told me about some time ago? Ever think of surprisin' your mother and bringing it home?"

Rose had thought of the tin plenty of times but hadn't bothered to go to the ravine. "Would ya want me to get it?"

He smiled. "Just sometime."

"All right, then. I'll try an' find it again." She gave a little wave and left for Hen's.

The morning was fair, slightly warmer

than a typical late October day. They'd had snow flurries yesterday, and the bright-colored leaves were nearly gone. Rose told Mattie Sue that a gray sky meant snow, and Mattie Sue clapped her hands with glee.

They made grilled cheese sandwiches to surprise Hen, who admitted she was quite uncomfortable. Mattie Sue said her mommy liked homemade tomato soup, and there was "a big batch of it" in the freezer. So Rose heated the soup to piping hot and sprinkled Parmesan cheese on top before serving it with dill pickles and cottage cheese.

After the noon meal, Rose encouraged her sister to lie down and rest while she took Mattie Sue out for a brisk walk.

"When do kids get to go to Amish weddings?" Mattie Sue wanted to know as they walked.

"If you're Amish, you go when you're courting age—at sixteen."

Mattie Sue seemed to think on that. "That's a long time away. Do you think Mammi Emma will be better by then?" she asked, gripping Rose's hand.

"The doctors don't think she'll ever walk again, if that's what ya mean, but she sure feels better than she used to."

Mattie Sue nodded, then pointed to an abandoned hornet's nest high in a tree along the road. "Lookee there!" she called. "Nobody's home anymore."

Rose had to smile. "They've all flown away."

"Where to?"

"The queen hibernates through the winter."

"Oh." Mattie kept pointing out things all around her, asking questions. Then she was quiet for a time, her short legs working hard to keep up with Rose's pace.

"You'll soon have a little baby in the house," Rose told her.

"Mommy says it's a boy. Do you think she knows?"

"Sometimes mothers do, I guess."

"Guess what else, Aendi Rosie."

"What's that, honey?"

"I'm putting my Amish dresses away."

"You are?" This was a surprise.

"I don't want my baby brother to get mixed up. He might think he's in the wrong house."

Rose chuckled. "Do ya honestly think so?"

Mattie Sue squeezed her hand. "He'll peep open his eyes and see me." She paused a second. "He might think he should be Amish, too."

"I see."

"Today's my last day to dress like you."

"Have ya told Mommy?"

"Not yet."

Rose leaned over and kissed Mattie's Sue cheek. "I'm glad you're my niece, honey-girl," she said, thinking how much fun it was to see Mattie Sue growing up and hearing her express herself so wonderfully. *Such a sweetheart.*

They turned toward home, the skies beginning to powder them with snow. Rose was glad for the scarves beneath their coats and reached into her pockets for a set of mittens for each of them. "Let's go home and make hot cocoa, jah?"

Mattie Sue raised her head and grinned up. "With marshmallows on top?"

"*Abselutt*—absolutely!"

~

The flurries had ceased by the time Rose was ready to head home. Hen offered to drive her the short distance, but Rose refused, urging her to keep warm at home. A black-and-white tabby cat and her three matching kittens scampered across Hen's front lawn as Rose headed out toward Salem Road.

The sky had cleared some in the west and the air was very still. She let her mind wander back to the many times she and Hen had walked this road as youngsters . . . and the times she had ridden here with Nick. *Good days.*

A fox crossed the road in the distance and a flock of geese flew in a V-shape toward the south. *Winter's coming fast,* she thought, recalling Mattie Sue's excitement about attending the Christmas play again—this time with her entire family. Soon they would be ice-skating on the deacon's pond and taking sleigh rides, too.

And caroling. Even though Rose was single, she wanted to go caroling this Christmas. She didn't fit in with the young couples going door to door, but she could take Mattie Sue . . . and maybe Beth Browning, too. It would be fun to have them over to bake and decorate cookies. Maybe the school-age Petersheim grandchildren would join them, too.

Dreaming up all sorts of interesting things to enjoy with the people in her life, Rose thought again of Hen's coming baby. How wonderful it would be to hold a newborn infant. Oh, and such a dear thing for Mamm, and Rose's widowed grandmother.

Ever so healing, Rose thought, making the turn onto the narrow road that led home.

In the distance, Rose spied the location where she'd often met Silas and Isaac in their respective buggies, a good stretch away from her father's lane. She was glad now that neither of them had lip-kissed her. Mamm had sweetly suggested some years ago that she and Hen save their kisses for the man they knew they'd marry. *"Not many do anymore,"* Mamm had said.

Clouds brewed in the north and covered the sun as Rose approached the all-too-familiar spot.

Nick met me here, too, sometimes ... with Pepper.

But she wouldn't allow herself to ponder Nick. The fact he was single was no business of hers. It seemed they'd kept missing each other. Some things just weren't meant to be.

She'd given her life and her future to God, so why should she fret now?

CHAPTER 40

*A*fter breakfast the next morning, while Mamm and two of her sisters did piecework for a quilt, Rose slipped away with her horse and retrieved the tin money box from behind the boulder in the ravine. No sense in letting it lie there another long winter.

She returned George to his stall and carried the tin carefully to the house. Inside, she gave it to Mamm, who smiled upon seeing it. "This old tin has been in the family a long time." Rose's aunts nodded in agreement. Mamm didn't ask how Rose found it, which was a relief, since her aunts were all ears.

Mamm pried it open and peered inside. "Well, what's this?" She held up a folded piece of paper.

Rose frowned.

"Goodness me." Mamm gave it to her. "It's for you, Rosie."

What? Had the letter she'd written to Nick somehow reappeared?

But no—her name was written on one side: *To Rosie.* In Nick's handwriting.

"Excuse me," she told them, her face growing warm. She slipped out the back door again and made a beeline to the hayloft for privacy, self-conscious at having her aunts and Mamm make such a discovery.

Quickly, she climbed the ladder and went to sit in the far corner, very near the spot where she'd cried after declining Isaac's marriage proposal. She cautiously unfolded the paper and began to read, her heart in her throat.

> *Dear Rosie,*
>   *I hope you find this note soon.*
>   *It may sound strange, but I don't want to be friends anymore.*
>   *Let's talk about it, jah?*
>   *Nick*

She stared at the words. "What on earth?"

Is this a joke? He doesn't want to be friends?

Getting up, she hurried to the hay hole and slid down. She dashed to the woodshop. There, she waited for her father to turn off the generator-run air compressor powering his woodworking tools. "Dat, why'd ya ask me to retrieve the tin box?"

He shrugged, but the twinkle in his eye was unmistakable.

"There was a note inside . . . for me."

"Well." A smile creased his mouth. "You'd better ask Nick Petersheim 'bout that, don't ya think?"

Then Rose began to laugh. She knew Nick better than anyone, and he knew her. She understood—Nick surely meant to say he didn't want to be *just* friends. Rose ran to her father and hugged him, getting wood shavings all over her dark dress.

"Nick's a worthy fella, Rose Ann," Dat said and motioned toward the door. "Better go an' talk to him."

Her heart swelled. "Oh, Dat! Denki ever so much."

Rose found Nick on the shaded path that linked the farms, walking this way. He stopped suddenly when he saw her. "You went somewhere with George," he said, smiling. "To the scary ravine, maybe?"

"Jah, and I got your note," she said.

"What note?"

She laughed as his eyes sparkled with mischief. The best part of the old Nick was still alive and well. "You don't have to write me notes. We can talk anytime, ya know?"

His eyes were fixed on hers. "Oh, Rosie . . . I love you."

Her throat closed up at his words.

"And . . . I've never stopped," he said, moving closer.

Her heart opened wide to what Nick had always meant to her. And try as she might to prevent them, tears sprang to her eyes. "I love you, too."

He reached for her gently. "Come here, my Rosie-girl."

She let him hold her, drawing comfort from his strength for all the lonely days, the sorrow-filled nights. She remembered the scruffy little English boy who had looked so forlorn that first day in the bishop's kitchen.

God must've planned this from the start.

She moved back slightly, looking into his eyes. "So you don't want to be friends anymore, jah?"

Nick smiled and drew her near again to kiss her hair, her cheek . . . every fiber of her alive at his touch. "Will you marry me, Rosie, and be my love?"

An autumn breeze rippled the last leaves overhead. "I will," she said. "With all of my heart, I surely will."

Nick's gaze lingered over her eyes, her

lips . . . and then he was kissing her—his lips on hers. She didn't hesitate, surrendering to his enthusiastic embrace. Oh, the incredible delight! Wrapped in his arms, Rose felt the old yearning. "Mrs. Nick Petersheim," she whispered.

He laughed joyfully as he cupped her face in his hands, his cheek against hers. And then he kissed her again, more times than he ought. His affection was like honey, and Rose was glad she'd saved her kisses for him alone.

Only God could have imagined this moment!

The sky lowered around them, and it started to snow.

"Look, Rosie," he said as the enormous flakes fell like a sacred canopy. "The Lord's in agreement, too!"

"I believe He knew . . . all along." Snug in Nick's arms, Rose smiled up at her handsome husband-to-be, amazed at what wondrous things a single day could bring.

EPILOGUE

October 1987

The treed pathway is covered again with leaves of yellow, orange, and shades of red. The path is a beautiful reminder of Nick's and my journey of love, and of his return to God and the People. Each time I take the shortcut between Dat's land and the bishop's, I'm ever thankful for divine mercy and grace.

Nick's baptism was certainly evidence of that. So often I think back to that inspiring day when my dearest friend, now my husband, said yes to Christ and His *Gemeinde*— the local community. A whole new spiritual world opened up inside his heart on that special Sunday, preparing Nick for possible ministry amongst the People. I secretly wonder if the Lord was showing him that someday he might serve as a deacon or preacher. If nothing else, Nick will continue to extend compassion to those in need, just as he did when he helped Mrs. Schaeffer at the homeless shelter where his mother spent her final days. Showing God's grace to others is one of our callings as husband and wife.

It has been heartening to see how warmly Bishop Aaron was received back into the esteem of the ministerial brethren after his silencing was lifted. Prior to our sunny wedding day in late November last year, my father-in-law asked Nick to go into partnership with him to farm the land. So we've been living in the large Petersheim farmhouse, and the bishop and Barbara moved to the Dawdi Haus. According to Barbara, who is truly my second mother, they enjoy having a son and daughter-in-law running things and living on the premises. Barbara and I have become ever closer this past year, although she still can't succeed in getting me to indulge in every single chocolate dessert or pineapple upside-down cake she loves to bake!

My parents, on the other hand, still reside where they've always lived. Mammi Sylvia moved to the Dawdi Haus where Brandon and Hen stayed . . . and Dat's eldest sister will live in the smaller house, come spring.

Ah, spring, that green and glorious season of new life! Like our dear friends Silas and Rebekah, Nick's and my first child will be a springtime baby. Nick is so anxious to hold our tiny babe in his strong arms. He says he can't wait to take him—or her—on a pony ride, or to show our little one how to make leafy sailboats, just like we did, growing up here on Salem Road.

Hen and Brandon's towheaded son, Andrew Solomon—named in part for Dat—is almost a year old and has an appetite "like a horse," or so Mattie Sue says with a giggle. She relishes her role as big sister. All of us were invited to attend Andrew's dedication at the little country church where Hen is content to worship with Brandon. Mattie Sue was also included in this lovely day, having never been dedicated to God as an infant. The four of them come to visit us often, and it's remarkable to see Brandon's keen enthusiasm for the bishop's companionship . . . the way he interacts with the man of God. Both he and Nick have embraced the call of the believer and are living accordingly. Ach, I've never seen Hen happier, which makes me smile, just as I do when I catch a wink from my darling husband.

It is a joy for Nick and me to live together in accordance with God's sovereign will. Patience plays an enormous part in perseverance as we wait and trust for what is to come—what God has in store for those who worship Him.

Take yesterday, when Dat, Mammi Sylvia, and I were having coffee with Mamm. Mamm's eyes grew wide all of a sudden, and her eyebrows shot straight up. *"Ach, I just felt some tingling in my legs!"* she exclaimed, her eyes bright with tears.

It made me want to cry for joy.

Dat leaned over and kissed her cheek in front of us. *"Well, glory be!"* he said. Then Dat charged out the back door, running across the field to the phone shanty, where he reported the good news to her doctor. Who knows what might lie ahead?

It's also a joy to think of how life has improved for the Brownings in the past year. Gilbert Browning married his longtime friend, Jane Keene, last Christmas. Beth was the maid of honor and delights in her father's choice of a bride—an understanding and loving stepmother. The timing worked out nicely, because, as is our way, I'd stopped working there when I married Nick. I still keep in touch with Beth, of course, who will always be precious to me. How can we ever forget the blessed role she played in Mamm's life?

Every day, Nick and I are overjoyed at the divine providence we witness around us. We marvel when we rise at dawn, when we eat, when we labor, and when we lie down to rest. Just as Dat and Bishop Aaron have always said—their life's theme—God is truly at work in all of our lives.

Oh, we can hardly wait to pass this precious truth on to our firstborn child . . . and to all of our *Kinner* yet to come, Lord willing.

AUTHOR'S NOTE

From my earliest days in Lancaster County, I have been intrigued by Amish tradition. The People themselves, their sense of tranquility, self-sufficiency, devotion to God, family, and community—and their remarkable work ethic—continue to draw and inspire me.

As for my research, I am gratefully indebted to my astute assistants and consultants, and to my husband, David Lewis, who enjoys brainstorming my story lines, and who reads my chapters hot off the proverbial press.

My great appreciation goes out to my

editorial team—David Horton, Julie Klassen, Rochelle Glöege, and also Ann Parrish and Helen Motter—for their skilled and tireless efforts. To the many wonderful people who are involved in publishing my books, thank you!

In addition, I wish to acknowledge the lingering effect the old English classics have had on my writing muse, especially in regard to THE ROSE TRILOGY.

Also noteworthy is the Amish table blessing referred to in chapter five of this book. It was taken directly from my book *Amish Prayers,* a newly translated collection of some of the treasured prayers offered by devout Anabaptists for the past three hundred years, now available for contemporary readers' enjoyment and inspiration.

Finally, as always, I give honor to my heavenly Father, who guides my thoughts and my steps, and forever has won my heart.

Soli Deo Gloria!

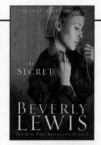

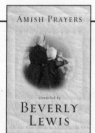

DON'T MISS THESE BEAUTIFULLY ILLUSTRATED CHILDREN'S BOOKS
FROM *NY TIMES* BESTSELLING AUTHOR

Beverly Lewis

To find out more about Beverly and her books, visit *www.beverlylewis.com.*

A delightful tale of a boy searching for answers, *What Is Heaven Like?* also offers suggestions for parents and educators to use when talking with children about heaven.

What Is Heaven Like?

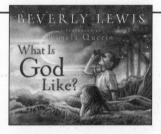

A charming story of a brother and sister spending a fun-filled day and night remembering all they know about their heavenly Father. The last page also offers suggestions for parents as they seek to teach their children about God.

What Is God Like?

With fascinating glimpses into daily Amish life, this book follows a girl trying to prove she can be just like her mama. Her gently amusing and genuinely touching results also encourage readers to be like the Lord Jesus.

Just Like Mama

⬥ BETHANYHOUSE